THE
WITCHING
NIGHT

BRUIN ASYLUM NO. 1

THE
WITCHING
NIGHT

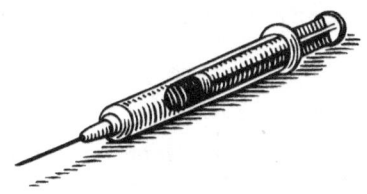

C. S. CODY

BRUIN ASYLUM
BRUIN BOOKS
THE EMERALD EMPIRE
EUGENE, OREGON

Published by
Bruin Books, LLC
September, 2013

This book was designed and edited by Jonathan Eeds

Cover design by Michelle Policicchio

Artwork appearing on pages vi and vii are excerpts from It Rhymes
with Lust, © 1950 by Leslie Waller and Arnold Drake

My ongoing gratitude to Mr. Tran Việt Húng for the cover art provided by
Viêthúng Gallery, 90 Nguyen Hue Street, Ho Chi Minh City, Viet Nam

Printed in the United States of America
ISBN 978-0-9883062-2-6
Bruin Books, LLC
Eugene, Oregon, USA

Visit the scene of the crime at www.bruinbookstore.com

Bruin Asylum is a division of Bruin Books, LLC

THE WITCHING NIGHT

INTRODUCTION

Leslie Waller, August 1963

Introduction

C. S. Cody intended *The Witching Night* to be the first in a series of supernatural novels, but he never got around to the second book. What we are left with is a stand-alone novel about a Satanic cult rooted in the heartland—an edgy, literate and groundbreaking thriller. What sets it apart from most supernatural fiction is that the protagonist summons the power of science, not faith or white magic, in his clash with evil. Dr. Loomis—a young, well-grounded MD who operates a small clinic in Chicago—draws on his medical training by using pharmaceuticals to keep himself buoyant and lucid in the midst of a direct attack by a malignant entity . . . *or is it a curse?* We are never quite sure what this dark power is, even when it assaults an intended victim. It's a killer, though, and likes to torture before it kills.

Although more suspense and mystery than white-knuckled horror, the story never flags, never fails to fascinate. Tension mounts as the invisible screws tighten on Dr. Loomis, and despite the searing pain in his head he has the strength of character to fight the madness, to stand up to it. At one point he tells himself, "When all seems lost, attack." It's something the string of victims before him could not do. Loomis has grit. When his battle with the invisible force reaches its most desperate stage, the story drops into a fever dream of journal entries reminiscent of Guy De Maupassant's famous horror story, *The Horla*. It's utterly gripping.

It may only be coincidence, but Fritz Leiber's witchcraft novel, *Conjure Wife*, was finally published in hardback the same year *The Witching Night* came out: 1953. *Conjure Wife* had been around for a while before that, though, first seeing print in the pulp magazine *Unknown Worlds* in 1943, then again as part of a hardcover omnibus of witchy novels called *Witches Three (1952)*. The two novels, other than sharing the same general subject matter (witchcraft in the modern age,) bear little resemblance to one another.

The Horla

Leiber's novel is by far better known, inspiring three movie versions, and has remained in print more or less since first appearing in hardcover.

Although less known, *The Witching Night* is the better book. The story sparkles with wit and ingenuity, and the writing style embodies a timeless quality that speaks to us eloquently. The reason behind the novel's neglect today may be because Cody never ventured into the horror/fantasy genre again. There was no follow-up, no expansion on the themes he puts forth. He came out of nowhere, dipped into the fantastic realm with a one-shot novel, and then bailed without ever bothering to build a following among horror fiction connoisseurs. Perhaps it just wasn't an abiding interest of his, and he preferred the venue of standard fiction to dark fantasy. The character driven style of *The Witching Night* would indicate it. We come away from the novel with a good understanding of what makes Dr. Loomis tick because we watched his character grow in the midst of conflict, and terror, and turmoil. Dr. Loomis is at the center of the novel. It's his story. The horror is secondary to his development. The narrative barbs sink deep because we really care about what happens to Loomis. We are *afraid* for him.

It is unjust that *Conjure Wife* spawned three (mostly bad) movies and *The Witching Night* hasn't been given a glance by filmmakers. It would make a great movie. The dark, sensual relationship between Joe and Abbie could be explored more openly if the film were made today. The book's shocking scenes would not have to be filtered. The hero's drug dependency—in this case a survival technique—could be plumbed for all its worth. In many ways, the novel is more suited for this decade than the one in which it first appeared. Lynch or Polanski are my picks for Director. They would certainly uncover what is buried beneath the surface.

Following *The Witching Night*, Cody wrote a straight-to-paperback potboiler for ACE Books called *Lie Like a Lady*. The enticement page in the front of the book reads: *A MINK-LINED NIGHTMARE! As the pampered son of a Midwest mogul, Hanley Kimmel, III, had everything. He could burn his candle at both ends and have plenty more left to light up. But beneath the personal charm . . . lay an abyss that no culture could reach. Girls . . . drink . . . exotic thrills . . . they alone kept him going . . .*

From witchcraft to tabloid drama, Cody was threading his way through the genres, his compass swinging in all directions, and then he abruptly gave up and went silent. *The Witching Night* and *Lie Like a Lady* comprise the only two novels Cody ever completed. He was never heard from again.

. . . But that's not at all true, is it? I've strung out the charade a little too long, and I apologize for that, but sometimes the facts are fun to play with, especially if they lead to something intriguing. C. S. Cody was himself a fabrication, a pen name adopted by Leslie Waller as an outlet for some of his early genre work, a ploy that was far more common among writers of the 50's and 60's than it is today. After dropping the Cody *nom de plume*, Leslie Waller (1923-2007) went on to write a series of bestsellers focused on organized crime and international intrigue. By the time his last novel appeared in 2001 he had written thirty-six books, including a number of movie and television tie-in's under a second pen name, Patrick Mann. Some of those novels should be immediately familiar: *Close Encounters of the Third Kind* (with Steven Spielberg,) *Dog Day Afternoon*, and *Falcon Crest. Hide in Plain Sight*, written under his own name, was based on a true story about the US government's Kafkaesque intrusion into an innocent family's affairs. It was later made into a highly regarded film starring James Caan. It gets a little confusing over which of his books are novelizations, and which are stand-alone novels that were later made into films. The point is that Waller was in high demand, both with general readers and Hollywood moguls.

Waller's skill over the decades grew, as did his popularity. Unfortunately his cannon of work lies in that period of time that seems to be ignored by publishers today: the 70's, 80's and 90's. Most of what was published during those decades, and there is some really good stuff in there, is languishing on secondhand store shelves and in garage sale bins. William P. McGivern, another fine writer, is trapped in the same literary vanishing point.

The Witching Night will be the first of Waller's works to see print in over a decade. The one exception, the one very notable exception, is a graphic novel that he coauthored with Arnold Drake called *It Rhymes with Lust*. It is still in print today and available from Dark Horse Comics. Anyone interested in 50's noir and in the history of comics should pick it up. *It Rhymes with Lust* is widely regarded as the first graphic novel, and it is a thing of beauty.

Small Press publishers tend to be crusaders, especially those publishers who focus on neglected works and underappreciated writers. In the case of Leslie Waller, *The Witching Night* is a good place to start. More of his novels deserve the smell of fresh ink and a crisp new cover, and so I hope some of the New York publishers take note and restore his name to the bookshelves. *The Witching Night* is our crusade.

Welcome to the Asylum.   —JE

From *It Rhymes with Lust* © 1950

'Tis now the very witching time of night,

When churchyards yawn, and hell itself breathes out.

HAMLET

fey [fā] ›**adj. 1a** unwordly and vague. **b** able to see into the future; clairvoyant **c** appearing touched or crazy, as if under a spell **2** *Scots* **a** fated to die soon **b** full of the sense of approaching death [Middle English *feie*, fated to die, from Old English *fæge*]

Intracaine in Oil for Caudal Anesthesia and Analgesia in Rectal Surgery.

Barnett A. Greene, M.D., Julius Barcham,* M.D. and Samuel Berkowitz, M.D., Brooklyn, N. Y.

Departments of Anesthesiology, Unity and Adelphi Hospitals

Received for publication September 20, 1950

 XPERIENCE with caudal injection of 5 per cent intracaine in oil** in 250 patients undergoing rectal operations is hereby reported. We have developed a technique during the past two and a half years and now regard it as a reliable and safe means of simultaneously producing prompt surgical anesthesia and significantly contributing to postoperative hypalgesia for anorectal operations.

Our study was stimulated by the work of Kenny[1] with the caudal injection of 40 to 60 cc. of proctocaine (procaine base 1.5 per cent, butyl aminobenzoate 6 per cent and benzyl alchohol 5 per cent in arachis oil) for the relief of intractable pain caused by pelvic carcinoma. A search of the literature then revealed that Odom and Kolczun[2] had long used 20 cc. 2 per cent procaine base in almond oil by lumbar epidural injection for sciatica; that Abajian injected 2 per cent intracaine in oil for six hours of peridural anesthesia,[3] that Turner used caudal injection of 10 cc. of 1 per cent procaine base in oil for the relief of lumbosacral sprains during the seven years prior to his report.[4] We were therefore assured at least that the epidural instillation of an oil-soluble anesthetic agent was safe inasmuch as none of these earlier workers had encountered any complications. Before arriving at our present practice we tried a variety of rectal oil-soluble anesthetic mixtures in a series of caudal, lumbar and thoracic epidural blocks for pain due to malignant disease. While many produced some degree of analgesia none produced a reliable and prompt depth of anesthesia sufficient to permit operation. Two per cent intracaine in oil was inconstant in securing intense surgical anesthesia and significant postoperative analgesia. The 5 per cent solution, however, has been found to provide both. In 105 cases we have added 0.5 to 1.0 cc. 1:500 epinephrine in oil to the anesthetic agent because (a) epinephrine is a proved aid in intensifying and prolonging the effect of an anesthetic solution; (b) epinephrine in oil has been shown to retard the absorption of other pharmacologic agents injected in oily vehicles, e.g. pencillin,[5] and (c) epinephrine slowly absorbed from an oily solution over a period of several hours[6] would ameliorate the hypotension sometimes produced by caudal anesthesia. Epinephrine in oil has been avoided in hypertensive, cardiac and hypermetabolic patients.

The property of intracaine to induce anesthesia more quickly and diffuse more widely[7] also made it more suitable for our purpose than

*Dr. Barcham is now associated with the Wifllamsburg General Hospital, Brooklyn, N. Y.

**Intracaine in oil was supplied by E. R. Squibb & Sons, New York, through the courtesy of H. Sidney Newcomer, M.D.

1 «◊» Prologue

THIS REALLY BEGAN, I suppose, when I first met Colin Jones. He and I were students in Chicago—he in political science, I in pre-med—and we became very good friends. Perhaps I should have realized at the time that something was bound to happen to me, simply because I was Colin's friend. You see, Colin was Welsh, and he was fey.

When I say he was Welsh, I mean he was an American-born throwback to every Welsh characteristic you could think of. He was obstinate to the point of stubbornness, honorable beyond all dreams of honor, methodical and full of a love for work, dour and playful by turns, fiercely proud. And one thing more: he was fey.

"You'll never understand it, Joey," he used to say in our student days. "I could talk of it all night and you'd be no wiser."

"There's nothing on earth you can't describe," I'd retort hotly. "Cut out the mystery and give me facts."

"A medical student for you," he'd chuckle, which was usually the end of it.

Now that everything's over and done with—at least I *think* it's done with—I've learned something new about facts, something Colin knew very well. I know that facts can mislead a man and that they can fail you, miserably, at the moment when you cry out to God for their help.

From 1942, when I finished my internship in time to enter the Medical Corps, to 1946, when I was discharged, I saw nothing of Colin. I had misplaced his address and my own changed so often that any correspondence we might have started would have been fruitless. When I got out of the Army, I took my severance pay, cashed my war bonds and set up a small office in Chicago's South Side. There was still quite a shortage of doctors at the time, and I often found half a dozen new patients waiting for me every day. I remember it was the end of autumn, early November I think, when Colin walked into my office.

He looked like somebody else; not merely five years older, no gray hair or facial wrinkles, but like somebody else. My receptionist announced Colin Jones, and another man walked in—same general appearance, same voice, different man.

"No, it's me, Joe," he said quickly.

"Prove it."

"The thirst for facts, is it?" he smiled. "I'm Colin all right."

There was something there, a turn of phrase or an inflection. At any rate, I suddenly saw Colin beneath the fleshy façade of this stranger. "What the hell happened?" I wanted to know.

"Well, now," he folded himself into a chair and got comfortable.

"There's the matter of five years, Dr. Loomis, and

the matter of a small war. The part I saw was *too* small, nothing but ants and foliage, a regular jungle of a war."

"Pacific?" He nodded. "Malaria?" He nodded. "Something more?"

He paused for a moment before answering. "No," he said at last. "Sorry to disappoint."

He flicked a bit of lint from his knee, negligently, and I had the feeling he was flicking away the war with it. I also had the feeling that I should be more effusive with him. We hadn't met in years—the whole war separated us—and here we were, talking like two Englishmen who hadn't been properly introduced. "Well, good," I said quickly. "It's fine to see you again." Then I stopped. I couldn't think of anything more to say. "Still . . . ?" I tried to remember something he could still conceivably be doing. Before the war he had been active in a labor union. "Still unionizing?" I asked.

He shook his head with heavy slowness, as though it were a globe as big as the whole world. "I don't have the stamina for that now," he remarked. "An unknown great-aunt died in the old country and I am now a man of small means, enough to save me from working for a living." He hunched his thin body forward carefully. "I've got something else on the fire, Joey. A little project of research."

"You? Research?" I laughed slightly. "But that's facts, isn't it?"

He pulled a very wry face and in the expression I suddenly saw the old Colin quite distinctly: the upraised eyebrow, the corner of his thin mouth dipping in humorous disdain.

"You've got a lot to learn about facts," he said quietly.

"That may be," I said, "but—"

"Anyway, Joey-boy," he cut in, "there I was, reading the alumni bulletin, and to my extreme surprise I find Joe Loomis listed among the illustrious sons and daughters of Chicago. Being in need of a medic's ministrations, I say to myself: 'I'll share my ill-gotten gains with old Joe. He'll know what to do with them.' So I'm here—*with* my checkbook—and I crave the service of a sawbones."

I was on known ground again and I smiled at him. "What kind of service?"

He sat up straighter in his chair, still with that same cautious, gingerly movement as though he were crated in with several dozen eggs. "A . . ." he paused and wet his lips. "A headache," he said softly.

The word surprised me. I had expected something more spectacular after Colin's curious build-up. "Headaches? That's all?"

"A headache," he repeated, his voice flat and dry.

"Describe it."

"It's constant, violent, and aspirin won't help it. Aside from that I know nothing more."

"Any particular part of the head?"

"All over."

"Any special time of day?"

"God, you don't even listen," he said loudly. "It's constant,man, *constant!*"

"Relax." I made a meaningless doodle on the pad, a line that looked something like a coiled snake. "Are they throbbing or steady?"

"Steady."

"Do you wake with them?"

"Man, I sleep with it. *When* I sleep!"

I glanced up at him. The violence of his words was somehow shocking, coming from that thin, steady, immobile face. "How much sleep do you get?"

"At night, none. I sometimes cat nap in the day when I'm too tired to go on."

"How long have you had them?"

"Not them, Joey; *it*. It's the same headache all the time, the same one that started out."

"Started out when?"

"Two weeks ago. Maybe three." He seemed to relax in the chair, his spare body sinking back into the leather cushions. "And that's it," he said at length. "Now do something, will you?"

"Is that all?" I asked, hoping to get some further symptom, some hint of a previous disease or a knock on the head or bad teeth, something more than the mere fact of the headache.

He was a long time in answering. Finally, when he did speak, the words seemed to linger on his tongue, hesitant, almost as though he had to scrape them out into the air. "Yes," he said, "that's . . . all."

There was very little to go on. The headache could stem from a variety of causes. The symptoms were unusual, of course—the seeming constancy, all that. But for the time being there was nothing definite to be said. "We'll take some urine and blood out of you, Colin," I said, trying to sound jocular. "And I'll send you to have some X-rays taken. Then we'll be able to get at this thing a little better."

I looked up at him in time to catch a grimace being wiped off his face, a tense, gnarled spasm, as in strychnine poisoning. "What's the matter?"

"Nothing," he mumbled, "only this pain. Is there something you can give me now? You know me, Joey, I'm not the one to run from pain. But this thing is splitting me apart. It's . . . it's like a wedge at the back of my head that presses in and down and won't stop until it cleaves me through the middle in halves." He spat the words out in a long stream, hardly pausing to give them emphasis or sound, as though they were less an explanation than a scream, a moan of agony.

I ripped the doodled page off my pad and scribbled a prescription on the clean sheet. "Have this filled right away," I told him. "It's codeine and it'll help."

"It will?" He reached out quivering fingers for the slip of paper. "You think it will?"

"It should."

"Damn it, Joe, it's *got* to."

I DIDN'T SUSPECT at the time that the X-rays would come back without any clues. The blood and urine analyses proved nothing more than that Colin still had latent malaria. His sedimentation count showed no trace of unnoticed rheumatic tendencies. An electro-cardiogram I ran indicated normal heart action; a dental check-up showed nothing; the oculist's report read 20/20, no astigmatism. Colin's basal metabolism was slightly below normal, but hardly worth considering. And most baffling of all, the codeine proved worthless.

"Then shoot me full of morphine," he begged the next Monday. "There ought to be some way to deaden this thing."

I had taken to dropping in at his apartment every other evening just before I had dinner. I would usually find him lying on his back with an ice bag crammed down over his forehead. "Does that give you any relief?" I asked.

"Absolutely none," he grunted. "How about that needle?"

It would have been the easy way out. I didn't feel like doping him, though, before I had some idea, no matter how vague, of what was causing the pain. When I told him as much he groaned feebly. "You're one hell of a doctor," he muttered and then, as if afraid of offending, he smiled up at me, a weak, nebulous kind of smile.

"Okay," I said, "you can have your needle."

The morphine drained out of the hypodermic into his bloodstream. I could feel his body soften and go limp. Although I shouldn't have been, I was immensely relieved. At least this was something morphine could deaden. I had begun to think it would resist even narcosis, but when he relaxed I relaxed with him.

"There we go," I murmured.

He sighed deeply, his thin lips trembling with the exhalation. We waited in silence for a long moment. There was nothing in his little apartment to break the quiet—no clock, no traffic noise, nothing to shatter the moment of waiting. Then he sighed once, harshly, and opened his eyes wide. "Please," he said, "listen, Joe . . ."

"Yes?" I knew what he would say, that the pain was gone, that this month of agony was ended, even for this fleeting moment of morphia-peace. "It's all right now, isn't it?"

"I don't feel any difference," he said, almost matter-of-factly, "I don't feel any difference at all. The pain's still there. My mistake, suggesting morphine."

The month that followed was almost as bad for me as it was for Colin. I had him hospitalized and called a consultation with some of the brain men then available in the city. We ran all the tests again, all the X-rays. When the month was out, we knew exactly what we had known . . . there was nothing organically wrong. Was he allergic to something? Could the headache be an especially virulent reaction? We tested him for everything; he was allergic to nothing. After talking it over with Colin, who pooh-poohed the idea,

I called for a psychiatric evaluation. The tests took some ten days, the interviewing another week. When it was all over, we knew nothing more. And the worst of it was, Colin's headache grew progressively worse. He slept so little now that I wondered how he could remain coherent. He had stopped complaining of the pain, never spoke of it unless questioned closely. His will power was amazing; it was miraculous to see him speak, think like a normal person while this monstrous, abnormal pain enveloped his brain.

"Tell me, Colin, is it still like a wedge?"

"Wedge? No, it's not that anymore." He seemed to be trying to take stock of himself, gathering with excruciating care the bits of information his pain had not yet blocked off. "It's stopped being a wedge," he said, "and it's something much different, Joey. It's an odd thing. It's . . . it's like the reverse of a wedge, like the split had been made and now a drawing-out had come."

"How do you mean, a drawing-out?"

"It's suction, as though I were being tapped like a maple tree."

"Drawing out your sap, eh, Colin?" I tried to smile at him.

"It's more than my sap," he muttered.

The really remarkable characteristic of Colin's symptoms was that all this intense pain had not thrown him into a coma. The human body takes just so much pain and then it goes into a state of shock, throwing up a buffer of unconsciousness between itself and the hurt. But unless Colin was lying, and he couldn't possibly have counterfeited such agony, his pain was severe enough and prolonged enough to blank him out a hundred times over. Yet it didn't. Day and night, as the hours marched by in slow seconds, he remained conscious, alert, rational.

"You never told me," he said one night. He had taken to speaking in a low, throaty voice that used little of his waning energy. "You never told me you knew Abbie."

"Abbie who?"

"Abbie," he murmured, "with hair like wings."

This began to sound like the delirium I had been expecting. "Try to think of something else," I urged him. "Think of swimming; think of a tall, cold drink."

"Hair like wings."

"Yes, I know."

"Wings of . . . of the Angel of Death." He sighed wearily and rolled over on his stomach.

This was it, then, the inception of coma. Soon his words would wander further and further, like those of a man falling into deep sleep. And then . . . unconsciousness, the blissful sleep of exhaustion. "Let it slip away from you, Colin. Submit to it."

He rolled over and sat up on the bed with one smooth movement. "What're you babbling about?" he asked sharply.

So it wasn't coma. I turned away from him and began playing with the compresses and glasses on his night table. "Nothing," I said. "You were talking about some girl."

Colin sighed and shook his head slowly from side to

side, moving it as though it were some huge, delicately blown glass bubble that might fracture in a thousand bits with rough handling. "You're no help," he said at last.

"Help for what?"

"For . . ." there was a sudden light behind his eyes, ". . . for the thing that I have in me. You can't help, not as a doctor, but perhaps . . ." He let his voice die away as he watched me, his eyes burning feverishly.

"If a doctor can't help," I retorted, "who the hell can?"

He let his body fall back against the bed. "Okay," he said in a peculiarly choked voice. "I should have known better."

"Known *what* better?"

"Known better than to ask something from a . . ." he groped for the right words, ". . . from a fact-worshiper." In his mouth the phrase had an ugly ring to it.

Then something came to me from the back of my mind, something sly and stealthy, a soft rap at the rear door of my consciousness. "Colin," I said harshly, "has this thing got anything to do with . . ." I didn't know the exact words for it, ". . . with your being fey?"

He closed his eyes and smiled up at nothing. "And if I told you it did," he said then, "would you be impressed?"

"Impressed enough to call back the psychiatrist."

When he spoke, finally, his words had a hollow

sound to them as if they were uttered inside some catacomb. "There's no test for what I've got," he said.

"Then you *know* what you've got?" My voice was almost a shriek. "You *know* what it is?"

Colin nodded slowly with that delicate head action he had taken to using.

"Colin, if you know, tell me."

The grin on his face grew taunting. "I won't," he said perversely.

"But I'll tell you something else, Joey-boy. I knew what it was from the beginning."

"Then, why—?"

"—did I call you in? Because I wanted to prove something. It's all part of the . . . the project I told you about. The research. I wanted to see if my good friend Joe Loomis, with all his hard-won U. of C. facts and his great scientific resources, could do something." He paused to regain his breath. "And now I know," he went on more calmly, "and now there's no doubt."

"Look, Colin." I tried hard to sound confident and assured. "If there's anything I can do, not as a doctor but as a friend, then tell me."

"Not you, Joey." He sounded much weaker.

"Why not me?"

He let his head press back against the pillows; his eyes roamed over the dull white ceiling of the hospital room. "I don't think you're the man for the job. You might be. I'm not sure."

I stood up and went to the window. The early March weather had brought unseasonable snow. It was sweeping in off Lake Michigan in thin flurries and gusts, rolling over the dull expanse of the Midway where in summer babies play on the grass, and where now warming sheds had been set up for skaters. A thought kept rising to the surface of my mind and I kept putting it down. As I watched, two girls went by on the sidewalk below, their books under their arms, their cheeks frosty red . . . students on their way to the Cottage Grove streetcar line, through with school for another day, home to warmth and dinner and peace. The thought kept nagging at me. I turned from the window and looked at Colin.

"What has Abbie got to do with all this?" I wanted to know.

"Abbie knows you," he responded quickly.

"But I don't know her."

"Then keep it that way," he said. "She's a lovely girl, really beautiful."

"Why should I keep it that way?"

"Joey, stop asking questions. Life isn't only questions. If you keep asking them long enough you get answers and then you're trapped."

There was very little to be gained in talking to him when he was in this kind of mood. I said goodnight as encouragingly as I could and left the hospital. My car was cold and hard to start, but after a while I got it going and drove along the Midway to the Outer Drive. The Drive wound slowly through Jackson Park, now thinly hooded in snow, the tree branches icy and glistening, the lagoons level and white. The

Coast Guard station stood lonely and lifeless, a thin thread of smoke whipping off in hasty patches from its red brick chimney, a flag of soot soon lost in the driving wind. Jackson Park was dormant, sleeping beneath a cottony blanket, saving itself for the tremendous burst of green that would shoot up in every shrub and tree when spring awakened in a few weeks. Abbie, I thought forlornly, Abbie.

I stopped for the traffic light at 71st Street and watched the Illinois Central electric line gates come clanging down. An express shot through the intersection waving a tail of snowflakes behind it. I pulled my car into the parking lot and went upstairs to my office. Abbie, I thought. I didn't know any Abbies.

The office was empty. I opened my file cabinet and looked through the patients' index there. Of the two hundred names there was one Abbie, a Mrs. Abigail Holmgren, age 63, a grandmother, since moved to Globe, Arizona, for a pulmonary condition. She wasn't Abbie.

There were my appointment books. I rummaged through the receptionist's desk, discarded two historical novels and a back issue of a movie magazine, then found the old books. The first one, the oldest, bore entries in my own writing. Those had been my early days when I couldn't afford a receptionist. No Abbie there. No Abbie in the newer book. No Abbie in the latest one on top of the desk. I was wasting my time.

I sat down at my desk and lit another cigarette. It tasted peculiarly Turkish, a flavor I've often noted in cigarettes during cold weather. There's something about the temperature or the climate that brings out the Turkish part of the blend. I made a mental note, as I'd done every winter for the last five years, to try an all—Virginia blend. Abbie.

There was a last chance: my private appointment book—the place I listed all my out-of-office engagements. It started in February of 1946. The first entry: "Buy two suits." My first civilian act officially noted down. I paged through slowly. On June 12th there was the notation: "Ray and Jessie, 24th, 1800." I was still using Army time and the note reminded me that I was supposed to dine with my friends on the 24th at six p.m. Methodical. On the 24th I had made another notation: "Apologize R & J." Ray and Jessie, that was. Apologize for what? I sat back to think. The 24th of June . . .

Suddenly my mind was clicking like a comptometer, ringing everything back in a neat sequence. The afternoon of the 24th, late, I was washing up before going to Ray and Jessie's for dinner. The phone, an emergency call on 67th Street, the girl tall, jet black hair, a figure that—

She was lying on, the living room couch, a towel wrapped around her left forearm. The towel was white in places but the blood had dyed most of it a mottled rust. There was a gash nearly an inch deep, longitudinal, starting below the inside of the elbow and running some five inches toward the wrist. The lips of the wound were black. The cut was at least twelve hours old. A thin rill of blood oozed up from its depths. I looked up in surprise at the girl and her face was drained white, bluish; her dark eyes black in huge, staring eyeballs, crescents of violet under her lower lids; her lips chalky, quivering; her long, glistening black hair writhing in crazy directions.

"Why didn't you call me before?"

"I—" She licked her lips but they remained dry.

"What did this?"

"A . . . a bottle." The words seemed to suck all energy from her.

"But how? You couldn't do this with a broken bottle."

She shook her head feebly and her lips pressed shut. "What kind of bottle? Was it dirty or clean?" She shook her head silently and I gave up. I had to cauterize. Her face was expressionless, blank. The nitric foamed, wisps of steam spiraling upward. She watched, curiously, without emotion. I neutralized the acid with bicarbonate, swabbed the cut clean, and began the suturing. It took eight stitches. I've known patients, especially women, to pass out after the first or second puncture of the needle, but this girl watched calmly, with interest, as though I were suturing my own arm, not hers. Then I loaded a hypo and gave her a *tetanustoxoid* injection. "Call me tomorrow," I said. "If it gives you a lot of trouble, call sooner."

She nodded and licked at her lips again, a feline gesture, as of a cat cleaning itself. Her tongue was pink, pointed, her teeth small and sharp. "My purse," she said then, pointing to the end table. It was the first time she had spoken at any length and I found

her voice deep and strangely resonant for a woman.
"Bring it to me," she said, her voice much stronger
now. She opened the bag and took out a twenty-
dollar bill. I reached for my wallet to get change and
she shoved the bill at me with an imperious gesture,
as though commanding me to take it without any
nonsense.

"Do you live here alone?" I pocketed the twenty.

"Yes."

"You'll have to rest very quietly for several days.
Move the arm as little as possible. In fact, make a
sling for it out of an old scarf."

"That's enough, Dr. Loomis," she said. "I'm not a
fool."

"Why did you wait so long to call me?"

"You've got your money. I'd like to be alone
now." There was a peculiar ring to her voice, the kind
of tone you sometimes hear in old master sergeants or
ancient cavalry officers, the square, blunt thrust of
authority that shoves its way around every word, like
the mortar between bricks.

"All right," I said. I had the urge to throw the
twenty in her face but I was a struggling medic. Who
was I to throw away money? "Come in next week," I
said as I went to the door. "If the shot bothers you,
take a few aspirins and try to sleep." I hadn't even
bothered to ask her if she was allergic to foreign
substances. We usually find out things like that before
shooting people full of tetanus. But, as she said so
coldly, I had my money. The hell with her.

And that, I thought now, that was Abbie. Abbie

Cowper, if I remembered accurately. She hadn't come in that next week. I never saw her again, neither her slash, her antitoxin shot, nor her stitches. I don't know who removed them. I never saw her again, nor did I find out what made the cut. It wasn't a broken bottle, I remembered that clearly. It was something thin and pointed, a slim knife, a curving knife, judging by the outline of the wound.

Now that I'd placed Abbie, I had to see Colin at once. I locked the office, hurried downstairs and into my car. Colin would have to tell me about Abbie now. I drove quickly back through Jackson Park thinking all the while that perhaps now I could crack Colin's maddening wall of silence.

I raced my car up 57th Street and was brought to a quick stop at Woodlawn by the traffic light. Abbie Cowper. I remembered the last name clearly because it had sounded like "Cooper" over the phone and I couldn't find it on the downstairs button panel for a few minutes. I remembered the name, but as I tried to remember the girl, nothing definite came. Tall, dark-haired, beautiful, yes; but what did she look like?

The light turned green and I jammed the gas pedal down fast, pushing the car along 57th past the Unitarian Church, the university's Reynolds Club, the block of dormitories, west to Ellis where I turned hard left and sped towards the hospital. I had to see Colin now, had to confront him with my new knowledge. I had questions to ask him, lots of questions."

I dashed up the long flight of stairs to the main foyer, nailed an elevator just as the doors were closing and shot upstairs to the fifth floor. I had brushed past the nurse's desk before I heard her call my name.

"Your patient's failing," she said matter-of-factly. "We tried to get you."

"What?"

"Here." She pushed Colin's chart toward me. Respiration down, pulse slowing, temperature 93.8.

"Ninety-three-eight!" I yelped. "You're crazy."

"We've been trying to get you for the last half-hour," she informed me stupidly.

I ran along the corridor of private rooms. Colin's light was on. An orderly was setting up an oxygen tent. Without pausing to greet him I shoved a thermometer in Colin's mouth and picked up his thin, fragile wrist. He let the thermometer slide from his lips to the sheets. "Ninety-one-four," he whispered. "Just took it."

"Can't be," I snapped impatiently.

"You mean, I'd be dead with that temp, eh, Joey?"

"Well . . ." I didn't want to commit myself, not to him.

"You're right," he said softly. "I am dead."

"You're delirious." His pulse was counting fourteen to the half-minute.

"I've been dead," he whispered harshly, "since November."

His wrist dropped out of my fingers. I started to pick it up again and then stopped. Somebody tapped me on the shoulder. It was Bernstein; he'd been in attendance all the time and I hadn't seen him. "*Coramine*," he murmured in my ear, "not three minnutes ago. Two c.c.'s."

"And it didn't—?"

He shook his head. "No reaction."

The orderly started to lower the oxygen tent over Colin's face. "Save yourself," he told the man. "I can't use it." The orderly looked questioningly at me. I could feel Bernstein's eyes on the back of my head. In the doorway Dr. Geffin and a nurse were standing tensely, their glances flicking back and forth between Colin and me, Colin and me. They were all waiting for me to say something, order something. The *Coramine* hadn't worked. Nothing had ever worked with Colin. And I knew the oxygen would be wasted too. I straightened up and jerked my thumb at the orderly. I motioned with my eyes at Bernstein and Geffin. No coma, no delirium, no treatment, no nothing. Silently they filed out of the room. This was my show, all mine.

"So," I said fiercely, bending over Colin's pale face. "You've been dead since November, have you?" He nodded listlessly. "I know who Abbie is," I burst out, "I know all about her!"

A flicker of light passed behind his eyes. He raised them slowly to meet mine. "All?" he whispered.

"I know all about her," I repeated stubbornly, trying to force him to reveal what he'd been hiding these months.

"You, Joey?" The idea seemed to amuse him. "My medical scholar?" A giggle shook his body.

"Listen, Colin, whatever you're hiding, whatever this 'project' of yours has been, it'll die with you. You know that?"

"Let it." His eyes glassed over. "It couldn't be otherwise."

"It could if you'd confide in me, Colin."

"You? Do you really want me to?" His shoulders heaved in a puny, feeble movement that was meant to be a shrug. "Joseph-child, I've confided in you more than you know. But you'll find out, later. Much later."

"You're dying," I snapped, "be sensible, will you?"

"Joey," he whispered, "sit down here." He patted the bed beside his frail body. "You're a man of facts," he went on more slowly, "and even though I've laughed at you, I understand. There was a reason, the project." He seemed to be summoning reserves of energy, from where I couldn't guess. "I've found nothing. No, it's different. I've found something but only the . . . the top of it, like the iceberg's crest. There's much below, hidden. I've failed. But I know why, which is something grand after all. I've failed and the reason of it is that I could never succeed. I'm not the man. The way I was heading, no man could succeed. Not even you, and you're—" He grew visibly weaker in that instant, life fading out of his face.

This was the strangest deathbed delirium I'd ever heard. It was so coherent, so rational, and yet so completely obscure, as though he was talking in another language. "Tell me more plainly," I said, as though I were a small child begging for a hint to an involved riddle. "Tell me so I can understand."

"No," he retorted flatly. "It would be only a passing on of error." He paused for breath. "I'll tell you

you no more, Joey. No more clues, no more facts."

"But I—!"

"—you're no wiser than before." He smiled a ghastly grin up at me. "Just a wee pep-talk before the coach passes on," he whispered. "Then carry the ball. You'll have to try to understand."

"I can't—"

"—don't try then. Just listen." A great sigh shook his upper trunk, deepening the huge shadows under his chin. "Men," he said softly, "have been fighting up out of the cave for a long time now, Joey. But there's something holds them back. Human nature, maybe. Some say God or the Devil. Yet they keep fighting all the while, as though some day they'll break through the veil of ignorance and step out into sunlight. It goes slow, Joey, by fits and starts." A trembling started in his mid-section and shook his mouth closed.

"Take it easy, Colin." I felt like a clod of earth, crumbling, useless.

"No matter." He had forced his lips open again and his tongue was thick between them. "I was a fighter, Joe, and you know that. The old Colin. And when I forsook that fight for another it looked like I'd gone soft, no guts." He was silent for a while, then cracked open the dry line of his mouth. "It's all one fight," he whispered. "Only I was over my head, outmanned, undone before I commenced. I made a mistake, I fought alone. Don't do that, Joey-boy. Fight together. They outnumber you, boy, and you need every friend you've got."

"Against who?" I flared suddenly. "Who am I fighting?"

"Them." He paused. "The Others," he added unwillingly. "They go by many names, Joe, and one's as good as another." His eyes closed slowly.

"Colin?" I was frightened. "Colin!"

"Yes?" The word was a quiet sibilance in his mouth.

"What about Abbie?" I waited tensely for his answer. "Where does Abbie fit in?"

"Abbie?" His eyeballs shifted from left to right under their closed lids. He worked his lips back and forth weakly, their motion hardly apparent in the cruel white light from his bed lamp. "So now I'll leave," he whispered quietly. "They've won and I go with them."

"But Abbie?"

"And now it's your fight, Joey-boy." He paused for the briefest of instants. "Goodbye."

His head seemed to sink a little deeper in the pillow. I felt his wrist. No pulse. My fingers awkward, I adjusted my stethoscope on his chest. Through its tubes I could hear a sound, a quiet unreeling sound, as of something being withdrawn. Then, abruptly, there was silence. I stood up from his bed. He looked the same as before. There was only one difference. He was dead.

From behind me now, from the black, empty, uncurtained oblong of night that was the window, came a rushing sound. Something tore past, something huge that hurtled through the night with a ripping, crashing roar. I ran to the window and threw it open. The night lay heavy and black over the Midway. The street lamps glittered faintly along snow-specked streets. The wind howled and moaned around the corners of the hospital, a high, hurrying wind that snatched at the heavy granite and shrieked its insides out on the sharp stone edges. It was the wind, I thought. The noise was the wind. Only the wind.

Colin was dead, the unknown battle had ended; the months, the endless months since November, the torture, the agony, the excruciating misery, the dark, unnamed opponent. Now Colin was dead.

And the noise at the window . . . that noise was the wind. Nothing but the wind.

2 «◊» The Black Host

I WAS SOMEWHERE WITHOUT CONTACT, sliding through a viscous, buoyant fluid like heavy syrup and my body had no weight, my limbs no feeling. There was a ringing in my ears and she had to laugh at that because it was funny. I couldn't hear the laugh for the ringing in my ears. I knew that she laughed as I knew she was naked, her hair a kind of shawl that dangled tauntingly before her and trembled with the vibration of the elevator. The nurse was watching me too and making fierce faces at me, her fingers pulling out the corners of her mouth. "You can't hear me make faces," she cackled. Then the girl swayed toward me and I could see her bare hips undulate like seaweed and her hair, buoyed by the medium around us, oozed out at my face like tentacles. "Stop the ringing," she cooed. She raised her arm and brandished it languidly before my eyes. I counted eight stitches in the soft white flesh, a good suture, healing well. I reached out to touch it and pressed the red nipple of her breast instead. The ringing stopped suddenly.

I was sweating, trembling, my body shivering in rhythm to the alarm clock. I opened my eyes and found my hand outstretched from the bed, pressing down hard on the cut-off button of the clock. I looked at its face. Nine forty-five. I shook my head violently and the trembling of my body slowed to a stop. I got out of bed.

When I got back from the funeral it was nearly three o'clock. Eight patients waited patiently. I took off my coat in the inner room of my office and something about me must have impressed my receptionist. She followed me inside, pushed her gold-and-plastic spectacles up onto her forehead and gave me a quizzical glance. "Rough?" she said.

"A funeral," I said by way of an answer. "Anybody phone?"

"I've written them down." She continued watching me. "You look terrible," she said at last.

"Who's the doctor in this office?" I asked peevishly.

"Physician, heal thyself." She laughed at her own hackneyed joke. "Anyway," she said, "this Jones case is over. It was getting your goat, wasn't it?"

"Could be," I side-stepped. "What do you mean I look terrible?"

"Peaked," she remarked, "beat, *ausgespielt.*"

"Danke," I muttered. "Give me the list of calls."

She handed me the slip of paper. "Why don't you get married?" she asked. Sooner or later every woman I know asks me that, usually from behind the protective barrier of her own marriage.

"Why don't *you* try it?" I asked nastily.

"Umm." She rolled her rather hyperthyroid eyes. "Too much trouble."

"I didn't mean *that,*" I said.

She shrugged her shoulders. "It'd do you a lot of good." She eyed me clinically. "Put some fat on you, take the lines out of your face. You'd love it."

I couldn't think of anything nice to say so I looked at the list of calls. "Who's this Paul Nelson?" I wanted to know.

"Lawyer. Sounded like it was important."

I sat down on the edge of my desk and dialed Nelson's number. After I hung up my receptionist looked pained. "You've got that peaked look," she warned me. "Like somebody stole your gal. If you had one."

"Jones left all his stuff to me," I told her. "Everything but his bank account. The money goes to a remote cousin in Billings, Montana."

"You have all the luck."

"He made the will last November," I added dully, "his first and only will."

"So?"

I told her to start shooing in the patients. Colin had been telling the truth. He knew he was dying back in November. He knew even before he came to me. And he knew, even then, that he would pass on his . . . his project to me. Why? What project? How could I carry it on? There were too many questions, and, frankly, I didn't feel like getting any answers.

I was worried about myself now. The fear for Colin had ended and now I was wondering what had happened to me. I knew I was rundown. The receptionist didn't have to tell me that I was getting five or six hours of sleep each night, sleep tortured by mad dreams like this morning's. My appetite was shot. Food tasted repulsive. My nerves were drawn tight. In the past two months I'd banged up all four fenders of my car parking it badly or nudging somebody in traffic. My coordination was poor, my complexion yellowish. I sweated more profusely. Surveying the symptoms now, I diagnosed overwork.

I had taken to watching the faces of people in crowds, turning suddenly to see who might be behind me. If I saw the same face more than once I fretted over it. The week before I had made a call on a patient in Hyde Park and as I parked my car at the curb I'd seen a tall, burly man pull up behind me in a battered old Chevrolet coupé. He was a gross-looking man with puffy cheeks mottled by pockmarks, a large, bulbous vein-netted nose that drooped slightly to one side. His lips were loose and full, like the flabby meat of a cut peach, soft and wet. He'd been sitting there when I left a half-hour later.

Then, today, driving back from the funeral, a battered Chevy coupé started following me on Ogden Avenue and trailed me into the Loop. I didn't see it behind me on the Outer Drive but the traffic was heavy, the visibility poor through the rain. When I stopped for coffee at the Walgreen's in my office building, I found the man sitting at the counter eating a sundae piled high with whipped cream. It was the same man, or so I thought. His build seemed heavier, his nose smaller, but his lips flabbed at the whipped cream with that same sensual palp. It wasn't the same

man. It was my nerves. There were thousands of
battered Chevy's and thousands of gross, bestial
middle-aged men. It was my nerves.

His lips had caressed the stiff whipped cream, slid
over its foamy, oleaginous surface with a smacking,
kissing motion, his thick tongue lapping at the
yielding mass as though it were another mouth.
Nerves. God, all nerves.

When the last patient left I lit a cigarette fast,
inhaling the sulfur fumes from the match and cough-
ing. I had to get some rest. I was seeing things. Yet I
couldn't leave my practice. All over Chicago there
were ex-Army men like me struggling to build up
their list of patients. I had to stick with the game and
play it out. My whole future depended on founding a
secure practice. I couldn't allow myself to think of
anything else—not the rambling death-thoughts of
Colin, nor imaginary men in Chevy coupés, nor faces
at a funeral.

I had to stay with my practice through spring, the
worst time of all, and into summer. Then I might
manage a week in the country somewhere. Then it
would be safe. And then it would be too late. I would
be a nervous wreck. There had to be some middle
ground to this thing. If I knew someone with a
summer place where I could drive weekends, leave
Saturday night, return Monday morning. None of the
people I knew had summer places and if they did they
certainly wouldn't be opening them till June. And by
June . . .

At ten-thirty the next morning, my stomach gnaw-

ing away at half a cruller and two cups of coffee, I left
lawyer Nelson's office with the key to Colin's apartment in my pocket. I needed rest, I needed relaxation;
instead I was mucking around with his affairs again. I
was a fool.

Colin's apartment was small—two rooms—and
light. A chill rain fell outside the two windows he
had owned. The rooms looked bare, the cell of a
monastic. The living room had two plain pine chairs
and a couch that opened up into a rather narrow
double bed. Two walls were lined with bookcases.
The other room boasted a sink, a tiny refrigerator, a
kitchen table and some grimy cooking utensils. There
was a damp, heavy smell to the atmosphere, a dank-
ness that even the light from the windows couldn't
dispel. I wandered back into the living room and sat
down on the edge of the couch. What was I supposed
to do? What did anybody do in such a situation?

My gaze ran along the bookcase to a corner of the
room I'd neglected. There, in deep shadow, sat a
small, sturdy desk that must have been hand-carved
from oak about the time Lincoln was splitting rails. I
grasped its brass handles and pulled up; the whole
front broke away into three sections that slid up and
back with silent, well-constructed ease.

There were a series of pigeonholes, four flat
drawers and a shelf on which a dozen books were
stacked. I read off some of the titles haltingly. *Das
Walpurgisnacht im Westphalialeben,* by somebody named
H. Schlomgresser; *Magna Mater: A.D. LXXCCL,*
written by Guglielmo Faresi and Paulo Chiappetti;

three volumes of *The Golden Bough,* labeled "Adonis," "Attis" and "Osiris"; a weighty tome in green leather titled *Den Nederwelt von Renaissanischer Zeit;* and another, almost as thick, with mottled oil-slick coloring on the page ends, *La Messe de St. Secaire et Autres Messes Sombres,* by a man called, simply, Religieux.

My command of languages evaporated shortly after my student days, but what little I could translate of these titles gave me a curiously oppressive feeling, as though books like this should be kept on musty library shelves for busy worms, not in the empty apartments of dead men.

I rummaged through the drawers of the desk. Three of them were empty, but from the fourth I lifted out a small, paper-wrapped package. The paper was peculiarly thick, with the script initials E.V. worked into the design at regular intervals. I unwrapped the package and found a flat paper box inside, the kind jewelry sometimes comes in. Inside was cotton batting. I lifted it off.

Beneath lay a disc, black, grainy, about the size of a poker chip. It had a slight indentation on one edge and three little horns set along its circumference, small triangles that made the disc look something like a gear with most of its teeth missing.

It seemed to be made of some brittle substance that left minute black grains on my fingers. One edge of the disc had a piece broken out of it, a small arc chipped or cracked away. I held it a few inches from my eyes. There were four indentations around the place where the piece had been removed. The impressions of four small, exceedingly sharp human teeth were there. A chill darted across my shoulder blades.

I left Colin's apartment quickly and drove back along 71st Street, hardly watching the traffic around me. The Illinois Central tracks flanked me on my left and a train full of people rushed past. The sudden roar jolted me back into attention again. I glanced in my mirror. A battered Chevrolet coupé was half a block behind me. I put on speed and lost it. Nothing there now, only nerves. I began to think more coherently. The disc was a host like those used in Catholic communion. I knew enough to realize that a black host was for a black mass. The book title returned to me, *La Messe de St. Secaire et Autres Messes Sombres*. Great. Swell. What in God's name had Colin been fooling with?

As I pulled my car in the office parking space I ran my glance idly over the back doors of the shops in my building. I seemed to be trying to equate myself with reality, lash myself to the earth with the sharp physical bonds of sight. There was Terry's Bar and Grill, three empty beer kegs lying on the concrete loading platform. I needed contact with the world around me, sensual contact to hold my mind in its place. Morton's Shoes, the janitor brushing some rubble out the back door, his wide push broom shoving puffs of dust ahead of it. This was crazy. This folderol with black masses, this hiding away of black hosts in desk drawers, it was all crazy, unearthly. A plump young man pushed open the back door of the Eloise Vogue dress shop and stood there in the shelter of the eaves smoking a cigarette. Eloise Vogue . . . E.V.

The initials on the paper were E.V. A florid, arty kind of paper, the sort of wrapping that exclusive little shops used. I dashed in the front door of the store, my overcoat flapping wildly behind me. The place was empty, peopled only by manikins. A chime sounded somewhere as the door swung shut behind me and a carefully coifed salesgirl materialized from behind a curtain.

"Can I help you?"

"The . . ." I tried to catch my breath, ". . . is the manager in?"

"One moment, please." She disappeared behind the curtain and after a moment the plump young man I had seen smoking a cigarette entered. "Yes?"

This had to be good. It had to sound convincing and yet innocent. I decided to play around with the truth very slightly. "I need some help on a problem," I said finally. I took the box out of my pocket and laid it on the glass counter beside us. "Is that yours?"

He picked it up and casually glanced at it. "It's ours."

"Well, here's the problem. My . . . my wife got this in the mail. It had a . . . a brooch in it and no card. We'd like to find out who sent it. We think it was an oversight on their part and we feel sort of silly not being able to thank them."

The man nodded understandingly and his glasses caught the glint from hidden fluorescent lights near the ceiling. "If it's jewelry," he said disgustedly, "I can tell you who bought it like a flash. We've only carried the junk for five months now and it sells like Cadillacs. Still got most of it in stock." He sighed heavily and reached behind the counter for a flat ledger book. "*If* it was delivered," he added. "Sometimes the girls just make a slip out to 'cash' and let it go at that." He started at the back of the book and worked his way to the front slowly, perusing each page with care. "Mrs. J. L. Dalkin?" I shook my head. "What kind of brooch was it?"

"Well . . . it was sort of . . . sort of round and . . . You know."

He looked at me quizzically. "Sure it *was* a brooch?"

"I'm sure." I felt the skin near my ears grow warm. Was I blushing?

"Sure it wasn't a lavaliere or a pendant or a clip?"

"It was a brooch."

"Hmm." He paged backwards slowly. "Mrs. R. Corey?"

I shook my head again. This was probably a wild-goose chase. I didn't even know what name I wanted. Colin had either bought something here himself or else found the box some place. It wouldn't prove anything. "Was it an M. J. Pearson?" I shook my head. This was ridiculous. How would I recognize the name? "Miss C. Stokes?"

"No," I said. "Look, maybe we'd better forget about it."

He kept on paging. "Won't be long now," he said. "I'm getting into November of last year."

"Well, let's just skip it."

"Wait . . . was it Mrs. A. A. Rothman?"

"No. Let it go, okay?"

"Last one," he announced. "Couldn't have sold any before this. Miss A. Cowper. That ring a bell?"

ONE GASTRIC UPSET, one dog-bite, menopause, one queer fluttering above the spleen, *spermatorrhea* acute . . . four-fifteen and visiting hours finished.

I put away my stethoscope, folding it carefully and laying it gently in the top of my traveling kit. I rarely take such care with my stethoscope because of all my instruments it's best adapted to hard knocks, being mostly rubber with some steel. I took special care with it today. I took special care with everything this afternoon. I caught my receptionist looking strangely at me about three-thirty when I welcomed old man Harkness (queer fluttering above the spleen) with more joviality than I'd greeted a patient since my first day of practice. I finished putting the stethoscope away and approached the moment I had been waiting for all afternoon, the moment when I would take the box out of my pocket and think about it.

The taking out of it was relatively simple. My motor mechanisms still functioned smoothly. In due course of time the box was transferred from my pocket to the top of my desk where it lay, untouched for a long moment. This was going to be the hard part, not the looking at it but the thinking about it.

The girl with the black hair, black as wings, with the voice like a coiled steel whip, low and throbbing, with the face like a . . . I couldn't remember her face, only the staring of her eyes as I worked at the slash in her arm, only the dryness of her lips, the way she'd licked them and then couldn't talk, the gesture of licking them, the sharp little tongue, the soft, wet lips, the sharp, tiny teeth. They were features but they didn't add up to a total face. All I could remember were features, separate features without a frame of reference. The eyes, the mouth, the teeth, the voice, the teeth, the arm, the teeth.

Sharp, small. The piece bitten out of the host. The black host.

"A Mr. Morelle's waiting," the receptionist said.

I looked up at her, then back hastily to the box on my desk. "Morelle?"

"No file." She shrugged her shoulders. "Okay?" I nodded and she ushered in the new patient. He was a young man, very dapper. His glen-plaid suit was cut perfectly and his short-tabbed collar framed a wide Windsor knot I would have paid five dollars to learn the knack of tying. He was good-looking, with a purity and fineness of face that was close to effeminacy. He smiled graciously at me and sat down across the desk.

"Frankly, doctor, it's my insomnia."

I pumped him for symptoms and then went into

my insomnia lecture, about the devious causes of it and how hard it was to diagnose. He seemed to take it all in without really listening, as though he were preserving a kind of wall behind his soft façade, a wall against which my words were mere gusts of breeze. There was something about him that irritated me. "So that's the long and short of it," I concluded rather brusquely. "If you want to put yourself in my hands we might get to the bottom of it quite rapidly. Otherwise . . ."

"Oh, I think it's simpler than that," he said.

"Really?"

"Yes, it's my character."

This was a new angle. "I see."

"Doctor, the fact of the matter is, I'm a very fussy person. And very ambitious. Did you ever notice how those two traits seem to go hand in hand? I'm an . . ." his voice lowered deprecatingly, ". . . an insurance salesman. Doing very well. The fact is I married rather young, nice girl and all that, but it was a mistake. She's . . . well, she's rather careless about things, untidy. And I'm at the point now where I can go on to big things. *But*— " He lifted a thin, pink hand to me. "But a new job means entertaining, social responsibilities. Flo, my wife, can't help me. She'd absolutely squelch my chances." He sighed rather prettily. "That's the whole point. I fret about it so much that I can't sleep." He gave me a wide, handsome smile.

"What you need," I said sweetly, "isn't a doctor. You need a lawyer."

"Perhaps," he tactfully agreed. "Meanwhile, I've got insomnia."

I got his drift finally. "You want a prescription for sleeping pills."

His smile broadened winningly. "That's it."

I scribbled a quick prescription. "This isn't a barbiturate," I said "so you can't get in any trouble with it." I got up from my desk and went to the door. "You can settle with the receptionist."

He sat there for a moment and then got up. "I hope you're not offended."

"By no means. After all, you could get something almost as good as this without a prescription." I smiled, rather triumphant at seeing through his story.

"Really?" He didn't seem impressed. He shouldered his way past me delicately, negotiating the narrow space in the doorway without touching my body. As I closed the door I could hear him pass a few words with the receptionist. Then I heard the outer door shut. I opened my door and grinned at the receptionist.

"Sweet boy," she said. "I heard about his trouble."

"I don't think he sells many policies," I replied. "Go home."

She began working on her lips with a brush and color. "If a guy like that's married," she mumbled past the brush, "why aren't you?"

"Look what he's married to."

"You wouldn't have his luck, though." She gathered her belongings together and I helped her on with her coat.

I heard her high heels click away down the corridor, heard the elevator doors wheeze open and snap shut. I was alone in the office. It had probably been a mistake to send her home. I needed somebody to talk to. I was always making mistakes. This whole day had been a mistake from going to the lawyer all the way to checking the box with Eloise Vogue. If I had the power, I would have wiped it clean and started over again. I would have ignored the lawyer. That would have been that. I went into the inner office to get my coat. Nothing came to me in the way of new ideas. I was fresh out, wrung dry. The business of the black host, the tracing of it to Abbie, had thrown my brain into reverse, backing away madly from the facts of the matter. That, I told myself as I shouldered into my coat, was what Colin had warned: facts trap you.

I reached for the box with the host in it. It wasn't on my desk. I looked under, inside the drawers, in my pockets, in the outer office. It wasn't anywhere. It was gone.

My nice young man with the insomnia had it.

3 «◊» A Better Key

WHEN I BEGAN WRITING this narrative I had it in mind to let the whole affair unreel naturally, as it actually did, one thing following the other in sequence. The virtue of this plan, I thought, would be to lend the facts of the case a solid, material basis. Otherwise, the whole affair would sound somewhat like a suspense story, full of odd occurrences shrouded in mystery and the supernatural. Looking back over what I have written, I find I've been too factual, if anything, too engrossed in the petty details of my life and thoughts. And worse, I find that with all its detailed accuracy, it falls short of the full truth.

I had begun to live on two levels. One, the material level, based itself in my work, in the daily swabbing of cuts and percussing of chest cavities. It went along smoothly enough, despite the fact that I devoted only half a mind to it. The other, the inner level, danced and sprinted about every corner and wall of my experience, a shimmering, impish thing that revealed itself momentarily, then slipped away from me into some remote, shadowy cavern of the mind.

About a week after dapper Mr. Morelle, with his

imaginary insomnia, had stolen the host from my office, I thought of confiding the whole peculiar business to my receptionist.

It was about ten in the morning and we were sitting in Walgreen's drinking coffee. I looked at her closely. "What religion are you?" I asked.

"Huh?" Her eyes widened behind their gold-and-plastic glasses. "You're not getting choosy at this late date are you?"

"No, I just wanted to know."

She seemed to think it over for a moment. "Lutheran," she said. "Lutheran Evangelical."

I was disappointed. At least she could have been a Catholic. "Do they have hosts in the Lutheran ceremony?"

"Sure," she said slowly, eying me with suspicion, "at communion."

"Tell me about it, will you? The communion and all."

She took a sip of her coffee and leaned back on the counter stool. "I haven't been to one in fifteen years," she said, "but there's usually a sermon and such. Then you go down to the altar rail and get it."

"Describe it."

She shrugged her shoulders. "You kneel at the rail and the pastor comes along with the hosts on a silver dish. He puts one in your mouth and says, 'Take, eat, this is the body of Christ given for you.' Then he gives you wine in a little silver cup and says, 'Take, drink, this is the blood of Christ given for you.' Then the benediction and home you go. Give me a cigarette, will you?"

I gave her one and held a match to it. "Is that different from the Catholic ceremony?" I wanted to know.

"It *better* be," she said, smiling. "Actually, it's about the same. Lutherans don't have much originality."

"Ever been to a mass?"

"Are you crazy? My grandpa'd have a fit."

"Like to hear one?" I showed her the book I was carrying under my arm.

"You know," she said, blowing smoke in my face, "there's something going on in that weird mind of yours lately. Go ahead, read it."

"This isn't a regular mass," I said as I paged through to the spot I'd marked. "In fact, no good Catholic would be caught dead near it."

"Cut the build-up and read."

I found the place. "'Gascon peasants,'" I read, "'believe that to revenge themselves on their enemies, bad men will sometimes induce a priest to say a mass called the Mass of St. Secaire. Very few priests know this mass, and three-fourths of those who do know it would not say it for love or money. None but wicked priests dare to perform the gruesome ceremony and you may be sure that they will have a very heavy account to render for it at the last day.'"

"Cut the build-up," she repeated. "I'm dying."

"Okay." I found my place again. "'The Mass of St. Secaire may be said only in a ruined or deserted church, where owls mope and hoot, where bats flit in the gloaming, where gypsies lodge of nights, where toads squat under the desecrated altar. Thither the bad priest comes by night with his light o'love, and at the first stroke of eleven he begins to mumble the mass backwards and ends just as the clocks are knelling the midnight hour. His leman acts as clerk. The host he blesses is black and has three points; he consecrates no wine, but instead he drinks the water of a well into which the body of an unbaptized infant has been hung. He makes the sign of the cross, but it is on the ground and with his left foot. And many other things he does which no good Christian could look upon without being struck blind and deaf and dumb for the rest of his life. But the man for whom the mass is said withers away little by little and nobody can say what is the matter with him; even the doctors can make nothing of it. They do not know that he is slowly dying of the Mass of St. Secaire.'"

She took a long breath and let it out slowly. "What's the name of that book?"

"The Golden Bough," I said.

"What's a leman?"

"You pick the key-words," I responded. "It's an illicit mistress."

"Goodness." She pushed her fingers against her face in a gesture of mock embarrassment.

I sighed. She didn't seem to have any idea of what I was driving at. She was a good kid, lots of fun, but she didn't have the imagination of a slot machine. I put the book away and finished my coffee.

"And you think," she mused, "that somebody was saying that kind of mass for Colin Jones?"

Some of my coffee went down the wrong way. "So," I coughed, "you're wise."

"Too wise. You don't think that mumbo-jumbo works, do you?"

"No. That is, I don't think I do."

"Well, get smart, doctor. That kind of thing died out with knights in armor." She tapped her cigarette against the rim of the saucer with a knowing air, as though knocking off the dead ash of history.

This was the moment to tell her about the black host, about Morelle's theft. She had a good head on her shoulders. Together we might make something out of the evidence, something further than the dark suspicions I already had.

"I've said it before," she went on, "and I'll keep saying it till you fire me. I've worked with doctors long enough to know when a guy's going off the deep end. That's you, right on the edge. Why don't you, knock off for a week? I'll keep the racket going."

I laughed slightly. "You will, eh?" We went upstairs to the office.

The mail was lying in a disorderly pile below the letter slot of my outer door. She scooped it up and filed through it quickly. "Something from Nelson," she said, handing me a thick envelope. "Also two bills and two checks. Also do you want to buy a shortwave diathermy machine second-hand cheap? Army surplus, it says here."

I shook my head and took the lawyer's envelope into my inner office. He was a methodical man, all right. As Colin's lawyer, he had to keep tabs on the loose ends of the case, and as Colin's heir, I got the loose ends, neatly packed in an envelope. There was a bill, weeks past due, from a New York outfit that specialized in old and rare books, a post card from the U. of C. alumni association asking for a contri- bution, two announcements of political rallies that had already been held, a post card reporting the post- ponement of the bi-monthly meeting of the Indiana Dune-Dwellers Association, a circular from some odd religious sect, the deed to a plot of ground designated as Subdivision 32, Line 16, Portchester Development A-41, State of Indiana, and a Yale lock key.

Only two things interested me, the deed and the key. I called up Nelson and he explained that Colin had bought the land in1945 just after his discharge. During the first months of his new civilian life he'd built a little cottage there, a one-room affair designed and hammered together all by himself. "Do I get it?" I asked.

"Of course," he said. "I'll give you directions for finding the place."

Colin had gotten me into this mess, had driven me half-crazy with doubts and divisions of purpose. Now he left me the way out. I could get away now, drive up to the cottage and loaf or, when the weather warmed up, swim and lie around until I was back to normal again. Good old Colin. He came through finally, with a key I liked.

I picked up one of the post cards, the one from the Dune Dwellers, and felt a proprietary pride in it. I was now, by proxy, a member of this property association. I was a Babbitt, a *rentier,* a bourgeois. I was back to normalcy again, back in the comfortable, lazy, protective lap of the propertied class. I had leisure, no worry, nothing to do but snarl about taxes and curse the radicals. I would play this role to the hilt. I would be a Dune-Dweller in spades, doubled and redoubled.

That evening, the deed in my inside pocket radiating a warmth that was positively physical, I dined at Burton's, a restaurant the university people frequent. It was not yet six-thirty and the place was filling slowly. I had a semicircular corner seat to myself, the whole table with its tall center candle, a monarch's view of the restaurant and, turning very slightly the other way, a fine view of the street outside. The weather was spring, finally. April was at hand and, in Chicago, April showers usually come in March or May. Wonderful weather. I ordered onion soup and sirloin with garlic sauce, and let a Bushmills-and-soda smooth my palate into receptivity.

This was living. Good weather, good food, good whisky, good surroundings and a radiant frame of mind. It was almost ludicrous, the change that key and deed had made in me. The onion soup was winey, sharp, the cheese-crouton delicious. I turned my attention to the salad. When the steak came, I would be keyed up to a keen pitch of appreciation. *This* was living.

I would eat many such steaks. I would get a little fatter. I would go to concerts, take women out, get married, have children. I would enjoy my youth and build out of it great memories for the years after.

That was the only way to live and tonight, now, I would begin.

The steak arrived on an iron grill pan, still spitting and sizzling with a gay, busy splutter. The baked potato opened up its flaky goodness and embraced the huge square of butter. I transferred a hot, soft, limpid portion of steak to my plate and watched its brown goodness well up. I lowered my fork to it and felt the tines sink in with hardly any pressure at all. My knife pressed down, juice spurting beneath it as it surged gently through. Then I lifted a piece of the steak to my mouth.

"Why, it's Dr. Loomis," a woman's voice said.

The meat turned overpoweringly oily on my lips, a slimy, fleshy taste that revolted me. That voice. I looked up into Abbie Cowper's large black eyes.

"Don't you remember me?" She seemed amused at my expression of shock. She smiled warmly and raised her left arm into the level of the candlelight. The flickering illumination showed me eight fine transverse lines, light and almost invisible on the soft, rounded flesh of her forearm. I stood up. "Miss Cowper," I said, the words very hard to get out of my mouth.

"What a memory," she laughed. "It's been a year or more, hasn't it?"

I nodded silently. The stink of the bloody meat was nauseating me.

"And I was such a bad girl about the whole thing. I never did call you back." She smiled again, depreciating the sense of her words to the level of a gay childish prank.

Was this the same girl? She looked the same—almost—the same lean figure, the same soft arms, the long, black hair that enclosed her oval face like a shawl of night. But she was so different now. Her voice was gentle, appealing, none of that sergeant-major ring in it, only the soft, low-pitched, inviting voice of a beautiful woman.

"Oh," she said in sudden dismay, "I think you're angry with me."

I smoothed out the querulous expression on my face. "Not at all," I said hastily. "It's just . . . well, I remembered you but I didn't recognize you."

"We met under rather strained conditions" she said reassuringly. "Oh, I beg your pardon; I don't think you know Dr. Khereniev." She stepped sideways with a lithe movement that had nothing to do with her legs or feet.

Behind her, less clearly seen in the candlelight, was a short, stooped man of perhaps fifty, built along the oddly contrasting lines one sometimes finds in European intellectuals the face and neck thin to the point of emaciation, the hands birdlike, the limbs almost stunted in their narrowness, but the mid-section bloated, layers of abdominal fat padding the whole lower torso in startling contrast.

"Good evening, Dr. Loomis," he said, his voice rather high and mincing. I am not fortunate enough to be a medical doctor but we are, nevertheless, brothers under the sheep-skin." He smiled genially at what he evidently considered a good joke.

"Were . . . were you about to have dinner?" I asked, my heart working queerly.

"That is correct," he replied.

"Well, then . . ." I made a churning motion with my arm indicating the rest of the curved corner seat around me. "Would you like to join me?"

Abbie Cowper's eyes hooded slightly and then opened wide in what seemed like genuine friendliness. "Thank you," she murmured, her voice vibrant.

I looked quickly away from her. Some force inside me seemed to draw my eyes from her, as though wanting to shield me from too much sight of her. Khereniev helped her to the seat and then, plumping down with a sudden pounce, he began reading the menu, his lips puckering in and out.

I wondered where I had seen him before. He looked very familiar. His head was large and inclined to sweep back to a bulbous lobe at the back. Whether he once had much hair I couldn't tell, but his forehead was enormously high, slanting back over a strong frontal ridge to meet the three stringy tufts of hair often left when men with erstwhile widow's peaks go bald. His nose was small, hooked, predatory. It lanced out over a tense mouth, the upper lip thin and pale, the lower full, with an unhealthy redness to it. His neat, pointed chin was accentuated by a scraggy goatee that drooped where it should have bristled. Where had I seen him before? I remembered then. I'd never seen him. He simply looked like Leon Trotsky's twin brother.

"Dr. Khereniev is at the university," I heard Abbie's low voice say.

I turned to her, let my eyes flick momentarily past her, and then settled on Khereniev again. "That's my alma mater."

"So?" Khereniev's goatee showed signs of interest. "I am there in the capacity of an assistant professor in the Social Sciences." His words came out crisply in neat patches well suited for recording in a student's notebook. He eyed me rather like a gamecock waiting for provocation, daring me to contradict him.

"I'm afraid I haven't kept in touch with the university," I apologized.

"Hardly a sin," Abbie said comfortingly. What had happened to her voice? Where was that steely ring to it, that note of command and imperious authority? She sighed and caught her breath. "Since we're revealing ourselves," she said lightly, "I think you ought to know what I do, too."

"Come to think of it, I don't."

"You mean," she began archly, "you don't listen to *The Loves of Bridget Flynn?*"

"What?"

"Or perhaps you're too busy during the day. Haven't you ever heard *Captain Carefree, Boy Pilot?*"

"Is that who you are?"

"No, I'm Sandra Weir, the mysterious secret agent trying to get the plans from Captain Carefree. I'm also Bridget Flynn . . . and Mrs. McQuilsh on the Fusfeld Prepared Mustard show."

"A radio actress," I said finally.

"Marvelous," Khereniev murmured mockingly, his

cheeks flushed. "Inductive reasoning?"

I was about to reply in kind when Abbie spoke up again. "Jacques has an international reputation for being a cynic," she said. "He just has to keep his hand in."

"I know you," I burst out, "you're Jacques Khereniev!"

"The sheer reasoning power of this man astounds me," Khereniev's thin, dental voice responded.

"Gentlemen," Abbie cut in. She favored us both with a brilliant smile that gleamed invitingly in the soft candlelight. "You'd better finish your steak," she told me, "it looks exciting."

I glanced at the steak, at the piece still impaled on my fork which only a moment ago I had been so ready to put in my mouth. I completed the process. To my surprise it tasted good. The aroma was weaker but the taste was still full and rich. I chewed it contemplatively, marveling at the mental sources of physical enjoyment.

Khereniev ordered for both of them, sautéed livers for him and the sirloin rare for Abbie. "I'm famished," she confessed as the waitress brought the first course. "They had me rehearsing for a new show all afternoon and I haven't eaten since breakfast."

"It must be interesting work," I said between bites.

"It must seem that way to other people. I think it's a very easy way to make a living. Nothing more." She spooned at her onion soup and tasted it appreciatively.

"Tell me," I began, "does your arm give you any

trouble?"

"My arm?" The full curve of her delicious lips seemed to negate the very idea. "It's healed perfectly, which I lay entirely to your skill."

"What is this of the arm?" Khereniev wanted to know.

She showed it to him. "Bad cut," I mentioned in passing. His small brown eyes narrowed as he inspected the minute scars. He seemed to be seeing them for the first time. He bobbed his head with mouth down-drawn, as if commiserating with her.

"Lucky the knife was clean," I said without thinking.

"Knife?" Abbie's black eyes caught a strange flicker from the candle flame. I saw Khereniev pause in the middle of his salad, an oily leaf of romaine on his red lips.

"Now, Jacques." There was a warning note in her voice. She brushed the tip of his goatee with a careless finger. He bridled under the touch but took it without comment. "He's so intense," she went on to me. "He has to hold himself in all day long. When he leaves the university he's like a . . . like a jumping bean."

I stared at Khereniev. "Why do you have to hold yourself in?"

"It's nonsense," he snorted. "Abbie, you're impossible."

"Why shouldn't I tell Dr. Loomis?"

He made a face at his salad. "I seem always to be forced to remind you that I am not public property like some quaint museum exhibit."

Her face fell and she looked very solemn for a moment. "I didn't mean to offend," she said in a chastened tone.

Khereniev seemed to think better of it. He patted her on the arm. "You know, doctor," he said then, "women are given to man to destroy his peace of mind, then join together the pieces again."

I didn't like the proprietary ring to his voice and it must have showed. Abbie pushed away Khereniev's hand and turned her face from him. Khereniev seemed to take it very calmly, well in his stride. He returned to the salad and began chewing at the romaine. "In case your inductive reasoning is baffled," he said, "Miss Cowper is my godchild. Her father and I studied in Paris together." A curious expression came and went across his face and he attacked the salad with increased vigor.

There came over the conversation one of those lulls, one of those peculiar silences that occur, quite naturally, when three people are eating. Not when they are comparative strangers, it's true; still the whole thing was quite natural. Yet it wasn't. The silence was tense. I could feel it as if it were something in the air, like the moisture or thunder that precedes a spring storm. The byplay that had just passed had the flavor, as it was acted out, of something completely normal and innocent, but beyond this air of casualness there were undertones, subtleties, that disturbed me. Did they have to establish their relationship? Had I asked for it?

I felt a kind of excitement building up inside me, the exhilaration of doubt, the tension of uncertainty that seemed to underlie our smallest actions. Khereniev's massive, bulbous head bobbed up and down over his salad. Abbie, her long, thin fingers holding her spoon with a careless flexion, sat perfectly still watching the rich texture of the soup, her huge eyes round and unseeing, a half-smile disturbing the full curve of her mouth. In their preoccupation with the meal there was a kind of identity between them, as though they were puppets controlled by the same hand. Every time I glanced at Abbie, furtively, I felt the tension within me grow.

There were so many contradictions about her she was like a signpost to many countries, arrows indicating all points of the compass, mileages that differed, names that canceled each other out. Suddenly I began to realize that I had been fooling myself. I had been playing tin-badge detective. The results were ludicrous. They were false. There was no positive line of identification between Abbie and Colin. The line I had so brilliantly laid down from Colin's death to the black host to the black mass to Abbie was mere dream doodling. Any competent lawyer could tear it apart in five minutes, any cop prove another and different line without so much as lifting a flat foot. I knew that now. And if I would ever doubt it, there was always Abbie's warm dark face beside me, brushing away mystery and darkness, giving the lie direct to my crazy intuitions. It was a lesson to me. Never would I trust to intuition again; the results were abominably wrong.

I looked up and found myself gazing directly into Abbie's eyes. "You're pensive, Dr. Loomis." She smiled chidingly." I think you're still pouting over my arm. I think it rankles you professionally."

"Well, it was a nasty cut and I . . . How long did it take to heal?"

"Oh," she gestured airily, "a week or two. I didn't let it bother me."

"That's amazing." I tried to stop myself, but the question came out. "How did you get it?"

"Dr. Loomis," Khereniev's words had a heavy, brooding tone to them, "I have a peculiar idiosyncrasy common to men of sensibility. I dare say medical men construct a certain immunity to it, but the discussion of wounds and other pathological matters is particularly distasteful to me at the dinner table." He stabbed at a flat, pale green disc of cucumber, missed, stabbed again.

"Jacques . . ." Abbie's voice died away strangely. In that one word there were conflicting nuances, entreaty, cajolery, indecision, almost fear. The voice of a radio actress, I told myself; a wondrously flexible instrument.

"I don't mean to be direct," Khereniev went on brusquely, "but I abhor medical discussions."

"But, Jacques," Abbie said, "it's all past now."

"Possibly." He pushed the salad away from him and sat back stolidly. A quizzical expression unfolded across his mobile face. "To me," he said, "the human body is a tool, cleverly assembled and adjusted, but a tool nevertheless. To me it is the physical extension of the mind, created as shelter and implementation, but highly secondary to its controlling force. And if our minds were not equipped with a corporeal adjunct, it would be necessary to invent one. Personally, I would relish the challenge of creating a new and more efficient housing for the mind. The present one has many disadvantages."

"It grows old," I put in meaningfully. "And it dies."

His cruel little eyes, hooded by thick brows, glanced up at me for an instant, then sought the middle distance. "The medical reaction," he mused. "The equation to fact and experience. In 1910, in Petrograd, I saw a man flogged with the knout. The flogger was an expert who had perfected his stroke so that the lash of the knout shredded his victim's shoulders and back with each blow, while—and this was the art of his efficiency—while the hard, heavy knob of the knout landed each time, with a crushing precision, on that area of the victim's back directly over his kidneys. This takes the unerring master touch of the great artist, you understand. With each stroke the flesh was slashed, but also the kidneys were hammered, the skin above them lacerated. Tell me, doctor, how many such blows, each accurate to the fraction of a millimeter, would you say a man can bear?"

I was watching him, fascinated. "I don't know," I mumbled.

"Say twenty? Assume the man to be muscular, in excellent physical condition?"

"Please, Jacques." Abbie's voice had a queer tremor in its lower register.

"I really don't know," I managed to stammer.

"Let us say twenty." He chewed the number over for the moment and found it to his taste. "Well, then. This man absorbed fifty lashes of the knout. Fifty." He savored the word. "The flogger was not quite at the peak of his prowess and somewhere during the fifty he missed his vital spot a number of times. The man's backbone, that is to say, two or three of his vertebrae, were pulverized. Being hard, they crumbled. The kidneys, being soft, resisted rather well. And then do you know what was done to this man?" He let the idea of more, still *more* torture, sink in. "Then, doctor, they poured brandy and beer down his throat . . . to revive him, ostensibly. Are you familiar with the diuretic effect of such stimulants? The man lingered for several hours."

I broke the silence that followed by clearing my throat, twice. "Did I understand you to say," I asked, "that you disliked pathological conversation at the table?"

He leered at me and I caught sight of a broken, brownish row of teeth. "You've managed to spoil my appetite completely," Abbie said.

I stood up and pushed the table away from me into Khereniev's fat gut. "Let's get away from this," I told her.

"Yes," Khereniev whispered, "leave with the eminent medico, by all means." His stare was fixed on Abbie's face and in his eyes was an unspoken taunt.

Dare to leave, they mocked. Just try it.

I took hold of her arm, the left one with the suture scars on it, and pulled her up on her feet. "You're getting away from here,"I muttered in her ear.

"I . . . I don't . . ." Her voice faltered and stopped.

"Let go of her," Khereniev said lightly, as though I had picked up the wrong golf ball in a sand trap.

Beneath my fingers, Abbie's arm was cold, lifeless. Deep in her throat, below her vocal chords, a murmur, a kind of grating sob issued. I pressed her arm harder.

I saw her eyelids swing up, her eyes dart sideways at me, then fix on Khereniev. "I'm leaving, Jacques." She picked aimlessly, blindly, at her coat lying across the back of the seat. Her
nerveless fingers finally found a hold in it.

"You're not." Khereniev's voice was abruptly soft, unbelieving. It didn't sound like the same voice any more.

"Yes." She turned to me. "Let's go, please."

She pushed me slightly in the direction of the door. Khereniev got to his feet, panting slightly. "But, Abbie . . ." His short, hairy hand stretched out to her and I noticed that his fingernails were ragged and black beneath the rims. "Listen, Abbie . . ." I pulled out some bills from my pocket, laid them on the table and started for the door.

"Abbie, dear." It was Khereniev's voice, soft, unobtrusive behind us. "Abbie . . .?"

We walked out of Burton's, my fingers still tight on her arm.

The Outer Drive was filled with cars as I drove along it. I steered in and out of traffic, avoiding the knots of automobiles that seemed to pile up behind a slowly moving car. I was weaving in and out, my speed just a trifle faster than the other, just about ten miles faster than the speed liIp.it allowed. A million questions nagged at me. I wanted to spill them out, fast, to relieve their unbearable pressure. "What kind of hold has he got on you?" I burst out.

"Jacques?" She was huddled against the door of the car, her eyes empty, her expression meaningless. "He's an old friend."

"Old something, but not friend."

"No," she sighed, "he's a friend. Believe me." She lapsed into silence and her attitude demanded the same from me.

I wheeled the car in and around the curves, skirting other cars, pulling ahead of them, finding holes in traffic and plunging through. I managed to scrape past a cab that was going as fast as I and almost nicked hisrunningboard. I glanced back in the rearview mirror just in time to catch sight of a battered Chevy coupé twisting around the cab and speeding on. I jammed down the gas, lurched forward, picking up instant speed. A traffic light loomed ahead, green. I meant to make it. There was a cop at the intersection and I braked quickly, passed him, slammed left and picked up speed. Then I glanced back. The Chevy had never slackened its pace. It hurtled around the corner, whizzed past the startled cop and kept hard on my trail.

"What's wrong?" Abbie asked suddenly.

"There's a car following us."

"Car?" She sat up quickly and peered through the rear window.

"I don't see any car."

"Old Chevy coupé," I said.

"That means nothing to me," she said. "But there is some kind of car behind us."

I flicked a glance at the mirror. "That's a Chrysler," I muttered.

"Well, then . . . ?"

"So I've lost him," I said in irritation. I couldn't have lost him, but I had. "No harm there," I muttered.

"Why should someone follow you?" She sounded a bit frightened.

"I don't know." I didn't feel like telling her it was the same

car I'd seen behind me for the last two weeks, the gross man inside it almost a friendly face by now. I was suddenly very tired. I'd had a hard day. All kinds of things had happened. I'd been happy, shocked, eager, angry, frightened, all kinds of unsettling things. Now I was simply tired. I made another turn and drove slowly up the street she lived on, watching the house numbers pass. I felt washed out, fed up.

"You really do have a good memory," she said then. "It's the third building from the corner."

I nodded without speaking and pulled into the curb. "Home," I said dully.

She smiled at me, and the expression on her face showed both melancholy and liking. "Would you see me to the door?"

That forced a smile out of me. "Sure." We got out of the car.

"Let me apologize for Jacques," she said softly. "He's got a frightful temper."

"Sure, I know." I opened the outer door and edged toward the inner, the locked door.

"Shall I see you again?" She sounded hopeful, inviting.

"I hope so."

"Call me any morning," she said. "I'm usually home until noon."

She'd never sent Colin a black host. She was somebody else, another Abbie, a tall, full-breasted, night-haired girl whose voice ebbed and flowed like some dark and wondrous fluid, soft, enticing, yielding and moving. But I was crazy. I was going to ask her about Colin, like a fool. I straightened up and leaned forward toward her. Her eyes were on a level with my mouth but as she stood there, her head tilted back, I could have brought my lips down on her by simply moving forward those few delicious inches between us. But I was crazy.

"Say," I whispered; "I met a guy once who knew you."

The full, heavy lids of her eyes slid up, like a curtain unveiling hidden mysteries. "Can I call you Joe?" she asked then. In her mouth the name was soft and melodious. It sounded like the rustle of the night wind through leaves.

"Call me anything at all," I heard my own voice

saying. The distance between us was diminishing, like a tendril of smoke that the wind dissolves away. "He said you knew me," my voice mumbled hazily.

"Sure I know you," she said, "I know you so very, very much."

I think we kissed. Looking back on it now, I'm almost positive we did. It seems to me that it was unlike any other kiss where you meet a girl's lips and feel them beneath your own and sense the pressure of her body on yours. It wasn't like that. It was different. It was like falling down into a cloud, into a pool of something dark that envelops you and surges up around you and wipes all reality from you, I felt my mind swallow itself up and disappear in the darkness.

The next thing I recall clearly was sitting behind the wheel of my car and watching the façade of her apartment building. After a moment three windows lighted up. I remember nodding sagely, as though this proved something tremendous. I was telling myself to stop hanging around like a high school sophomore and leave, with dignity, like a thirty-two-year-old sophomore.

I remember steering the car slowly up the street toward the corner. And then I remember one thing more. I remember looking, idly, stupidly, at the battered old Chevy coupé sitting under the corner street lamp. The man inside was sitting quietly with his eyes closed. He was a heavy, gross-looking man. His nose was bulbous and lumpy. And his lips . . . his lips were as soft and as wet as a cut peach.

He hadn't followed me. He'd known where to go.

THE STREETS that took me home were probably as well populated and as busy as they ever were. But as far as I was concerned, they were empty of life. I imagine my eyes registered minor matters of distance; I got home safely. But as I sat huddled in my small apartment, coat and hat still on, a forgotten cigarette on my lips, I couldn't remember how I'd gotten home. I didn't even bother trying, I was too busy thinking of other things.

This man, this gross, bestial slob of a man with an obscene nose and moist faun's eyes that seemed constantly to be weeping . . . how had he known where to find me? Why had he been following me for two weeks; why had he followed me tonight; why did he lose me in traffic when he had successfully trailed me that far; why did he then go to my destination and wait? And finally, another why: why hadn't he followed me when I left Abbie's apartment?

What had there been about that kiss? I thought for a long while, trying to assemble my wits. One thing was clear: Abbie was innocent. She didn't know Colin. She couldn't possibly have gotten mixed up in whatever it was that surrounded Colin. That she knew people like Khereniev was unfortunate but meaningless. That my gross follower knew her address was a matter of mere chance. That the memory of her kiss, a kind of sensation halfway between a wound and a taste, was still with me proved nothing. She liked me, so she kissed me. She had a peculiar way of kissing and I wasn't used to it. So what?

When I reached this point in my reasoning, I got up, put away my hat and coat and picked up my mail. In it was a post card, a typewritten notice that: "Due to the weather, the Indiana Dune-Dwellers Association meeting is postponed at least one week. Call Dora or Sam Olson for a new time and place." A Samuel L. C. Olson was listed in the phone book but when I called I got, evidently, Dora.

"My name is Loomis," I said, "I'm a friend of Colin Jones."

"Oh yea-ess," she chirruped. "How is he these days?"

That stopped me, but only for a moment. "Then you haven't heard," I asked, "that he's dead?"

"Goodness no-o-o. Dead! Goodness." She seemed genuinely affected.

"I was his doctor," I went on, "and also his chief heir. He left me his cottage out in the Dunes and I was wondering if . . ."

"Why, I simply can't believe it," she exclaimed. "Colin Jones is dead."

"That's right."

"I'd never believe it," she let me know. "You're his doctor *and* his heir?" A carping note had crept into her voice, as though perhaps I'd poisoned him for his inheritance.

"That's right, Mrs. Olson. I was also his friend for many years."

"Dead." She was silent for a very long while. "Well, for goodness' sake, what did he die *of?*" she wanted to know.

"A head injury."

"Well . . . He never mentioned you to us, you know."

"I'm his legal heir, Mrs. Olson, extremely legal. I own his cottage and I've been receiving his mail. That's how I learned about the Dune-Dwellers."

"Receiving his mail?" Wasn't that, her tone hinted, a federal offense or something?

"That's right, Mrs. Olson." A threatening note had crept into my voice.

"Well, then," she said after a long pause, "I guess that makes it all right." I failed to follow the logic of this remark but it seemed to smooth over her ruffled mind immeasurably. She became downright chummy. "I suppose," she went on, "that you'll be wanting to join the Dune Dwellers. As a matter of fact, you're probably entitled to join just by taking over Mr. Jones' cottage. And that's all right with us. I mean, we'll have to vote on it, everything democratic of course, but if you're Mr. Jones' heir and that sort of thing, why, goodness, there won't be any trouble. Would you like to attend our next meeting? It's more or less a business meeting and not everybody'll be there but we planned it as a first-of-the-season Dune-warming as well, to officially open the season you understand, and I don't see any reason why you can't attend providing you can make it up there this weekend. I know how busy doctors are and, of course, I'm not the president, Sam is, but I'm the corresponding secretary and I'm sure it'll be quite all right."

I put my ear back to the receiver and cleared my throat. "I was planning to look at the cottage this Sunday anyway," I said.

"But I haven't even told you where we're meeting or anything else vital, as Sam says. Vital. Well, it's eight o'clock. If you come a bit late it'd be best so that I can break the news to the rest of the members. Nine would really be best. Let's make it nine."

"All right," I said patiently, "let's make it nine."

"Fine," she caroled. "Well, if that's all, I'll say goodbye and welcome to the Dune-Dwellers. Poor Mr. Jones. I know we'll have loads of fun, all of us, and it'll be just grand having a doctor among us. Goodbye."

"Uh, Mrs. Olson?"

"Yes?"

"The address. I haven't got the address."

"Aren't I the limit? Of course Sam says my tongue's got a self-oiling hinge, but I *do* carry on, don't I? The address."

"Yes."

"Certainly." She seemed to be thinking hard. "It's just after Stop 51 on the lake bus route. You ask anybody and they'll tell you. A little green-and-white cottage perched right up over the lake practically, and there isn't another place for nearly a mile. It's quite a lovely spot. Stop 51 on the bus route. They'll know."

"That's swell," I said calmly. "And the name?"

"The name?" She indulged in another whinny or whatever she used to indicate mirth. "I'm just awful," she confessed gaily. "It's Abbie Cowper. C-o-w-p-e-r."

4 «◊» **Just Like Mr. Profit**

THE SMALL TOWN of Michigan City is neither in Michigan nor is it a city. It happens to be in Indiana and, other than boasting one of the country's better-known cough drop factories, it has few claims to the title of city except that traffic on the main streets is regulated by stop lights.

It happens, however, to sit almost athwart two large federal highways, D.S. 12 and 20, arterial giants that feed all of the Northeast and industrial Michigan into the Middle West . . . and probably vice versa. Michigan City is the gateway to one of the most heavily concentrated vacation areas in the nation. I've never been up in the Catskills, nor have I sojourned among Florida's beach resorts, but for downright concentration of people I think the territory that begins in the Indiana Dunes and reaches northwest across Michigan's lakeland counties until it ends, politically speaking, at Detroit's Canadian border, takes the cake.

And yet, despite all this concentration of humanity in a bi-state area, there are long stretches of open farm-land here, empty regions where the dunes creep slowly toward the lake, where the grasses struggle against wind and sand, where the trees and houses tip precariously, then begin their long slide into the waters.

I used to know every town from the Chicago city limits east and north to Kalamazoo. My parents drove out to the Dunes every week during the summer months and I remember leaning out a side window of the car spelling off signboards as we shot past, breathing monoxide and hot metal as the traffic stalled, piled up, loosened and stalled again.

Now I was driving my own car and there were no kids in the back to watch the passing sights with wide children's eyes. There was no one in the back of my car to ask me about the big Lux plant with the five-story-high model of a Rinso box, or the meaty, musky smell of the Mazola factory, or the acrid, biting, nose-gnawing fumes of Whiting, Indiana, where Standard Oil and Sinclair perfume the air with the world's largest refineries. I remembered the questions of my childhood clearly. Why do the liquor signs say "Last Chance"? Why does the air smell so funny? Why are they advertising the Stevens Hotel way out here? What is that fiery stuff the railroad cars are dumping? How long is that freight boat? Will they lower the bridge soon? Why are those fires always burning?

The scab, the flaky rind that surrounds any huge urban concentration, was here in the Indiana border towns that huddled up against Chicago. Gary, Hammond, Whiting, Indiana Harbor, East Chicago . . . steel towns, oil towns, industrial towns, ore boats down from Duluth, tank cars speeding east, truck fleets trundling heavily out of company gates and nosing off across the nation . . .

And then, suddenly, open country. After Gary all the industry falls away, the scab drops off and the flesh of the country is seen again. Trees hem in the highways, side roads twist invitingly out of sight, signs advertise summer cottages, boat rentals, lakeside hotels. The city is gone and the country arrives.

There are men along the roadsides repainting Burma-Shave signs, little girls arranging pottery jugs on display counters, two state troopers on motor-cycles passing the time of day, ancient Ford trucks jogging along washboard roads with feed for cows. And everywhere, especially on a bright, intensely wonderful Sunday morning, everywhere, there are cars full of people, whole families with their dogs, young couples parked under wayside trees eating sandwiches, mothers pointing off to the left where their husbands should have driven.

There's something atavistic about a Sunday morning in late spring when the leaves have burst forth and all the grass is high in the fields and the plowed furrows show dark, crumbly earth, porous and rich between rows of plants that seem to grow skyward as you watch them. This is the threshold of summer, the brink, when the earth is gathering itself for the full, thrusting rush of its fertility under a warming, coaxing, all-pervasive sun.

I left Michigan City behind me and kept to the highway that runs along Lake Michigan's shore through summer colonies that seem to be small enti-ties complete unto themselves. Yet they border so closely on their neighbors that the average tourist would never know where one ended and another began without the help of roadside signs.

You Are Entering Morton Groves, a Restricted Suburban Area. No Peddlers Allowed. Also, the knowing tourist adds to himself, no Jews, Negroes, Italians, Mexicans or, very probably, anybody but white Protestants with Anglo-Saxon names. Half a mile out of friendly Morton Groves one passes a small, comfortably crowded general store whose window sign proclaims: *Kosher Delicacies Our Specialty.* Another mile, another sign: *Rocco's Place: Pizza Today.* The thoughtful tourist finds himself wondering where the most fun is to be had, where people get more out of life and then, quite unexpectedly, he catches sight of another sign as he speeds past: *Are You An American? Think, Act, Be American!*

About ten minutes after I'd passed that sign I found the first landmark Nelson had described to me—a huge estate bounded by iron fences, its long road barred by a high, ornate gate, its twenty-room villa set well back from the road in a mass of leafy trees. The place had been empty all winter and it showed signs of neglect. One of Al Capone's trusted lieutenants had built this estate in the twenties and now, resting after a more than active youth, he often repaired here in spring to seek solace in the eternals of nature.

Something struck a responsive chord in my mind, something about the beer baron's huge estate, crusted with filigree-and-iron lawn deer. Then I remembered what the spring morning with its familiar, long-forgotten scenes out of childhood had wiped from my mind. I remembered now about Abbie.

During the two days since I'd talked with the garrulous Mrs. Olson I had decided to face the fact that I was mixed up in something shady, something underhanded that had been left to me in Colin's legacy. Coupled with this was the realization that Abbie was irrevocably entangled in the whole affair. There was no point now in fooling myself like some youngster after his first kiss. She simply wasn't pure of mind. She wasn't above such goings-on. The tenuous line of identification I had traced by means of the wrapping paper was as strong and as rigid as a steel bar. She knew Colin. She was involved in his death.

Yet the sight of the gangster's estate stirred to mind a factor I had overlooked. There was an organization here; all the facts proved it. Yet why? What was it all about? People organized for *something*, not out of sheer whimsy. The Capone syndicate, for example, was out for money, power. Everybody knew it. Yet where was the money in this group of Abbie's? If, as I suspected, they had been involved in Colin's death . . . why? He had a small estate, but it had all gone to strangers, to a Montana cousin and to me.

There are only a certain limited number of motives in human conduct, only so many spurs that goad men to action. There are three: money, hunger, love; and all the rest, fame, power, security, satiety, revenge, all the rest are simply facets of the central trinity.

Then what was the spur that drove Abbie and her—

her associates onward? I knew very little about them, nothing more than a few obscure facts and some suspicions that seemed, on the face of them, absurd. Actually I knew only that there was an organization, undoubtedly called the Dune-Dwellers, but what they wanted or how they worked or why they were banded together I didn't know.

I slowed the car to a halt at the top of the high dune. This was the spot Nelson had mentioned. From it I could see for miles in every direction. To the south of me I saw rising smoke, a thick haze that blanketed Gary and Whiting. To the east a belt of pines and small trees locked the shifting, ever changing dune sands into some semblance of order. To the north, miles away, I could see a red-roofed mansion with a sparkling glass porte-cochere . . . either a millionaire's private home or, what was more probable, the house of some country club. To one side of me, now, a giant dune spurted up out of the sand and underbrush, a huge waterspout of a dune, like the central pillar of a tornado, towering and slim. How could mere sand have formed itself into such a barren, tapering tower? It stood apart from its smaller, gentler neighbors, a pariah-dune, different, aloof, almost of another race. What an odd, lofty thing—as though nature had revoked its laws to mold only this one, this up-shooting pillar of dust and dazzling, glittering silica, molded, as it were, out of subterranean fires.

I turned left, as per instructions, and steered the car along a narrow rutted road, half sand, half dune grass,

half—if you'll excuse the arithmetic—no road at all.
There hadn't been a car along it, evidently, since last
autumn.

There was a strange loneliness about this dune trail
with its commanding view. The road I was traveling
led due west toward the lake and I knew it would stop
at the crest of this dune, probably peter out into the
nothing from which it came. I saw no cottages, no
signs of life, no refuse along the way, no felled trees.
This was the place Colin had chosen for his country
retreat, miles from what civilization there was, miles
from any sign of human activity, surrounded by
woods and the sparse; spiky dune grasses that clung
precariously to a sliding, slipping base, edging ever
closer, as rain and wind did their work, down the
slope to the water. I wondered, vaguely, when nature
would tear down that great tower of sand I had seen.
I was watching the passing scene carefully, alert for
signs of life. It was only by such caution that I caught
sight of Colin's cottage, set back some hundred yards
from this excuse for a road, surrounded by tall pines
and shrubs, huddling close to the sand in an attitude
that cried out for isolation and solitude.

I pulled the car off the road and got out. A faint
suspicion of a path led down the slight incline to the
cottage door. I stopped a few yards before it and
surveyed the place, Colin's retreat, now mine. It was a
cozy affair, well designed in a severely functional style.
Colin had evidently sunk piles into the shifting sand
and built a strong foundation of roughhewn logs on
them. The log foundation rose upward to the level of

the two shuttered windows I could see, and was followed by white-painted clapboarding. The roof of the cottage was flat and slanted downward from the front for rain drainage. The eaves jutted out widely on all sides and cast heavy shadows on the clapboarding. I walked up the three steps, fitted my key to the lock and opened the door.

I was immediately struck by the freshness of the atmosphere, a surprising airiness that one seldom finds in shut-up rooms. I unfastened the window shutters and let the sun in. Up near the eaves was a reason for the freshness, ventilators whose slanted louvers let in air but kept out rain and light. There was no back door to the place, only a third window at the rear that was also shuttered from the inside, locked by a sturdy brass bolt. A low partition divided the cottage into large and small areas, the smaller filled with a sink, a primus range and cupboards, the larger furnished with a stove, two chairs and a single bed that looked suspiciously like an old Army cot. Nothing else. No pictures, no rugs, no curtains. Yet there was one thing more, I saw now.

Over the doorway, unnoticed as I entered, was a branch of mistletoe. It was nailed to the rough wood wall, a large branch of the stuff, its paired leaves still thick and green, its waxy berry clusters spotted but fresh. I looked at it wonderingly for a moment and then smiled. What kind of kissing games had Colin been enjoying here? Then I looked at the windows and the ventilators. Each of them had a sprig of mistletoe over them, some of the branches still bright and fresh, some beginning now to fade into a bright golden hue. At the base of one window I stooped to pick up a small white berry that had dropped off. What a curious decorating scheme.

I tossed my overnight bag on the cot and began a more thorough inspection tour. In the kitchen cupboards I found a half-full box of salt and an empty pepper shaker, an unopened can of beans, a kerosene lantern and a box of sodium fluoride powder for killing ants. Under the cot in the main room was a large wooden Army footlocker without a lock. Inside were only two things—a pair of 7x50 Zeiss night binoculars and a .22 caliber Colt Woodsman pistol, empty.

I picked up the binoculars. They were a large, powerfully built pair, heavy and massive, their leather covering rubbed away from long usage. I stepped to the front windows and trained the glasses out across the dunes. The sunlight played on trees and grass; distant pines were brought into instant, sharp focus that almost blinded me. These were night glasses, engineered to pick up faint details in darkness. The harsh brilliance of sunlight was too much for my eyes to accommodate all at once. I squinted and felt my pupils contract hastily.

I swept the binoculars around in a half circle, surveying the landscape. I could see my car, the door handle glinting brightly, the air above the engine cowling warped and shimmering with rising heat currents. I moved my glasses past the car and up slightly, focusing their delicate mechanism. They caught sight of another cottage, almost invisible behind a screen of pines and poplars. As I watched, a man came out of the foliage and set a ladder against the wall. He mounted it with a window screen in his hands and began nailing the screen into a window frame. He was a tallish man, sparsely built, in his tan pants and undershirt, a pink bald spot gleaming out from his tuft of gray hairs like an egg bedded in straw.

As I turned from the window I remembered the .22 pistol. It was a small caliber for anything but target practice or, at the very most, bird hunting. I had never remembered Colin as a marksman, nor interested in such matters. There was no ammunition for the gun anywhere in the cabin. I put it back in the footlocker and shoved the whole thing under the cot. I looked at my watch. Noon. I got two sandwiches out of my overnight bag, washed them down with the iced tea in my thermos and settled back on the cot to enjoy the very thing I'd driven all this distance for . . . sleep.

A tarry smell seeped down from the roof over me, warmed and spread by the intense sunshine. Somewhere two birds called to each other. A soughing, whispering sound came from the trees outside. I had the momentary thought that all this sunlight and all this wonderful country air shouldn't be wasted by a tired medic with thoughts only of sleep. The thought flicked past me, returned once again to peck at my mind, then fluttered off with a sound like a bird flitting from one tree to another. I smiled at it as it disappeared into the soft, deep green of . . .

IT WAS DARK outside and my shirt felt wet and clammy under my armpits. I sat up on the cot and tried to read the dial of my watch. I struck a match. Eight-fifteen. I stumbled to my feet, yawning and trying to work up saliva in my dry, evil-tasting mouth. I felt my way into the little room, found the lantern and jiggled it. Something sloshed around inside. I raised the glass shade and lit the wick, then turned it down. Perfect. I wondered, in my muddled fashion, whether a newfangled electric light, dependent on power lines and fuses and wiring, could have come to life so instantly after a winter of disuse. I held the lantern over my head and returned to the front room.

The night outside my windows was black, in-pressing, full of movement. There was a shimmering in the darkness behind the glass, a wavering, fluttering movement that seemed as though the night was some huge, oily sea monster, trembling and oozing in at me. I pulled the shutters to and bolted them. There was a definite chill in the air; the cabin would make cold sleeping tonight unless I bundled up securely.

Something bright caught my eye then and I looked

up above the shuttered window. In the light from the lantern a fading sprig of mistletoe, yellow and sere in the daylight, now glowed brightly, almost as though afire with an inner flame. I pushed my fingers through my hair, took the lantern and left the cabin, locking it behind me. I started the car, jockeyed it around and drove off in the direction I had come. Mrs. Olson's information was easy to follow. I found the little green-and-white cottage perched right up over the lake. It was a low-slung one-story affair with a back balcony that jutted out into the air in *echt* modern style. The mailbox at the roadside said Cowper. I turned in the drive and parked the car behind an old Hudson sedan.

The cabin's windows were brightly lit. I could hear people talking and laughing. My thumb on the door-bell summoned forth a peal of low-pitched chimes, closely followed by high-heeled footsteps and Abbie, opening wide the door.

"We were afraid you'd lost the way," she said. "Welcome." She sounded sincere enough, I thought. I followed her inside.

"This must be Dr. Loomis," a woman's familiar voice shrilled. I saw a thin, wiry little woman, hen-like and inquisitive, whose sharp black eyes surveyed me in a series of swift, pecking jerks. "I'm Dora Olson," she explained unnecessarily. "And this is my husband Sam. Sam, meet Dr. Loomis. He was a very good friend of poor Mr. Jones and he's got the cottage now. Isn't that nice?"

I shook hands with the man I'd watched through

the binoculars, still sparse and gaunt despite the rough-textured jacket he was wearing. "Glad to welcome you," he mumbled. Evidently long association with Dora had robbed him of his full powers of speech. I could understand that.

"And this is Maida Teufler," Abbie said. I shook the proffered hand of a squat, dumpy woman of perhaps forty or less. Her short blonde hair was set in rigid waves and her moon-face was pink, scrubbed.

"A pleasure, doctor," she murmured. The accent was heavily Teutonic and the mouth that uttered it was a hard one, as though long years of coping with gutturals had whittled it and firmed it down to a double line of steel.

"And this," Abbie concluded, "is Jason Flye."

"Greetings," Flye said, and giggled peculiarly. He uncoiled his lean body from a couch and stood erect to shake hands. He was so impeccably clad that I suddenly felt like a brake-man in from Butte with whisky on my breath. He was wearing a bright navy blue jacket with flat silver buttons, trousers of dark gray flannel and blue-topped tennis shoes with white rubber soles more than an inch thick. Under the jacket was a shirt of some wondrously soft material. His mouth was set in a rigid, mechanical smile, exactly four teeth showing white against pink.

I shook hands. His palm was moist and his fingers trembled slightly, yet with a kind of basic depth to the tremor that bespeaks not an organic disturbance but rather something of the mind. I glanced at his face but there was almost nothing to see there that might reveal the source of that fine, steady tremor. His face was rather thin and topped by crisp brown hair in a crew cut. If he'd been five years younger he would have spelled college to me, but he was very nearly my age. And that tremor . . .

I found myself musing, his hand still in mine. He seemed curiously tensed-up, not ill-at-ease, but fundamentally hyper-tense, as though he were high explosive waiting for the snap of a percussion cap. "Hope you'll be happy here," he said abruptly. I let go of his hand. It dropped listlessly to his side and he giggled again, a strangely disturbing sound, like sewer water gurgling through some hidden opening deep inside the earth. Abbie led me to the couch and we sat down.

"How do you like Colin's cottage?" she asked.

"Hardy but nice," I replied.

"We were all very saddened to hear of his death." Her face went sad to suit the words. "But I'm very glad you're here to take his place. You know," she caught her breath for a moment, "it was quite a pleasant surprise when Dora told me you were joining us. I didn't dream you knew Colin."

"Very well," I said heavily. She didn't seem to notice my tone.

"And you are a medical doctor?" Maida Teufler asked then. I turned to find her seated beside me on the long couch. I hadn't heard her come over and I hadn't felt her sit down. Her voice came as a surprise to me and I think I might have jumped slightly.

"That's right," I said after a moment.

"We are so isolated here," she went on placidly. "It is good to have a doctor." She nodded sagely. "Is lonely but beautiful," she said. "I love it. My work keeps me inside all the year and when comes summer, I love this place."

"Maida's very talented:" Abbie put in. "She's a handicrafts instructor."

"*Ach.*" The woman laughed depreciatingly. "You, Abbie. I only teach knitting, small embroidery and quilting. It is nice, but I like better the outdoors. In Germany," she went on quickly, "there is always the forest for vacation, but seldom so close to the cities. I . . . I love this place."

I looked up in time to catch Dora Olson eying our group apprehensively, as though unhappy at not sharing in some precious talk. "Will you get up here often?" she asked me.

I thought for a moment and in that time I watched Jason Flye's face sharpen to trembling intensity. "Only weekends, I'm afraid."

Flye sat back jerkily on the couch and seemed to merge into its overstuffed cushions. As he did so there was a yowl, an animal shriek of terror. I jumped up. Maida let out a gasp and Dora Olson, her button eyes bright, whirled in her chair. From behind Jason's thin body the head of a cat emerged. I heard Abbie's throaty laugh and saw her scramble up, dash over and lift the cat in her arms.

It was a small black kitten, its furry breast marked with a slash of white beneath the throat. Abbie fondled it to her, cradling it in her arms. "Naughty puss," she crooned. "Did he hurt you?" The cat lashed a paw at her in play, then settled back comfortably and began licking its fur.

The room was lit from three sources: a brass kerosene lamp on the table, another one pendant from the ceiling, and a small fire burning on the hearth. In that light I saw Abbie clearly for the first time. She was wearing a long white dress of some nubby material whose texture changed constantly in the unsteady illumination. Her hair was let down to its full length without ribbons or combs and it fell in long black waves over her shoulders onto the white cloth. It was, I realized, the precise color of the kitten's fur. Abbie's face seemed young and vibrant in this light, the face of the girl I had dined with in Burton's, a young girl warm and alive, sharing her love now with this ridiculous little kitten. No one said anything for a long moment. Then Jason Flye giggled again and I glanced at his face. Behind the set smile on his lips, behind the slightly glazed eyes as he stared at Abbie, was a look of devotion, an unnatural, imbalanced kind of adoration. It reminded me of the face of a fakir I had seen once. He had been plunging the filthy, burred hook of an old fish-scaling knee into his forearm at the time. His eyes had looked as Flye's did now.

Flye seemed to sense me watching him. Turning away, he cleared his throat. "Mother and child," he said lightly and giggled again.

Everyone laughed politely. I watched Flye, hoping to see that fanatic look on his face again. His voice betrayed some of the tremor inside him at times. It

was edgy and faintly British, but there was an uneven-
ness to it, as though it were produced under incredible tension. Again, without conscious effort, the
memory of the fakir returned to me. His voice had
been something like Flye's, thin and brittle, with
strange rhythms to it as he plunged the knife again
and again into his arm. His face, too, had been set in a
mechanical smile, a grin of masochistic fervor and
devotion.

"Did I interrupt the meeting?" I asked Sam Olson,
feeling a desire to evoke words from his immobile
mouth.

"Not at all," his wife assured me before he had
gotten his lips in motion. "We're waiting for Mr.
Kelk. He's got the bylaws with him and we can't do
anything till he comes. He's the treasurer but somehow he holds the bylaws too although I never knew
quite why since I'm the secretary and I should be the
one to have them. Don't you think so, doctor?"

I was about to say something, I hadn't decided
what, when Abbie cut in and spared me the trouble.
"He probably didn't make the right train," she told
Dora Olson. "He's probably on the nine-five."

"As long as we have to wait for Kelk," Jason
spoke up suddenly, "how about a little refreshment? I
brought a fifth of—"

"Not now, Jay," Abbie cut in hastily. She smiled at
him and then at Dora Olson. "Perhaps some lemon-
ade? Or is it too chilly? Some nice hot tea?"

"Tea would be fine," Dora agreed. "I don't understand how young people can poison their stomachs

and blight their health with hard liquor. Do you, doctor?"

"Well . . ."

"Neither Sam nor I touch the stuff," she assured me, "and two healthier people you never saw, for our ages, of course, but we manage to keep fit and have fun without alcohol. Isn't that so, Sam?"

"What?" Sam lifted his large pale eyes to her. He had been in another world. "Sure thing," he said and I knew he hadn't the slightest idea of what he was agreeing to.

"Then we'll have tea," Abbie said decisively. She put down the kitten and was starting for the back of the cottage when Maida got to her feet. Again I didn't know it until I saw her, erect and speaking.

"No, Abbie," she said. "I make tea. You are hostess, no?" She gave the girl a gentle shove and disappeared into the other room.

Abbie knelt by the fireplace and sat there, legs tucked out of sight, the firelight picking out strands of brightness in her hair. "Maida's been busy all day," she said softly. "She baked two lovely *linzertorte* this afternoon, absolutely airy, like clouds, and so delicious."

"*Torten*," Jason corrected her. "Plural ends in 'n.'" He giggled softly.

"Full of nuts and strawberry preserves," Abbie went on without noticing. "I could absolutely stuff myself with them."

"We'd better eat them before Kelk comes," Jason sighed.

"I just love good food," Dora Olson said, stroking her oar into the conversation. "I don't bake German pastries but I *do* have a recipe for Swedish meatballs Sam's mother gave me and I must say they're delicious. Of course they take a lot of *things,* spices and what-all, and they're a lot of trouble to make but what I say is, life is short and you have to get some pleasure out of it. It's a problem knowing whether to spend your time making good *food* or not. Now I love good food but I do think some people make gods of their stomachs. Sam used to, always moaning about how his mother cooked, but I say food isn't all. It's *some,* but it isn't all. Don't you agree, Dr. Loomis?"

"Some people overeat," I said, committing myself to nothing.

"Dig their graves with their teeth," Dora latched on neatly. "An uncle of Sam's died that way, over-eating, all that *rich* Swedish food, y'know, it's enough to put five *pounds* on you with every bite. Just dug his grave with his teeth. You know what I mean."

I glanced at Abbie, hoping for rescue, but she was leaning back the fire warming her shoulders, her eyes closed. Jason was watching her with an interest close to adoration. "I know what you mean," I said then.

"That reminds me of poor Mr. Jones," Dora went on. "Now there was a man who *didn't* eat enough, not half enough. He'd take a bit of meat and a teensy potato and call it quits. Now I don't call *that* eating, not for a man his size."

"At least," I said idly, "he didn't dig his grave with his teeth."

"Well, maybe not." She seemed a bit disheartened by this observation. "Just what did he die of?" she pounced.

I waited for a moment, watching Abbie's face. She was so relaxed that I thought she might be asleep. But she shifted her body slightly to get closer to the fire. No response. I said: "Head injury."

"Well, yes, I know," Dora assured me, "but what *from* is what I'm interested in."

"I'm sure Dr. Loomis would rather spare us the details," Jason interrupted with jerky quickness.

"But Mr. Jones was a *friend*," Dora persisted. "I'd really like to know because he was . . . well, sort of one of the family. And I didn't even know he'd died. I felt *simply* awful not being able to go to his funeral."

"Well then" I said "there's nothing much to tell. He had acute head pains that nothing, neither narcosis nor anesthesia, could relieve."

"Really?" Her voice positively gobbled up my information.

"We tried everything, we ran down a thousand diagnoses, but in the end the thing escaped us. If it happened again I still wouldn't know what to do with it."

"How dreadful," Dora gasped. "Do you *know* something?"

She paused impressively.

I felt a curious squeeze inside my chest. Something in her voice suddenly fascinated me. "What?"

"That sounds *just* like Mr. Profit," she said.

My eyes were on her, watching closely, but I

thought I caught a flicker of movement from the fireplace. "Who's Mr. Profit?" I asked.

"Why, he used to be a Dune-Dweller," she explained. "He lived in Mr. Kelk's cottage just down the beach a ways. Well, as I was saying, he died two years ago in exactly the same way."

"I doubt it," I said. "This was unheard of in the medical profession."

"But Mr. Profit didn't *have* a doctor," she told me. "He just pined away and died, just *exactly* like poor Mr. Jones. Headaches and all. Same thing."

That clutching feeling was in my chest, harder. "When was this?"

"Just after the war," she said. "It was . . . well, he *got* sick in—"

Abbie stood up suddenly before the fireplace. The kitten pawed at her high-heeled sandals. "It's very warm in here, I think." She smiled at me. "How'd you like a guided tour of the Dunes?"

"Now?"

"No better time." She took hold of my arm and lifted it. "I'm an excellent guide." Jason blinked and looked quickly away
from her.

"Well . . . what about the meeting?"

"Oh, Mr. Kelk won't be here for a while. If he took the nine-five we've got half an hour before he arrives."

"Okay," I said, rising. I stood there, waiting for more of the gathering to join us but no one made a move to leave. Abbie, still holding my arm, led me out the front door and along the path . . .

"Will they vote on me while you've got me out?" I asked idly.

"While I've . . . ?" She laughed gaily. "Lord, but you're suspicious. Come on."

The night was still dark but the stars spread across the sky in a wide belt that I hadn't seen in too long, the full display that smoky city air cuts down to a frugal twinkle. Yet despite their brilliance the stars were cold, distant, aloof. They hovered high above us and seemed to be shining for somebody else, not us, not me. I felt strangely sad. Abbie had so obviously drawn me away before I learned about Mr. Profit. A low wind hummed in the foliage along the deserted road and swept little spirals of sand across the empty concrete strip. It seemed like a ghost highway, shimmering with a phosphorescence as of some dead, decaying thing. The roar of the surf was a muted hushing sound behind us as we walked along the road and cut up over the crest of a low dune. I heard a hooting noise in the trees ahead of us, a kind of hollow whistling, as of a flute blowing hollow and low.

"What's that?"

"Owls," she whispered. She had hold of my hand and was walking slightly ahead of me, finding it hard going in the loose sand. "I'm going to take off my shoes," she said. "Hold onto me, will you?" She braced herself on my arm and removed the thin-strapped sandals.

"Won't you be too cold?"

"Without these?" She laughed and gave the shoes to me, mere scraps of leather. "Put them in your pocket, will you?" She took my hand again and led the way.

She seemed to be much more comfortable without the shoes. I watched the curve of her back, bright and shining in the night, as she walked before me, the shifting play of the white fabric that swathed her hips rising and falling firmly around her as she traversed the sandy path. The light was uncertain, dim, and the only thing I could clearly see was her body, shifting and twisting in the night. It was not corporeal; it was more like the wisp of smoke that hovers over a fire, or the steam from some hot liquid that rises in an ever-changing plume, swirling and swaying from side to side.

"Where are we going?" I whispered, wondering then why I was whispering.

She stopped and turned toward me. "You never ask a guide where he's taking you," she said. She took a deep breath and let it out slowly, in a kind of sigh. "It was so oppressive in the cabin. Don't you feel something stirring and grand about the night?"

"It's . . . it's a bit eerie." I said after a moment. "I mean, there seems to be movement all about us, yet I can't see anything move."

"It's the wind," she said. "The wind is moving."

"I know. But it's eerie."

She chuckled and the throaty sound evoked a strange tenseness in me. "You're too impressionable," she murmured. "We'll just go on a little way and then we'll stop."

"Where? I mean, we can't just stop, not in the middle of the woods."

"You're impossible," she said. "Weren't you ever a boy scout?"

"Nope. And you don't look like a campfire girl either."

"Ah, but I am. I'm a campfire girl from way, way back." She squeezed my hand and started walking again.

I was watching her closely now, my only point of orientation in this moving blackness. I could see, just beneath the low hem of her dress, which almost touched the sand, the faint shape of her foot as it drew back, then disappeared to go forward again. High overhead, screened by the trees, I caught glimpses of the stars. We were walking down a slight incline but all I could see was the shimmering white shape of her body before me. Suddenly she stopped and turned to me. Stars caught highlights in her large dark eyes. "End of the line," she said.

"Where?"

"Have you the key? It's your cabin, of course."

"The cabin!" Suddenly I understood. She had led me through the woods, along a trail I probably couldn't have found in broad daylight, right to the door of my cabin . . . Collin's cabin. "But it's further than this," I heard myself say in disbelief.

"By car, following the roads. It's only a few minutes overland."

"Oh." I fumbled for the key and she guided me

forward to the door. I was within a foot of it before I finally saw it distinctly. I unlocked it. "Welcome," I said, trying to sound slightly sardonic. It didn't work.

She went inside ahead of me and immediately I heard her gasp a quick nervous intake of air that echoed shock or amazement. She stepped back with a convulsive movement. "It's cold in there" she muttered, "deathly cold."

"What?" I walked in past her. The cabin had a certain clamminess in its atmosphere, but it wasn't very cold. Not much colder than the out-of-doors had been. "Nonsense," I said. "Come on in."

"No." She drew back from the doorway and I could see her eyes bright and luminous with star reflections. "Can't you start a fire in the stove?"

So she knew there was a stove. "No wood," I said. "I'd have to rustle some up and in all this dark it'd take a year."

"Just a little fire?" There was a pleading, plaintive note in her voice, a small, little girl's voice. "Don't you have a few bits of wood . . . or branches inside?"

"You really want a fire?"

"I do, Joe. Remember?" Her voice went soft and appealing, "I'm the original campfire girl from way, way back."

I smiled at her in the darkness. "Okay," I said, remembering the mistletoe sprigs. "I'll start you a fire, a very special one too." I felt around in the dark for the branch over the door. "Come on in while I get it started."

"No, I'll wait."

"Well . . . okay." I found the branches and tore them down, felt my way to the little cast-iron stove and shoved the mistletoe inside. It lit quickly from my match, sending out puffs of thick gray smoke. "It's started," I called. "Come on in."

"I *am* in."

I looked up startled. Her voice had come from only a few feet behind me and as I turned to see her she was standing, tall and slim in the doorway, her eyes fixed on me, the fire picking hard, brilliant lights in them. There was a distinct rim of white around each iris. I looked away nervously. "I'll get some more fuel," I said. I reached up in the darkness and plucked a mistletoe sprig from one of the windows. "You'll never guess what it is," I said, trying to sound light and bantering. I brought it from behind my back and pushed it toward her. "Mistletoe," I said and laughed.

Her eyes went wide and wild as she recoiled. "Put it in the fire!" she hissed.

"It's just mistletoe."

"I said burn it!" She had taken a step back. *"Burn* it!"

"Okay," I said rather testily. "Sure." I threw it in the fire and watched the feeble flames lick at it. When I turned around I found her sitting on the edge of the cot, leaning back on her arms, her glance intent on the fire, her mouth open as though listening to a far-off sound, something faint and distant.

"That's much better," she sighed in relief. "Thanks awfully."

"Sure. What's a little mistletoe between friends . . .

as long as it isn't Christmas, of course."

"Christmas?" She looked at me blankly. "I don't . . . Oh, Christmas! Oh yes, kissing."

Yes, I thought suddenly, and it took you long enough to remember it. Was there something else about mistletoe that I didn't know?

"You seem to be allergic to the stuff," I said.

"Kissing?"

"No." I grinned. "Mistletoe."

She looked away for a moment. "I'm not allergic to kissing, though."

"Oh." I sat down next to her on the cot.

Her arms came up from behind her and went around my body, pulling me down as we both sank back on the cot. I felt her lips tremble momentarily and then open. It was the same as the time before, exactly the same. It brought the blood to my head with a thrumming rush, as though I were suspended upside down miles above the crust of the earth, dangling in space while the winds howled and shrieked past me in a constant, ceaseless, never-ending, roaring rush. My body had no weight, floated, was buoyed up in the viscous fluid of my dreams . . .

"JOE." It was her voice. "Joe?" Her breath had a spiciness to it, a tingling flavor that stirred me.

"Yes?"

"You don't say anything."

"Don't feel like it."

I could feel her throat pulse with a chuckle. "I'll have to be more careful of you," I heard her say.

"Yeah." I opened my eyes. I was back in the cabin. "Wear asbestos or something."

"I warned you."

"I know," I sighed. "Campfire girl from way, way back. And no mistletoe."

Her eyelids quivered open. "What?"

"You know . . . Christmas."

"Oh, that." She looked past my head at the fire in the stove. I was surprised to find it still burning, the sprigs of mistletoe hardly consumed. By my reckoning, hours, days must have passed. "You know," she said in a low voice, "Christmas used to be horrible for me."

"Horrible?"

"Yes, I-I never told you about me, did I? I come from North Dakota. My mother was Norwegian and my father was Welsh."

"Welsh?" I seemed to remember something important about the Welsh but I couldn't place it at the moment.

"Christmas was so much different for me than for the rest of the kids. We lived in a little town near Fargo and my dad had a farm . . . wheat. At Christmas all the other kids had parties and got gifts. They had trees with lights and they sang carols and . . . but I was never allowed any of that."

"Then what'd you do at Christmas?"

She thought about it for a long time. "You know something," she said at last, "I don't remember. Whenever I try to bring back the old days, there's kind of a blank that shuts down over my mind. I can't remember Christmas at all. I remember some things, little things, but the big events, the things a child cherishes, I can't remember."

"None of them?"

"No, it's as if I started living when I left home. My parents died, I remember that, and everything after is very clear. The way a life should be. But nothing before."

"It's nice," I said, "to forget things once in a while. Not everything is worth remembering, or good to remember either."

She sighed and her eyes were fixed on the fire with a hooded, distant gaze. "I always have the feeling" she said slowly "that each new thing I do is going to add to me. Do you understand? I feel like a . . . like a piece of paper with the top torn off, the beginning, and I have to live the rest of my life so that good important things will fill out the rest of the page . . . to make up for the part that's torn away."

"That's a wonderful ambition."

She shook her head. "How can anybody be good and important when they have no foundation? I . . . I began to live without a childhood, without an adolescence almost."

"That's too—"

"No it's not," she cut in suddenly. "I have the

feeling that if I could remember, I wouldn't like it at all. There's something . . . something peculiar and frightening about my childhood and I think that's why I can't recall it."

Her voice was strangely empty in that instant. "That's all past," she whispered, "and this is right now. Isn't it?"

"That's what I say."

"Say it some more," she told me harshly, her voice urgent and compelling. Tell me *all* about it." She lifted her face to me and I felt her mouth crush against mine with a hard, twisting movement. Sharp needles of pain shot through my lower lip. She was biting me, biting me, her teeth biting me, her . . .

I found myself sitting up on the cot, my chest trembling, my eyes watching the foggy, shifting outline of the stove before me. "Darling?" Her voice. "What's the matter, Joe?"

I shook my head unsteadily. "Nothing."

"Did I . . . ?" She let her voice die away.

"No, it's nothing." I got up woozily. What the hell was wrong with me? Was I some kind of moon-sick idiot or was there something terribly, frighteningly strange about her kisses? I shook my head dazedly from side to side, trying to clear it. "Darling? Are you all right? Is anything the matter?"

"No." Standing up I felt better almost immediately. The earth was under my feet. I could sense its rock-steady, unwavering support. I felt much better. "I'm fine," I said. "Let's get back to the Dune-Dwellers."

"So abrupt?"

"What?"

She got up and smoothed out her dress. "We hardly know each other." She laughed. "This is so sudden. I wonder if there are any more comfortable clichés that cover the situation?"

"Millions."

"Then let's let them cover it. We've got the whole summer to find more."

All the way back, I was floating along behind her in a night fog, the slim wraith of her white body flickering before me, the touch of her hand my only contact with reality in the shifting, nebulous, rustling wilderness of blackness about me. After what must have been only a few minutes, I saw the lights of her cottage through the trees. We stopped at the front gate and she let go of my hand. "Will you help me on with my shoes?"

I knelt in the sand before her and tried to get the tiny bits of leather on her feet. The straps were all mixed up and the buckles were too small for my fingers to operate properly. I remember seeing her toes, long but small, their nails shining in the light from the cottage, no polish on them, the rims white against the warm pink of her skin. She flexed her foot delicately and it seemed to melt into the sole of the sandal, the leather merging with the soft skin like a kiss.

I buckled the strap and fitted the other shoe, feeling her hand on my shoulder shift slightly as she balanced her body. Done, I stood up and brushed off the knees of my trousers. "I dub thee Sir Knight," she said softly.

"Thanks, kind lady."

"And the accolade." She moved toward me, her body pressing against mine. I could feel the whole length of it, the curvings, the firmness. Her lips were bright and moist and soft, how soft I could never tell.

"Uh-uh," I grunted, stepping back out of range. "We've got to face company."

She looked at me blankly. "No accolade?"

I shook my head. "Later," I said wistfully, "all summer, remember?"

"I remember." She took my hand and led the way into the cottage. Maida was serving tea.

The room was warm and comfortable, filled with the cheering heat of the fire. "Well, *there* you are," Dora Olson chirruped. "Mr. Kelk's just arrived and I guess we can start the meeting fitting and proper, as they say."

A tall heavyset man stood before the fireplace, his back to the room, the outline of his body etched with bright fiery tongues of flame. The black kitten played around his feet. He was a great hulk of a man who dwarfed Jason Flye standing to one side made Sam Olson's gaunt body seem like a gnarled branch.

"Mr. Kelk," Abbie announced. "Here's our new member."

He turned around and smiled at me. His face was bloated thick, pockmarked. His huge nose was spotted and veined, it drooped to one side. His jowls were wide and flabby, a kind of bestial cruelty in their jellying bulk. His lips were wet and loose . . . like a cut peach. I knew him instantly. I knew all about him, even the car he drove.

"Dr. Loomis," I heard Abbie say, "meet Sebastian Kelk."

5 «◊» Money, Hunger, Love

I GLANCED AT MY WATCH, saw it was after one in the morning, wound it carefully and rolled over on the cot. My eyes hurt. I had been scribbling on little bits of paper by the light of the kerosene lantern and I didn't have to be a doctor to know why my eyes hurt so. I had been making notes ever since I returned from Abbie's cottage half an hour before and now I was going to study them, like an intelligent man, and make some conclusions. I had the feeling that this weird business might be resolved by setting it down in orderly form. The man of facts.

On the back of an old prescription blank I had written Dora Olson's name. Beneath it was the following: "Inquisitive, garrulous, harmless. What part in Dune-Dwellers?" Below this tremendous bit of observation I had written her husband's name and this notation: "Capable, awkward, president of D-D. Brains behind organization? Not likely."

I selected another slip of paper, a piece torn from the wrapping of some surgical cotton I'd found in the car glove compartment.

"Jason Flye: Nervous, watchful, devoted to Abbie, subordinate in D-D. Seems always about to explode.

Handyman or hanger-on?"

On the back of an old check stub: *"Maida Teufler:* tough, efficient, great love of traditional. Both nurse and keeper to Abbie." Below this: *"Sebastian Kelk:* gross, cunning, sensuous, brutal. Sadist? Muscle-man of D-D?"

On a business card given to me by an X-ray equipment salesman: *"Abbie:* very confusing. Masterful and weak by turns. Insecure in relations to other D-D's. Gives but also takes orders."

I had decided not to list the larcenous Mr. Morelle. I was certain that he belonged somewhere in this group, but for the purpose of collating known observations, he would have to be held in reserve.

I shuffled the bits of paper into order, trying to reach that single insight that would link them in some common denominator. To date there was only one link, the Dune-Dwellers. Tonight's meeting had shown me that there was at least a legitimate basis for its existence. The talk had all been of tax rates, a water line they were planning to build cooperatively, the encroachment of a new subdivision behind them and the control of mosquitoes in some of the backwoods pools and streams. All perfectly legitimate, no matter how hard I tried to find ulterior motivation.

Reading through my collection of notes again I was struck by a thought both whimsical and time-wasting. There were animals that resembled each of my new confreres. Names slid into my mind almost instantly. Dora Olson, of course, was a magpie. She could be nothing else with her snapping, inquisitive

eyes and endless, reeling conversation that made an
art of monotony. Her husband Sam? A giraffe, obviously. Didn't they lack the power of speech, those
sedate, gangling, introspective animals? Sam, to the
life.

Jason Flye was even easier. A jackal. But as soon as
I labeled him I wondered why. He was alert, watchful,
but many animals are that way. Perhaps it was the
subtle air of subservience about him, the way he
seemed to fawn on the slightest desire of his friends,
eager to be of service. And yet some terrible tension
inside him showed in every movement he made. It
was as though his façade were dangerously thin, a
shell hiding some secret.

Maida Teufler, with her stocky, well-knit bulk,
reminded me most forcefully of a small elephant, cunning in the ways of old, worshiping the past, that part
of the present that reminded her of the past, staking
her life on *status quo*. Yes, she was the elephant.

As for Sebastian Kelk, that powerful apish man
with his tremendous inference of carnality and greed
was hard to tab. To my bridge between former experience and present immediacy, the unconscious had
delved back into its files and brought forth Abbie
again.

Lying on my cot in the cabin, I felt my inspiration
run dry. I yawned and felt the hinges of my jaw crack
loudly. I looked at my watch. Two a.m. I had planned
to leave at eight, be home by ten and at the office
before eleven. The way I felt now, I'd probably sleep
till noon. The first thing on my list to bring to the

cabin next trip was an alarm clock.

I rolled over and sat up, my bones stiff, my throat sandy, my eyes closing with fatigue. I took off my glasses, removed my shoes, slipped the blanket off the cot and got underneath it. I had never felt so tired. The mattress had no sheet but I wasn't in the mood for anything fancy, only sleep. I reached out my hand and turned the lantern down till the flame guttered. It wouldn't go out. Then I remembered something I'd seen in a Western movie once. You were supposed to blow these damned things out. I drew a deep breath and puffed it out across the top of the glass chimney. The flame died and I was in total darkness.

I sank back on the cot and let the rest of the breath out of my lungs. The atmosphere was briskly cool, fresh, spiced with the odors of the woods. The night noise outside had died away to nothingness, shielded by my shuttered windows. I sighed again and rooted deeper in the cot. Sleep would be easy, the easiest thing in the world, nothing to do but—

I sat bolt upright in bed, staring at the darkness around me. There had been a sound outside my window.

A rustling sound, a whispering sound, a sound of something soft brushing against something softer.

I was wide awake, wondering, listening. It came to me now, in my aroused state, that the night had been quiet as the grave. The movement of the trees and bushes had died away long before, the birds had quieted. Yet now, a moment after my light had gone out, I heard a sound.

I got out of bed and padded quietly in my stockinged feet across the floor to the front window. Gently, my fingers as sensitive as eyes, I felt for the shutter bolt and drew it back softly, slowly, without a sound. Without the slightest creak, the shutter swung back against the wall. I blinked.

The night was no longer night. It was a panorama of tree and sand illuminated by the staring brilliance of the moon. Had it just risen or had the clouds obscured it before? But there hadn't been any clouds; I had seen the stars quite clearly. This sudden intense moonlight was unnerving. I tried to accustom my eyes to it and then, in that instant, I saw movement.

Above me on the crest of the roadway, a few yards to one side of my car, I saw something that had been there vanish. I didn't see the thing; I merely saw the sudden absence of it.

I strained my eyes in the direction I thought it might take should it follow a regular line, holding my breath as if to intensify the acuteness of my tired eyes. Then I saw it again, clearly.

It was a white thing, about the size of a human being, that traveled at the speed of a walking person but seemed not to have contact with the ground. It was a wispy, shimmering kind of thing suspended a few inches from the earth, yet moving and shifting along it like . . . like . . .

I knew what it was. It was Abbie.

And the sound identified itself, too. I had heard the sound before but it had been masked by the murmurous noise of the woods. The rustling sound, the whisper of something soft against something softer . . . Abbie's bare feet, treading lightly through the sand and grass.

Whatever Abbie had come for, it hadn't been to see me. She could have knocked at any time when my light was on. Instead she had stood motionless and silent outside my cabin and waited for the extinguishing of the lantern that signified my readiness for sleep. She had been posted as a lookout to determine the moment when I should remove myself from the night's activity. A campfire girl from way, way back.

I laced on my shoes hastily, fumbling at the strings with nervous impatience. Whatever they wanted me to sleep through, I was going to stay wide awake for. And I could, too. I was as alert and restless as though I'd just wakened. In fact, I was much too alert; a kind of hypertension jiggled my nerves. Could it have been my long nap of the afternoon? Could it have been the tea Abbie served? I was ready to believe anything now. My body was responding crazily, every nerve tightly coiled, begging for sensation. This wasn't the way a normal nervous system reacted after feeling so deeply, so languorously fatigued only a moment before. Had they put something in my tea?

I shouldered into my jacket and started for the door. If they drugged the tea they were rank amateurs. There are very few depressants that will put a man to sleep if he fights against them. I know of none that can be administered orally, none at least that the average layman has access to. And the curious property of most soporifics is that a certain percentage of the time they have a reverse effect. I've known patients to become so restless and edgy under barbiturates that they want to climb walls and do pushups.

My hand was on the doorknob when I noticed the glint of moonlight on an object in the cabin. The twin lenses of the binoculars lay on a chair, their large glass eyes moonstruck, idiotic. I snatched them from the chair, unbolted the door and stepped outside.

Now for the night. I sprinted up the incline to the roadway and started off along it in the direction I thought Abbie had taken. With all her uncanny knowledge of these woods, I could trail her if only I caught sight of her white dress. I raced on along the road, feeling the sand give under my shoes.

I was running in the direction of the turn I had taken to find the cabin this morning. It was a perfect vantage point from which to survey the area. I tried to remember what I'd seen from there . . . Gary smoke, country clubhouse, that peculiarly stark dune, woods. No help there. If only I'd examined the closer areas instead of finding how far I could see.

I padded along the sandy road, my lungs pumping fast, my body jolted from the sudden effort. At last I stood at the turning point of the road and looked about me. No Abbie. Then, suddenly I realized that I was spectacularly visible on this high place, bathed in moonlight and silhouetted against the sky. I dropped to my knees in the soft roadbed, then scrambled along the sand to the brink of the dune. The moonlight flooded the scene with a hard, bright light that seemed to separate every individual leaf and branch from its component mass.

I focused the binoculars, swept them in a wide arc. Nothing but sand and trees. If I were to find anything, I would have to locate it first with my naked eyes. And they were so tired. They smarted and ached. If Abbie were anywhere here she was hiding. And that meant she knew I was watching. *If* she were here. *If* she hadn't turned some other way. *If* I'd seen her at all. I was beginning now to doubt even that.

I sighed wearily and tried another sector of landscape, more barren, less likely. My aching eyes traveled slowly across its surface, their motion in my eye sockets gritty and almost painful. Abruptly, I noticed movement. For the first time I saw something that wasn't part of the silent, immobile night.

It was a thin wisp of something—smoke, perhaps —that filtered upward in the still air from the peak of that huge dune, that upthrust of sand almost bare of vegetation but crowned at its summit by a thicket of bushes and trees. I trained the binoculars on that fine thread of lighter stuff trailing skywards in a moon-struck night.

The powerful glasses brought it into immediate clarity and although the illumination was tricky I was sure it was smoke. I knew the area was under the surveillance of a fire station somewhere in the Indiana Dunes State Park, twenty miles or so to the south of us. If this were a manmade fire, its thin smoke could never be seen at such a distance. Then, obviously, its flame was being shielded deliberately, purposefully.

I scrambled down the slope of the hill, slipping

and sliding, trying to catch hold with one free hand while my other held the binoculars. I had to get close enough to bring the fire itself into range. I had to get close enough for my night-glasses to distinguish the people around the fire, if there were any. This was a problem in woodcraft. I had been through enough approach problems at Sicily and Normandy to know something of the technique, even though most of our medic detachment advances, trailing as they did the first shock wave of troops, had been relatively safe. The technique was sudden burst of action from one bit of cover to another, choosing the nearest and best cover at hand, even if it didn't lead directly toward the goal. I thought of the .22 Colt back at the cabin, unloaded and useless. I didn't know much about using it anyway, but I had the feeling that I would have to learn . . . and then buy a box of cartridges.

I was a perfect target in this bright light. From their superior vantage point on a higher dune, they could spot me no matter what cover I took. It was clearly a matter of luck.

Nobody let out a yell. Nobody threw rocks at me. I scrambled along a ravine, then ducked behind a large bush on the slope of another dune. I focused the binoculars. I was closer, but all I could see was the smoke and a vague shifting movement in the bushes atop the dune. Something was definitely going on there. It wasn't Abbie by herself, it was more than one person. This dune of mine was smaller and lower than the one with the smoke. Yet its summit was no more than two hundred yards from the fire if that. I could scuttle along the base of the dune until it shielded me from them, then climb up its hidden side in perfect safety. Once at its crest I could lie flat and enjoy a ringside seat.

I stuffed the glasses in my jacket pocket and started. It was rather like walking up a "down" escalator. My feet moved industriously but the sand kept slipping out from under them.

As I gained height, the going was easier; the angle of the slope became more gradual and there were plants to grab. By dint of pulling myself up and trotting industriously through the yielding sand, I finally reached the rounded summit, an oval-shaped bit of dune with one or two scrubby trees and some coarse sand grass to give me cover. Peeping up over the edge of the top, I sighted on the other dune. The tall grass practically blocked my field of view, giving me tantalizing glimpses of movement and a telltale flicker of flame. I shoved the glasses in my pocket and began crawling snake-wise through the grass. I hadn't done anything like this since the overseas training they gave me in the Army. This so-called Infantry Crawl, a complicated movement in which nothing, not the torso, the elbows, the feet nor the buttocks must rise above the level of the head, was punishing exercise for a tired and possibly drugged medical man in poor condition.

I snaked my way through the grass, skirted the base of a tree, spit some sand out of my mouth and wriggled into a position on the very top of the summit. Taking out the binoculars I remembered some more Army training. Night glasses are built with large lenses that must be shielded from reflecting light. I cupped my hands around the lenses and decided that this would do the trick. Awkwardly, with a stray finger, I shoved at the focusing knob. The fire pulled into needle-sharp brilliancy.

I was startled. I hadn't realized how powerful the binoculars were. They seemed to bring the fire within a few yards of me. As I had guessed, I had a ringside seat.

A ring of huge boulders surrounded the fire, hemming in its light a rough circle of large, chalk-white stones that looked from where I lay, very massive. They hadn't dragged them up there just for one night, had they? It didn't seem likely. The fire itself was made up of half a dozen branches, a few leaves still clinging to the unburnt ends. As I watched, a hand thrust into the shielded area of light and dropped another branch on top of the blaze. I followed the hand back, the binoculars shaky in my hands.

As soon as my eyes adjusted to the difference in light intensity I could see the owner of the hand quite clearly. It belonged to my follow Dune-Dweller, Jason Flye. He was seated before the fire in a squatting position, hunched back on his hams, his sartorial elegance masked by a peculiar kind of garment a sort of loose-fitting robe with short sleeves out of which his bare arms poked. His face was blank, emotionless, his eyes wide and glittering in the fitful glow of the fire.

Next to him, directly opposite the fire from me, sat Maida Teufler, her stocky body swathed in a robe similar to Flye's. Her hands were folded patiently in her lap, one over the other and her face was as impassive as one of the boulders that shielded the fire. Yet there was a change in her face. A kind of intense expectation shone behind her marble-like eyes, a half-open, waiting, eager cast to her small hard mouth.

To one side of her, his back to me and his body outlined against the flames, I saw the gross bulk of Sebastian Kelk. A glance at the immense width of those shoulders, at the thickness of the neck and the jellying bulge of one cheek told me that it was my fat friend of the battered Chevy coupé. He was as motionless as the others and I wondered if on his animal face there were a reflection of the eagerness of Maida and Jason.

I had expected to find the Olsons here too. But I had no time to ponder their absence; I was wondering what had happened to Abbie. She must be here, somewhere. A sudden chill pricked the skin along my back. What if she had seen me? I had been a perfect target at least twice in the last few minutes. Was I the watched, instead of the watcher? What if this were a trap, if she were even now behind me, ready to spring and strike?

With a convulsive movement I peered into the foliage behind me. Nothing. Or was . . . ? No, nothing. I turned back to train the binoculars on the fire again. Nothing had changed. As I watched, Flye placed another branch on the flames, his long bare arm moving with delicate precision as though the placement of the fuel were an important consideration. As I watched, the scene darkened, and the figures grew less distinct. Looking up I saw a cloud over the face of the moon. It seemed to have materialized out of nowhere. I leveled the binoculars on the fire again. Something had changed.

In the moment I'd looked up at the sky, Maida had disappeared. The two men remained motionless, but where she had squatted only a black hole in the night remained. Where had she gone? Where was Abbie? Were the Olsons in this? Could this be a trap? It had all worked too well so far. I wasn't that good. Were they drawing me into something? The back of my neck had a tingling, creeping feel to it as though someone were training a gun on the base of my skull. I wanted to look back but I couldn't miss whatever was to happen at the fire.

Then, suddenly, Maida emerged from the blackness and stepped into the fire-lit circle. I saw her powerful figure fold up on itself as she sat down in her previous place. And then I saw the reason for her disappearance. She had returned with Abbie.

The girl stood there, erect and tall in the flickering flames. She was still wearing the white dress and her feet were bare. Her hair, disheveled but still beautiful, fell in two long black wings along the sides of her face, swooping outward and covering her shoulders with a mantle of glossy black. Wings, I thought then. The wings of the Angel of Death. Colin's words.

She stood there in the firelight, her head high, her chin out, her eyes closed. She held her arms down at her sides, half-hidden in the voluminous folds of the dress. Then, as I watched she took a step forward and I saw her bare foot plant firmly on one of the huge white boulders. As it did so, her hands shot aloft and each of them held something blurred that I couldn't distinguish. Her eyes opened wide and I felt fear in meas I saw them. They were the eyes of a madwoman.

There was something in them, something utterly maniacal and not of this world, a thing I had almost seen in them back at the cabin, in that moment when, playfully, I'd shoved the sprig of mistletoe at her. Each iris was ringed with dead white a huge, monstrously dilated area of glistening eyeball that showed frighteningly clear through my binoculars. They were wider than human eyes had any right to be, not bulging, not staring, but wide, wide as the night, wide as the moon now masked by clouds.

Then I saw her mouth. I've seen such contortions of the lips on Greek sculpture, on the faces of suicides, madmen and the victims of sudden deadly assaults. The corners of her mouth were down-drawn, bedded in monstrously deep wrinkles that bit into her skin and seared upwards to the base of her nose. And through her bright distorted lips I could see her teeth distinctly. They gleamed and danced in the flames of the fire as her hideously wide eyeballs did, flickering and convulsing . . . completely and finally mad.

A sudden movement distracted me. Maida's chubby arm had dropped something into the fire, not a branch, but something small that I didn't quite see. After a moment Abbie's taut body stirred and I could see her breasts surge and rise beneath the thick white material of her dress. Her lips twitched, grimaced then moved rapidly. She seemed to be speaking, but I could only see the motion of her mouth. It was like watching a silent movie, but such a movie as no sane man had ever dreamed of making, a movie of a girl speaking, the word's curling and distorting her wet red lips spitting, mouthing, grinning.

At last they were still. They rested, full and moist, close tightly as though she were waiting now for a reply. Kelk's massive body stirred, and his thick, hairy arm shot up out of the folds of his cloak. His burly hand was closed in a fist, one finger pointing at Abbie, pointing at her arms, at what she held in them.

There was a flash of light, a quick lancing gleam of something shiny that caught the firelight as it slashed downward in her right hand. She held it out before her. It was a knife.

She held it point down, a short, ugly blade, curving and double-edged, not steel, but some yellowish metal that hadn't the high polish of brass. It protruded from the balled fist of her hand, trembling, quivering. As I watched, I heard a rustle in the bushes behind me.

I whirled, jerking my body around in a hard, quick movement. There was nothing there, nothing. I stared, chills racing along in chest and stomach, and felt the cold touch of the wind in my face. The wind, nothing but the wind. I turned back hastily and leveled the binoculars again.

Nothing had changed. It was as though the group had been carved in some porous kind of limestone that only gave the impression of human flesh, simulating the warmth that should be a body but translating it into something unreal and ghastly. Kelk's arm fell back to his side and I saw a tremor pass over Abbie's body, a ripple that seemed to start in her bare foot, planted firmly on the boulder, shimmer upward like the flex of a cracked whip and snap her head back violently on her slim neck. She opened her mouth once, as though taking in a long, deep breath. She paused, tense, waiting, poised . . . Then her left hand swooped down out of the darkness over her head. For the first time I saw what it held.

It was the black kitten. Her fingers encircled its furry little body just back of its forelegs and I could see it scrambling futilely in her grasp, its dainty paws lashing out at the air, its pink mouth opening and shutting spasmodically. She held it straight out from her, as far away from her breasts as her arm could reach. I knew what was coming. I felt sick in the pit of my stomach, a kind of tumbling nausea that built up upon itself like waves rolling over each other to the roaring surf.

With a quick, sharp motion, she brought the knife across the kitten's neck once, fast, with efficiency. I could see a stain of blood well up and ooze over the long white marking there, flood it with crimson and then fade off into the black fur. The kitten's back arched once, high, then its little body went limp, stringy, dead. I tried to look away but it wasn't in me to stop. I was hypnotized by Abbie, under a compulsion stronger than fear or disgust. I had to watch.

I wish now that I hadn't. As I stared, Abbie brought the body of the slaughtered kitten to her mouth. I could see her lips curl and her teeth gleam fiercely until the furry black corpse masked her face. But I could see her throat, that long, smooth white column, so soft, so delicately modeled in sweeping lines. I saw it pulse as a regular muscular motion within it drew up and down in measured rhythm. I knew what Abbie was doing. She was drinking the kitten's blood.

Then I did look away. I let my face fall forward into the sand and I could feel the gritty grains between my teeth. Around me now the summit of the dune was filled with whispering and strange sounds. The wind seemed to be rising, mounting in intensity. It felt cold and soothing as it blew through my hair. I took a breath and spit the sand out of my mouth. I leveled the binoculars and looked.

Abbie had taken the dead kitten from her mouth. Her lips were intensely red now, a heightened shade of crimson that no lipstick in the world could match, oily, thick-bodied redness that accentuated her lips to full, lolling bestiality. She passed the back of her hand over her mouth and wiped some of the blood off, smearing some on her cheek. Then she dropped the knife into Maida's outspread cloak. With her free hand she grasped the kitten's head. I could see its dead eyes, wide and staring. She made a quick, twisting movement and the head was torn from the body.

She dropped it into Maida's cloak. Then, with exqui-
site care, she reached forward into the fire, her lips
moving, her mouth working back and forth, and,
plunging her hand into the very center of the flames,
she deposited the headless body of the kitten there.

I watched Maida's eyes. They were empty, dead. I
looked at Jason Flye. *His* eyes were alive! They
gleamed with something more than firelight. They
were wild and questing eyes, staring up into Abbie's
blood-smeared face, yearning, as though she were
about to present him with a boon beyond price.

I looked back at Abbie. Her face was blank, her
eyes closed.

Her hands, still wet with red, were busy at the folds of
her dress. Her fingers worked quickly and then, with
an abrupt movement, she pulled at her dress. It came
away in one piece, whole. She was perfectly naked
beneath it.

As I may have mentioned before, firelight was
kind to Abbie. Although she was probably in her
thirties, she looked like a slim young girl in the light
of a candle, a lantern or, as now, a wood blaze. The
flames of the fire had risen by this time above the
level of the shielding boulders. In the confused scene
I could almost swear they were licking at her long
firm legs. She stood in the firelight, her stance erect
yet loose, her legs parted slightly, her arms at her
sides, her chin firm, eyes closed full breasts taut and
swelling, the white outline of her smooth lips soft
against the dark background. She seemed to be
waiting. They all seemed to be waiting. Maida's stony

face was set in an expressionless pose, her eyes dead yet waiting. Jason's body was tense, his lips parted expectantly. And even Kelk's brutish hulk seemed alert and ready, his bulging neck muscles in hard wrinkles as he craned up at Abbie's naked body. I could imagine what his face looked like.

Again they were all like statues carved of some chalky stone. And then, with a gesture I cannot hope to describe, Abbie's arms stretched out . . . toward Kelk. Her eyes were still closed, but toward her bloody mouth there played an expression, a kind of smile if one can call such a shifting, obscene expression a smile. She sank down on her knees, her arms still outstretched to Kelk. Then, with a movement I couldn't follow closely, she fell sideways, her white body hidden by the boulders. A campfire girl from way, way back.

Kelk's huge body stirred and rose in the flickering firelight. His back was still to me but as he circled the fire I got a look at his face. His soft, flabby lips were trembling like the bladder of some ruptured beast, his tongue playing back and forth over their slobbering redness. His coarse-grained jowls quivered insanely as he stood there, thick legs spread wide, stood over Abbie's unseen, prostrate body and devoured her with his evil stare. Then, his fat body jellying with the movement, he looked up at the sky, at the clouds gathering fast across the dim face of the moon. I saw his brutish lips curve and writhe in a laugh, a bellowing shout in which all foulness and brutality were gathered. With a sudden, heavy pounce, he disappeared from sight behind the fire-lit ring of boulders. A monstrous bolt of lightning split the sky overhead, slashed downward across the air in one steaming stroke of violent release.

I jumped up as though stung by the bolt. Thunder rolled and shouted in my ears, pounding at my brain, howling and blasting through my body. Heavy, biting rain thrummed on my head. I turned and ran . . . ran as though cloven hooves were pounding after me. I dashed across the summit, jumped over the edge and slid crazily down the deep slope of the dune, crashing through sharp grass blades and brambles, slipping and sliding in a headlong rush to the ravine at the bottom. Behind me, I thought I could hear the crazy, high-pitched sound of Jason Flye's mad giggle.

I can't remember the next few minutes clearly. All that comes to me now is an agony of flight, eyes blinded by rain, lungs pounding, mouth dry and gaping, legs bursting with pain as I scrambled and fell, climbed and slid back, finally to reach the turning point of the road and stumble along it to my cabin. The rain made a slushy muck of the road underfoot. I remember climbing into my car, ramming the engine into shrieking life, slamming the wheel about in a frenzy of passion and rocketing down the treacherous road to the highway . . . that smooth, glossy, blessedly ordinary highway that led back home to Chicago.

6 «◊» The Better Part of Valor

IF I HADN'T BEEN A DOCTOR, if I'd been an artist or a writer, someone whose work depends on himself alone, I very probably wouldn't have lived through the next week a sane man. What saved me was the steady influx of patients, the day-by-day parade of dog bites, strained ligaments, acne, all those happily mundane afflictions of human flesh. If I had been thrown on my own resources, seeking work and thought within myself, I would probably have taken to drugs. But as it turned out I had a very busy week.

Around Thursday, I had steadied down enough to decide something. After all those months of Colin and these past weeks of his deadly legacy, I reached a decision that anybody less close to the affair—you, for instance—would have made long before. I decided to forget the whole thing.

Simple, uncluttered, completely rational. I would turn my back on it once and for all. What business of mine were the goings-on atop that high dune? What did it matter to me that Colin had been trapped by his infernal feyness into something dark and hellish? I had a natural curiosity about the whole affair, but beyond that I had no business going.

But, as I may have mentioned before in the course of this narrative, I am a methodical man. If I had been less methodical, perhaps I would not be writing this now. But, as I re-read the events of the affair, I realize they signify nothing without some explanation. Since this is to be the last chapter, I must, in all fairness to you, clear up the matter to everyone's satisfaction. I think I can do so. At least, after you have read this final chapter, I hope you will think I have done so.

On Friday, finding my practice had slowed down to an average tempo, I took the morning off to knot the last loose ends securely in place. Let me ask you to forgive the sporadic, rather disorganized nature of the narrative. A variety of events took place, some confusing, some all too enlightening, in the space of only two days.

It is now Sunday evening as I write this . . .

Friday: 9:30 A.M. *County Building.* I presented myself at the coroner's office and talked with a middle-aged, rather officious clerk who at first was reluctant to let me see the records on Mr. Profit's death. Since it was a fatality unattended by any physician, I felt sure the coroner's office would have a record of it, but I had to think up several fancy and not too choice lies before the clerk would give me access to the books. What I found was brief and to the point.

The entry read:

"Profit, Thaddeus J., white, 51, April 7, 1946, approx. 4:20p.m., 1421 E. Superior St., 3rd floor. Reported by: Anna Balough, landlady, same address. Verdict: heart failure, senile decay. No inquest."

I thanked the officious clerk, tucked my notebook away and left.

Friday: 10:15 A.M., 1421 *E. Superior St.* I found Anna Balough sitting in the living room of her basement flat, her huge, flabby body squeezed into the narrow confines of a chaise longue that would have fitted a normal person with room to spare. A boy of nine or ten answered the door and ushered me in, then disappeared into the rear of the house never to be seen again, at least by me.

"Sure, I remember Mr. Profit," she wheezed. "Care for some beer?"

I declined the open can of beer she indicated on the table near her. "Too early in the day," I explained.

"Friend," she gurgled, "when it gets to be ten am and I ain't had my beer, I just as soon turn over and sleep till tomorrow. A series of huge jellying movements surged up along her body and vibrated against each other in the bulging folds of her neck. She was evidently laughing. I found myself wondering which was to blame, beer or glands. "Little scrawny fella," she said by way of amplification, "never had much to say."

"Do you remember much about his illness?"

"I remember everything," she replied. "I got a

memory like an elephant and a build to match."
Laughter wobbled her body again. "First tell me why,
then I'll tell you how."

"Why is that I'm a doctor," I explained. "I'm
doing some work on diseases like Mr. Profit's and I
can't find the doctor who attended him. So . . ."

"I remember everything," she repeated. "I remember when I was thin, and that takes a lot of remembering, friend." This also amused her. I laughed with
her.

"Sure," she said, catching her breath, "I remember
Mr. Profit. He just sickened away and died. One day
he was healthy, the next day he was lying around the
house with a sick headache. My Lord, I only thought
us women got sick headaches." She threw a monumental wink at me and I had to smile, couldn't help it.
"Seeing's how you're a doc," she went on, "I guess I
can get free with you. Hey?" Another wink.

"I guess you can."

The gurgles subsided in her throat and she continued: "He tried to keep going, headache and all, but it
was too much for a little fella like him. Pretty soon he
took to his bed."

"Why didn't he call a doctor?"

"Fact is, I called Doc Prohaska all the way over
here and Mr. Profit, he wouldn't let him in. Now,
what do you think of that?"

"I think he was a little goofy, if you ask me."

"I asked him once, one evening when he came
down for a walk—I don't get enough gumption to go
traipsing up three flights of stairs, not any more—and

I asked him right out what was wrong with him."

"What'd he say?"

"Said, 'Miz Balough, there ain't nothing in heaven or earth can cure me.' Just like that."

"But what was it he *had?*"

"Exactly what *I* said. I said, 'What is it you got, Mr. Profit?' And he just sort of cuddles up on himself and looks away from me and says: 'I wouldn't want to tell you, Miz Balough, it'd ruin your digestion.'"

"Nothing more?"

"Oh well I told him what Father Konski always says. Put your faith is Jesus Christ and you will be saved. That's what I said to him and you know what he did? He laughed. Not real hard, but he sort of laughed, dry-like, like he was choking. And he says: 'You tell the priest there's one lamb of God won't be saved.' And away he walks."

"How soon after did he die?"

"After that? 'Bout a week, maybe ten days. It made me a little sad because if a man like little Mr. Profit can be taken away before his time, why, what's to say any of us can't the same? Of course the good Lord'll have His hands full carting *me* off, I can tell you that." She started laughing again, a huge, mounting spasm of mirth that engulfed her in its tidal wave.

Friday:. 11:30 A.M., *University of Chicago*. I hadn't been in Wieboldt Hall since 1936 or '37, when I was an undergraduate still only toying with the idea of a medical career.   On the first floor there's a small foyer, off which lead doors to classrooms and offices. It was in one of the latter that I found my man, Lenihan, the professor who was responsible for guiding me toward a medical career.

"Loomis you'll never learn how to parse a sentence," he'd muttered in 1936. "Why don't you leave the English language alone and be something else . . . a doctor or something equally innocuous."

Which was all the encouragement I needed. I remembered him as a thin, spare man in his thirties, already partially bald, already affecting a pipe in which he burned, it seemed to us, rubber bands. He had studied in the East somewhere, the kind of college that specializes in inspirational professors, men who draw out their students by sheer personality and podium dramatics. Lenihan had tried his best but somehow his weak gray eyes and wispy figure weren't suited to pedantic quips and the kind of veiled give-and-take insults with which the inspirational professor kindles his class.

I recognized him without much trouble. His encroaching baldness had, in ten years or more, left little of the gray hair. But his pipe! It seemed to be the same one, still stinking of that particularly tarry, malodorous aroma that comes of inexpert lighting, strong tobacco and, I believe, a tendency on the part of the smoker to drool back into the pipe, thus giving the more acrid byproducts of combustion a liquid medium in which to perpetuate their odor.

"You don't remember me," I began, "but I'm Joe Loomis. English Lit in '36."

He peered at me out of those pale eyes and then shook his head. "Sorry," he said. "You don't expect me to remember everyone, now do you? I realize that it may come as somewhat of a disillusionment, but . . ."

"You told me I should be a doctor," I said, smiling. "You said I wasn't fit for anything else. So I'm a doctor now."

"Splendid." He packed some more tobacco into his pipe but mercifully paused before lighting it. "I wish more of my literarily-inclined students had followed your lead."

"I looked up an old catalog of mine and I found you listed as teaching English historical background, the—"

". . . folktale in literature," he finished for me "the influence of primitive beliefs on literature, myth in poetry, supernatural backgrounds to English drama and the epic. I know." He waved his pipe and I had the feeling that he was postponing the lighting of it until he was on safe ground with me.

"That's what I've come about," I said. "I've recently become very interested in primitive religions and . . . and devil-worship." The words fell hard and flat in that quiet little room.

"If you're a doctor," he said, "you're probably making enough money to afford the tuition required for English 712, a course I'm teaching next quarter. I believe the registrar will acquaint you with the fees."

I had to pause for a moment to invent a lie. Lenihan took advantage of my silence to strike a kitchen match and apply it to the tobacco in his pipe. "I don't think I'll be in Chicago next quarter," I said at length. "I expect to be in New York all summer."

"Not a bad excuse," he said, winking slightly. "I've been sitting here trying to nerve myself. It seems I assigned a class the writing of a long paper. Now I must read said papers. If you have any questions to ask me, please make them as long and as complicated as possible. Anything to delay the ordeal."

"Primitive religions," I repeated, "and . . . devil-worship." I still couldn't get the pause out of that phrase.

"That all?" He seemed disappointed. "There's nothing much to know except that primitive peoples have always worshiped in more or less the same ways. Babylonia, Mexico, every corner of the earth. You see, people have to eat."

"What's that?"

"Eat. You have to feed yourself. That means the crops have to grow. So all primitive peoples have practiced fertility rites to pray for rain or the end of rain, for sun, for fish to run and deer to fall dead on their spears. Very businesslike. Practical."

"Just fertility?" I asked. "Where's the religion in that? And where's the devil-worship?" I got it out quite neatly this time.

"Look," Lenihan explained, "when you pray to the sun to make it shine, it's a short step to praying to the spirit of the sun. The sun god, so called. Pray to corn, pretty soon you pray to the god of corn. After a few thousand years or so, you've got a religion. In fact, every religion we have today is based on those primitive rites."

"Yes," I said quickly, "but those are . . . well, what you might call benign religions. Not malignant ones."

The professor nodded. "Just the reverse of the coin, that's all."

"I don't quite—"

"See here," he said, leaning forward to emphasize his words, "no matter how diligently you worship, things go wrong. I mean, sometimes the rain doesn't fall, no matter how many virgins you sacrifice. Sometimes the sun doesn't shine. The sea *will* swamp your fishing boat. If your faith is rather weak you begin to wonder why you're wasting your time in prayer. You begin to think; Well, now, perhaps I've got this backwards. Perhaps there is a god who *ruins* everything. If I get on the good side of *him* I'll be on easy street. So you invent a devil. And you worship him."

"In what way?" I asked. "That is . . . by what means?"

Simple enough," he said, sniffing slightly at his pipe. He tamped down the tobacco with a pencil point, stabbing the coals into place. "You just reverse your worship. Now you take a black mass."

"Yes?" It was my turn to lean forward now.

"What happens there? Why, you reverse everything. You drink real blood, not consecrated wine.

You read the service backwards. And then, instead of getting a feeling of good will and peace—as a communicant does in a real mass—you proceed to indulge yourself in quite the foulest acts your over-heated brain can imagine."

"Then what about the fertility?"

"You see, nowadays devil-worshipers don't bother with fertility at all. Except," he added, winking again, "in a perverse sort of way. Nowadays I imagine it's purely the sexual license of the rites that attracts communicants"

"And nothing more?"

"Nothing," he said quietly, "that I know of."

"I'm not sure I understand."

"Well, let me sum up a few things for you. There's the sex business for one thing; the license to engage in all sorts of obscenities under the guise of ritual. Then there's the business of knowing a secret no normal person knows, a knowledge certainly as old as any other religion, but so hidden that not one in a million understands it. And thirdly, perhaps most important is the business of getting on Satan's good side."

"You mean, because he's winning out?" I asked. "Is that it?"

"Roughly. Mind you, I'm simply guessing now. But it would seem that fertility has very little to do with the matter these days." He paused, glanced at me. "And sex has almost everything to do with it. Sex and insecurity."

Something stirred at the back of my mind. Why, I

asked myself did he use words like "these days"? I leaned back and tried to affect a casual air about my next question. "In short," I said, "devil-worship still exists. You know that for a fact?"

"I don't know it for a fact," he responded tartly. "But I would stake my life on it anyway."

"But why?"

"Let's put it this way; how old are you?"

I glanced up, startled. "Thirty-two."

"And tell me, how many of your cherished plans have gone a-glimmering in those thirty-two years?"

"Why . . . quite a few, I suppose."

"Exactly. And so they have for most people at most times and in most centuries. Sometimes, however, things are worse than at other times. Do you follow me? Some eras of history are much harder on the individual than others. Take our own times, for example."

"I begin to see it," I said slowly. "It's the insecurity, then. Everything is falling and the average person feels that God is losing out. So he turns to Satan. Is that it?"

"Not the average person, certainly not."

"Well, the neurotic, then."

Lenihan puffed quickly at his pipe. "Everybody wants to be on the winning side," he said. "If you think God's losing, naturally you switch to Satan. Mentally, that is. But your neurotic does the thing physically. Have you ever read or heard of what happened in Germany after the First World War?"

"Why . . . I know things were unsettled."

"Unsettled." He laughed quietly. "The state of public morality sank to levels we haven't seen since ancient Rome. Public morality, I mean. God knows what happened in private."

"I see. And today?"

"Pick up this morning's newspaper. See if you find any security in the headlines."

"So you feel certain that devil-worship exists today?"

He laid aside his pipe and squinted at me. "It seems to me that there are three kinds of people involved in devil-worship. Those who don't know any better. Those who simply get a kick out of it. And those who cannot live without it. I'm sure all three categories still exist. What bothers me is why you want all this information." He frowned for a moment and then his face cleared. "I imagine it's none of my business, eh? And, in any case," he winked at me, "you've helped me escape the grading of these abominable papers."

I thanked him and started to leave. As I opened the door, a sudden thought crossed my mind. I turned back to Lenihan. "One thing more," I asked. "Where does mistletoe fit into all this?"

He pursed his lips thoughtfully. "It was sacred to many early peoples, of course. They considered it a sovereign protection against evil of all kinds."

I thanked him once more and left.

Saturday: 5:15 P.M., *The apartment.* I had just finished taking a shower and was getting dressed to go out for dinner when the phone rang. I knew what it would be. Whenever a doctor is getting ready to eat and the phone rings, it's always an emergency case fifteen miles out of town. I made a face at the phone and picked it up.

"Joe?"

My fingers gripped the telephone hard, with a kind of galvanic response.

"Yes. Abbie?"

"What on earth's happened to you, darling?"

"Nothing," I heard my voice say. It sounded fairly normal to me. "I'm fine, as a matter of fact."

"Well, I'm glad to know the earth hasn't swallowed you up. You know, you left in a most dreadful hurry Monday and I've been expecting you to call all week."

"I know," I said haltingly. "Things have been popping at the office."

"Was anything wrong last week, darling? I mean, I went by your cabin Monday morning and you'd left the door unlocked and the bed all rumpled."

"I left early," I told her. "Overslept and had to run."

"I guess it's safe to leave your cabin unlocked around there," she continued, "but it did look odd. I made your bed for you."

Oh, you did, I thought savagely. And did you wash the cat blood off your hands before you touched the blanket? Aloud I said: "That was very nice of you."

"Joe, I thought if you hadn't eaten, you might like to have dinner with me." She paused for the proper length of time. "At my place," she added.

"Oh?" That was the last thing I wanted to put in my stomach, food prepared by her. "Well, I'm afraid I'm busy until pretty late. I've got a rush call out to Oak Park . . . possible appendicitis."

"Then later tonight?" she asked. "For a drink or two? I haven't seen you for a whole week, darling."

"Yes, I know." And she wouldn't be seeing me for a whole lifetime if I could help it. I had to let myself out of this permanently. "I'm afraid I can't make that either," I started to say.

"Oh, Joe." Her voice sounded dispirited, empty. "I thought . . ." She let the rest of her words die away, meaningfully. Suddenly I realized that if I were to tell her off it might arouse her suspicions. Above all they mustn't know I had seen their ghastly ritual or that I suspected them of anything. I decided to string her along.

"Darling," she said, "it isn't as though we were strangers."

"Well, look," I began rather lamely, "suppose we leave it at this. I'll drop by when I finish my calls . . . if it isn't too late. Before midnight, let's say."

"I'll be waiting."

"Don't count on me," I said hastily. "That is, I

may not be finished by midnight."

"That's all right, darling. You come over any time. I'll be waiting."

7:30 P.M., The apartment. I was lying on my bed, thinking. If only I'd made it clear that I wouldn't come. If only I'd cut the whole thing off then and there. But that would reveal everything.

In the kitchenette, I took the bottle of Bushmills from the cupboard and poured myself a fairly stiff peg. I sat down on the living room couch. I sipped a little and thought a little.

9:45 P.M., The apartment. Perhaps I could handle the thing like an ordinary affair nipped in the bud, the romance that never got rolling. After all, there hadn't been much between us, nothing binding, no commitments. What was I worrying about, then?

I sipped a little and thought a little.

11:00 P.M., The apartment. What the hell could she do to me, anyway? Throw me out? Big deal. If she got mad and threw me out, that was fine, perfect. I wanted out, but fast. I sipped a little more and I thought a little more.

Sunday: 1:00 A.M., The apartment. The Bushmills ran out. Nothing was left in the bottle but memories. I got up and walked, very steadily, I might add, to the kitchenette. Then, taking careful aim, I shied the bottle at the trash can. It made a loud noise when it hit and I found this amusing. I laughed to myself in the sudden silence of that room.

I combed my hair, checked my tie, and left the apartment.

1:50 A.M., Abbie's apartment. She was wearing white again. Don't all priestesses wear white? No, some wear black. I noticed that this white thing of hers was silk or something equally *chichi*, or froufrou, or whatever, and it clung or fell away, as the flesh beneath it dictated, very invitingly.

"Where was your last patient," she asked, smiling and crinkling her nose at my breath. She took a deep inhalation, the front of this white thing, this peignoir or gown or whatever, in silk or whatever, spread sideways across her breasts until I wondered why I'd wasted time in anatomy class. She took another deep inhalation. She knew.

"In a bar," I said nastily. "He fractured a tibia tapping a keg."

"What's the matter, darling?" she asked. We were

sitting on a couch, the same one she'd been on the day I fixed her arm. "Are you worried about something?"

"Yup." I felt that my tie was on too tight. She crossed her legs beneath the white thing and an opening that was invisible when she stood up now split away along one side and showed me one of her legs up to a few inches below her pelvic arch, not too few inches, not too many. Not as many as Sebastian Kelk had seen. The tie was choking me.

"Why don't you relax, darling?" She began stroking the back of my head, the point where the spinal column enters the skull, a point fairly lousy with nerve-endings. I loosened my tie.

"Just relax," I could hear her purr. "Let yourself go."

Not to put too fine a point on all this, nor take up valuable space in this concluding chapter, the next half-hour was made up almost exclusively of such byplay. There is a curious thing about me, as there is about a number of people who drink only occasionally. We build up a kind of tolerance for alcohol by which we can achieve tremendous relaxation through an overdose while preserving, relatively untouched, the centers of our reason. That is to say, we can act and talk as though we were drunk while at the same time there remains one kernel in our mind, one spot of sobriety that acts as the spectator, moderator and judge of our actions.

I will say this for Abbie—she did very well, all things considered. But she was playing right into my hands. By forcing the issue, by pushing ahead this way to the culmination, she was making it easier by the minute for me to break off our whole relationship. She was giving me good grounds for that final action when I would rise, disgusted, into one some humbug like, "I didn't think you were that kind of girl," and leave. It sounded corny, but it might work.

And it did. After half an hour of byplay, Abbie yawned once, hiding it from me, and tried the assault frontal. We had kissed a number of times and the sober part of my mind recorded with satisfaction that alcohol gave adequate immunity against the queer magic in her kiss. The sensory systems it usually set in motion had been effectively blocked off by the liquor. Abbie probably understood this. With a terse, almost businesslike candor, she played her last card. I don't remember what it was too clearly, but it took the form, as I recall, of a straightforward invitation couched in veiled terms.

This was my cue. I remember getting up, straightening my tie and fixing her with as steady a look as I could muster. She had played into my hands with a precision that did my heart good. She could fail. She could be beaten. I had beaten her.

"What're you getting up for?" she wanted to know.

I grinned crookedly at her. This was the payoff. She had been so dense, so bemused by her own prowess at this sort of thing, that she'd never imagined how she'd been outmaneuvered.

"Sit down here by me," she purred. Her voice, that low, throaty instrument that could invoke any mood, was inviting, enticing.

"I have something to say," I announced.

"Whisper it," she said. "In my ear."

What a laugh, this Theda Bara stuff, pure hoke, the traveling saleswoman and the farmer's son. I had outsmarted her. I was about to cut off this business with surgical precision, with a scalpel thrust, the way . . . the way she'd sacrificed that cat. The idea gave me strength and a tremendous feeling of mastery.

"Well, what is it, darling? Tell me."

I told her. Standing there rather unsteadily, grinning maliciously.

I told her off. What I said escapes me now. It was something brutal and to the point, something well-calculated to do the job I had in mind.

Her face went blank. I remember that. I can't remember precisely what I said, but I remember with perfect clarity the effect it had on her face. Her eyes lidded halfway, looked down at the floor. Then she got up and went to the door. In the previous half hour this white thing around her had been maneuvered off center. As she walked I could see her long legs flash in and out of the slit. I followed her.

"That makes it pretty clear," she said, opening the door.

"Precisely what I had in mind," I said. I bowed courteously and left. I remember getting into my car and driving away. I remember something else important that doesn't come back to me now. And that, just that, is all I remember.

Sunday: 1:30., The apartment. I awoke with a fierce hangover, one of the few I'd ever experienced. There was a tremor in the pit of my stomach and a perfervid quivering in my fingertips. I took two bicarbonate tablets and an aspirin, then drank down two glasses of tomato juice. I promptly gave them up.

This was bad. I should never have finished off that much whisky. I was getting old, out of practice. My head throbbed like a cut nerve and I had to go through the bicarb-and-aspirin routine again to replace the wasted dose. I lay down on the living room couch and tried to relax. The refrigerator went on with a grinding hiss and the top of my head rattled sympathy with it. Some Sunday idiot honked his horn outside in the street and my neck arched spastically, snapping my aching head forward with an agonizing lurch.

I had to get food inside me. I had to sit down at the typewriter and finish off my account of this business. *Paraldehyde* was what I needed, that or *sodium amytal.* I had neither in the apartment and I didn't feel like getting dressed and trekking over to the office. The very thought of getting outside in that blinding sunlight was painful. I sipped a few ounces of tomato juice tentatively. They stayed down.

I lowered all the shades, turned the student lamp

away from the typewriter keyboard and began. The previous parts of this chapter are what I finished. As I said at the beginning? I want to apologize for their disorganized appearance. They give the effect, as I page back through them now, of a patchwork quilt: many designs, many colors, no apparent plan welding them together.

And, frankly, I don't much care. I've written them down the way they took place, spasmodic, unrehearsed, and the writing of them has cost me a great deal in nervous energy. I feel therefore entitled to some measure of self-pity because I have been successful at last. As I write this now, I realize that I've finally severed myself from the whole gruesome affair. And the instrument of my deliverance has been this narrative.

If I had let the events of the business linger and rot in my mind, they would have driven me mad before long. The tension of holding such dark things in the mind is overpowering, as though the brain were a closed vat in which the black, stinking, maggoty grapes of some night wine are fermenting in their own foul juices. Writing all this down, though it may never be read by anyone, is enough release for such nocturnal secrets, miasmic vapors of a dark fermentation.

Perhaps you think I protest too much. I have the feeling I do. What I accomplished was very close to cowardice. The thin line between good judgment and craven fear is often less a line than a shading that slants off imperceptibly from one extreme to the other. There are only blacks or whites these days. Yet I prefer to think that what I have done is a lighter gray than the rest. I think that what I've done *is* the better part of valor and that he who fights and runs away will live to fight another day.

I would like to close this succinctly, drawing a number of conclusions that will give the narrative a meaning and point. Yet, in the interests of accuracy, I must record here that I haven't the mind for it today. My typing, even as I write this, has become haphazard, filled with errors. It would be unfair to you and to me if I continued this much longer.

9:00 P.M., The apartment. I've been resting. I gave myself two codeine tablets, put the pillow over my head and tried to sleep. My mind is perfectly clear as I write this and yet I haven't the stamina to finish typing. This is what comes from playing the fool, I suppose. I haven't had that much hard liquor in years.

10:20 P.M., The apartment. I've just returned from the office with a 10 cc. vial of paraldehyde. It seems a shame to let this writing go when I'm so close to finishing it. I have all my conclusions in mind and if I can get my nerves to stop perking, I'll wind the whole thing up.

10:45 P.M., The apartment. Success! The paraldehyde, medicine's gift to hung-over souls, has worked. I feel infinitely better. My fingers have stopped dancing about and a few minutes ago, when another imbecile saw fit to blast away in the street outside. I merely smiled. I still have the headache, but I mustn't waste any time now that I've settled my nerves.

The primary conclusion to be drawn from this whole affair is probably best expressed by Professor Lenihan. The central fact lies, of course, in the insecurity of our civilization. I'm not familiar with the emotions of a Frenchman, a Russian or an Arab. But I know something about myself and the people who live in this country. Through a series of incidents that began, I think, at the turn of the century, we have been seduced into a position of leadership, yet robbed of the qualities that would make us leaders.

The ignorance spawns fear in us. We common people, shoe clerks and riveters and masons and doctors, we feel our guts gnawed by this monstrous fear. Each newspaper headline chokes us, each radio newscast hammers us down into our cells like rats, trapped in the dungeon of our fears.

Is it so incredible, then, that we turn, blindly, despairingly, to the unknown? That we embrace it with a ghoulish fervor as of vampires greedily siphoning off the blood of the ages? That we plunge ourselves into excesses of mind and body, reveling in a hideous bacchanal of dark, forbidden things? It seems to me that . . .

11:30 P.M., The apartment. My nerves are equal to the job, but the very exercise of thought sends waves of agony across my head. I've taken two more codeines.

The parallel to devil-worship, the innocuous

parallel on normal, mundane levels, is escape of a less dramatic nature, escape into the past, into the novels, the songs, the ideas of the past, flight to vague philosophies of despair, existentialism, quietism, obscureantism, the brute cult, the action cult, pessimism, cynicism, defeatism.

When you destroy rationality, the dark night-fears of the unknown spring up from its shattered pieces. When you hamstring the mind of man, bind up his power and mastery of the future then you unleash the babbling, overpowering fears that man holds deep within him, the heritage of his infancy.

When you take from man the one tool he most needs that . . .

Midnight, The apartment. I've just read what I've written above and it doesn't make good sense. It's what I want to say but it doesn't say it coherently. The agony of wrenching my thoughts out of the pain that locks them in . . . the . . .

Monday: 1:10 A.M., The apartment. I'm beginning to be sorry I ever tried to write this with such an abominable hangover. My head is racked with aching; rest seems to do it no good. Yet something is making me finish this now. I have the feeling that I must conclude this affair here, on this page, or be defeated. I'm going to try a moderate dose of *Nembutal*. If it works, if I can get a bit of sleep, if I can remember what I'm trying to say and continue it to its conclusion, then I'll return to this page. Again, let me beg your pardon for this messy business. I'll cut it out of the manuscript when I revise it. I must remember to do that.

2:25 A.M., The apartment. Am doubling *Nembutal* dosage. Must watch drug intake.

3:00 A.M., *The apartment.* Ten per cent solution, morphine.

9:15 A.M., The apartment. Morning. The sun is streaming in through the slits between my shades. Outside I hear birds whistling. Some children call to each other on their way to school. A plane goes overhead, bound east probably, east for New York, or perhaps through Newfoundland and Ireland to England. Perhaps it is bound farther east than that, to Pans, to Rome. The morning is bright and gay. The whole world seems to be beaming with early summer.

And I am quite sure now, categorically certain, that they have said for me—as for Colin and Thaddeus Profit—a black mass, a mass of St. Secaire.

7 «◊» I'll Remember Her in My Will

PERHAPS YOU CAN TELL ME. You may have a wider range of experience that can supply a likely metaphor. The suspicion of being doomed is unlike any other feeling in the human mind's vast arsenal of emotions. I believe there is no one in the world who has not felt the eternal clutch of this emotion.

Yet to be doomed before our time! To be snatched off, like a casual mail sack gripped in the steel arms of a passing train, to be at one moment alive in the expectancy of many years, and then to be extinguished, to vanish, to dissolve in the space of an eye's wink.

Yes, it was futile, *and* sudden, and above all things, senseless. I could find no reason for it, no motive. I had been so clever, so circumspect. Where had I failed? How had they found out what I knew, and with such satanic efficiency? I called my receptionist and canceled all appointments. She knew something was wrong but I didn't have the heart even to hint at the root of my trouble. She led a fair-weather, completely uncomplicated life. She kept up with the world, but she wouldn't want to know about something as old as the world, something unbelievable out of the universal nightmares of the race. I told her I had a bad cold.

Then, in that first day of realization, I began to make plans. Like a man in a death cell planning out a career in the shadow of the electric chair, I sat down and conjured, once more, with facts, trying my blind best to ignore the one, the central fact that loomed enormous and devastating above me.

I had a few months to live. My first thought was to find out the exact nature of this curse on my body. I could pump people like Lenihan only so far, extract only so many additional facts from the few books on the subject, and then I would be at the end of my inquiry. It seemed certain to me that I would get no further with this plan than Colin had. If only I could find out more about my own particular case. What had caused it exactly, how had *they* found out, what exactly had they done and could anything be done to counteract it?

I knew partial answers to some of my questions. They were trying to destroy me for the same reasons they had destroyed Colin and Mr. Profit. I knew too much. They had a foolproof, detection-proof method of murder that no policeman would believe, no jury convict. It was the evidenceless murder with no fingerprint, no telltale odor or taste, no ballistics marking, no clue for the coroner, nothing but the final fact of its accomplishment.

What they had done and why seemed obvious to me as I sat there planning. How they had found out was puzzling but not tremendously important. They *had* found out, and that, irrevocably, was that. But the final question was the most pressing of all. Was it irrevocable? For Colin, yes. For me . . . no!

Colin's mistake had been his reliance on instinct. When it failed him, he sought study and that, too, failed him. Mr. Profit's mistake was surrender, without the slightest sign of struggle. I had that much to guide me, then: not intuition or study or surrender would succeed. Then what? The one thing neither of them had tried was direct action. The best defense is offense. When all seems lost, attack. Action would be my solution.

But what action? How can a man struggle against the suffocating night-phantoms of his dreams, against the entrenched powers of fear and evil? It seemed to me, as I sat there in futile thought, that I was a man fighting against demurrage in some dark elastic medium, a nebulous swamp of emptiness and invisibility. If action was the answer, what action?

Mercifully, I slept for a few hours that night. Where the urge for sleep came from, I cannot tell. But the pain that engulfed my brain and swathed its tentacles about my head like some malignant sea monster lessened and I slept. No, it was not a lessening. It was rather a retrenchment, as of some potent enemy digging in and waiting, retreating by plan to some heavily-fortified emplacement there to watch and wait and starve my aching soul into the final submission of death. I recalled every day of Colin's illness with a clarity that appalled me. He had enjoyed a few months of comparative ease, the pain ever present, yet never rising to the full, thundering cres-

cendo of its ultimate power. I would have to use my
time to some advantage. I would write this narrative
until I could no longer see the keyboard of my
typewriter. I would record the events of my borrowed
existence until the last, the ending moment.

And yet I knew, with a knowledge deep inside me,
that this satanic curse could never kill me. Colin had
been headstrong, Profit weak. But I was knowing,
alert, forewarned and highly unimpressed by their
machinations. They might overwhelm someone more
believing, more impressionable. But I didn't believe. I
wasn't impressed. I would beat back this foul thing
the way any malignant thing is defeated, the way I
would vanquish any other disease or pain. I would
win. They would lose. I knew that.

The next day I went to the office. Evidently the
sleep my pain had given me, as a bone to a starving
dog, had smoothed over the lines of anxiety in my
face. With only a little effort I managed to present the
calm facade of normalcy to my receptionist and my
patients. But the day went slowly. I caught myself
glancing at my watch every hour and wondering
whether it had stopped. Time seemed to drag on
endlessly. Events that seemed to take up hours were
in reality encompassed by minutes of my time. By my
mind's reckoning I had been in this office, treating
sprains, prescribing for anemia, taking blood pres-
sures, percussing chests, for days, weeks. My eyes were
set in baskets of pain. My forehead was beaded with
nervous sweat. My fingers trembled as I pushed up
my cuff and glanced, one more time in that eternity of

a day, at my wristwatch. Four-thirty. I was through for the day.

I got up from behind my desk and leaned against it for support. I heard the outer door open and voices in the reception room. Not another patient, I cried inwardly. My office door opened.

"He's here again," my receptionist said, winking broadly.

"Who, for God's sake?"

"That pretty fellow."

"What pretty fellow?" I snapped, almost loud enough for the sound of my voice to reach the person in question.

"Morelle," she sighed, "Mr. Morelle."

I don't remember waving him in. All I remember is one thing my mind saying over and over to itself, "He's here to check, he's here to check." Morelle was the trouble shooter, the man who stole hosts who was sent out to scout around and report back. He wanted to know whether the . . . the curse or whatever it was had fallen on me as they planned. I watched his dapper body enter the room, his curved mouth smile, his elegantly-shod legs cross as he sat down.

"And how are you, doctor?"

The audacity, the sheer nerve of this—this advance man for the devil! He must know that I linked the theft of the host with him, must know that I had added him to my private list of the Dune-Dwellers, must know that already I understood the nature of my accursed headache. Yet he sat down and smiled and asked after me solicitously. I had to hide my pain. I had to lie to him and lie with the perfection of an accomplished actor.

"Never better," I replied. "How's the insomnia?"

His big, round eyes opened wide. "I thought you'd forgotten about my trifling ailments," he said softly. The colossal audacity of this worm!

"Once a patient," I heard my voice say in a jovial tone, "always a patient. Did you get much relief from the prescription?"

The flicker of a smile disturbed his perfect lips. I sensed a kind of bored amusement in his mien, as though he were observing the dying activity of a gaffed fish. "Unfortunately," he said, taking his own good time, "it hasn't done much good."

"Then perhaps my original diagnosis?" I asked lightly. "A lawyer?"

"Divorce isn't the answer," he replied in kind. He seemed to be eying me with a kind of clinical detachment, as though we were both engaged in some covert operation, both wrapped up in something that our conversation merely cloaked with an air of reality. "Perhaps you've another suggestion?"

"Well . . ." I hunched my shoulders and leaned over the desk in an apparent attitude of deep thought. The action sent a twanging burst of pain up my spinal column into the aching recesses of my head, but somehow I was able to control the expression on my face. I kept it rapt, thoughtful. "Perhaps we'd better get to the real source of the trouble," I said.

"Which is?"

"That's something we'll have to find out slowly," I

said. "We'll take a series of tests. Insomnia can be an organic thing in itself, or it can be simply a reaction to some organic difficulty. As I said before, Mr. Morelle, if you want to put yourself in my hands for a few weeks, I think we can accomplish something."

Again that faint, malicious smile crossed his mouth. "Could you really spare the time?" he asked. A man in your dying condition, his tone added.

"I have a world of time," I said. "Often patients are outraged by the slowness of my treatment. You see, I'm being frank with you. We could find our answer in days, or it might take months. Or we might never clear it up satisfactorily. But there you are. No other physician could promise more . . . truthfully, that is." He seemed to be surprised. I could have been wrong, but it seemed that way to me.

"I don't know if I've impressed you with my situation, doctor," he said slowly, emphasizing each word. "I have a career a promising one. I simply cannot spare time and money."

I shook my head and smiled. "You're impossible, Mr. Morelle," I told him. "You give me a problem that takes both time and money to solve and then you as much as tell me you don't want it solved. I really think you're wasting your time and mine."

He nodded and his eyes watched me closely. "I thought you had a world of time," he responded softly.

"I do," I retorted, "but you've told me *you* don't."

"I see." He seemed to consider my answer for a long time and I felt the tension growing about us.

How long could I keep this up? Had I given myself away already?

"Tell me," he said, and paused. I waited tensely. He sighed and crossed his legs the other way. "Tell me," he went on after an agonizing moment, "have you had much experience with psychological ailments?"

"A practical knowledge," I said. "Quite a few of my cases have a psychosomatic basis."

"Of course," he rejoined. "But tell me . . ." Again he paused and I sensed what was coming. The direct attack. I knew it. How would I meet it? What facial expression, what words, what tone of voice? This had to be perfect. ". . . tell me," he continued at last, "is there much psychological background for insomnia and . . ." again he paused, ". . . and headaches?"

"Some," I said, making my voice sound thoughtful but not too interested. I had a blank expression on my face, not too blank, but holding only a slight amount of interest and conjecture. "Insomnia and headaches are often the result of anxieties, as any layman can tell you, and, on the other hand, as any doctor will testify, they are primary symptoms of organic disturbances. A bad tooth, faulty digestion, blood pressure, cardiac condition, almost anything can produce either insomnia or headache. And, I might add, there are other disorders with a similarly confused origin: intestinal upset, lack of manual coordination, profuse perspiration, skin eruption . . . many things." I paused just long enough for him to frame a reply, and then I spoke again, taking the initiative away from him.

"Do you understand your dilemma?" I asked briskly. "You've given me practically nothing in the way of evidence, but even so can you see how complex the problem really is?"

He nodded thoughtfully. I had the feeling that he was confused. Perhaps I had thrown him off the track. I hoped so. And then, when he spoke, I realized that he had not forsaken the direct attack, only modified it, shifted it.

"By the way," he said, "you were recommended to me by a friend of a patient. Dr. Khereniev? Remember him?"

I thought I handled it fairly well. I let my eyebrows rise slightly and my mouth open as if pausing in readiness to utter a response when my mind should remember Khereniev's name. "Of course," I said at length. "He's a friend of Miss Cowper. Abbie Cowper?"

"That's right," he said. Did I detect failure in the dying fall of his words? Was he convinced that either I knew nothing of their plot, or else that I was in some strange way immune to it?

"But Abbie's not just a patient," I said, thinking that this might strengthen my case. "She's a good friend. We have adjoining cabins in the Dunes."

"So I'd heard," he remarked. "My wife and I were trying to rent a place near there but there doesn't seem to be an available cottage. Do you know of any?"

The real question he'd asked was, did I intend to get rid of my own cabin? "Not that I know of," I said. "It seems to me that you'd either have to buy a cabin of your own or live as a guest of someone. I don't think you'll find any cabins for rent."

"It takes quite a lot of money," he said at length. I waited. "I understand a wealthy automobile magnate from South Bend is building in your area." What was he driving at? "Works for the Studebaker people, I understand. He's taken an option on one of the best locations there." Get to the point, I thought feverishly. I could only stand so much more of this cat and mouse business. Plans a pretty big house, eight or ten rooms." I felt perspiration begin to ooze down my forehead. Could he see it in this light? I didn't dare wipe at it. "Dr. Khereniev was telling me about it yesterday," he said. "It's to be on the tallest dune there, a whopper of a thing half a mile from the beach."

So that was it. The high place. He was probing my guard with the agility of a swordsman, trying every crevice. Did I know about the high place? Was I aware of its significance? My best tactic was silence. I shifted in my chair and looked a trifle bored. I waited.

"Do you know the place?" He asked directly.

"I don't know," I said offhand. "I've only been out there one weekend and I spent most of it sleeping."

Then he pounced. "Sleep's a wonderful thing," he said quickly. "I hope you never suffer from the kind of insomnia I have."

"If I do" I said, "I won't be as casual about it as you, Mr. Morelle. Insomnia can be a tremendous drain on the body. If I were you, I'd get to the bottom of it without delay I sat back fairly well satisfied with the tone of my admonition. It had the flavor of sound medical advice, of the single-minded approach a doctor would have toward Morelle's mythical problem . . . providing, of course, that he didn't know it was mythical.

He was silent for a long moment. Then, when he stirred to life, it was the movement of a man about to conclude his business and leave. I felt tremendously relieved, yet something at the back of my mind warned me to remain on guard. This might be another tactic. I pulled my prescription pad toward me. "Supposing" I said, "you give the matter some thought. I don't want to rush you, but I do not want you to make a decision as quickly as possible . . . for your own good. Meanwhile, if you'd like to refill the prescription it can't hurt. The stuff's harmless. But remember one thing: a sedative won't cure it. As long as you let it persist, you'll never get complete relief." Highly unethical, but it served to keep the conversation alive.

"Never mind," he said. He stood up. "I'll think it over," he went on. "And you'll probably hear from me in a day or so."

"All right." I stood up and smiled at him. I could afford to.

"Nice day," he said suddenly "It's great to be alive in this weather."

"It certainly is," I agreed. I managed to put as much enthusiasm into it as I could without seeming unnatural. I think it worked. At any rate, he looked at me with a veiled, slightly baffled expression, started to say something, stopped, and then came up with: "Thanks for everything."

I sat down and waited for the outer door to close behind him. When it did, I slumped back in the chair and felt unused muscles in my body begin a delicate fluttering. I let out a deep sigh of relief. I had won the first round, or so it seemed. As much as it could ever seem in this shady, uncertain affair. I leaned back still further and suddenly, with a white-hot intensity, a pain lanced upwards from the back of my head, hard, sharp, brutal. Perhaps I had won a round, but the battle, who would win that?

THAT WAS THE DAY BEFORE YESTERDAY. I am writing this now out of an almost frightening sense of total recall. Everything returns to me with brilliant clarity, like a sharply focused cinema film reeled off in the private theater of my mind, details accurate as to shape and placement, everything tremendously clear, with that absolute perfection no human being has a right to enjoy. And I am not, believe me, enjoying it.

I had been reading a little in some of Colin's books about the various kinds of savage or primitive ideas that underlay the whole concept of curses, spells, remote murders, etc. The business was childishly gruesome, a mélange of faulty logic, primitive fear and not a little fraud. The basic tenet of such black magic was the belief in an indwelling soul, not the philosophic abstraction of later religious conjecture, but a positive, often tangible object, a soul, that resided in the body of every living thing.

This "soul" sometimes took the form of a *homunculus*, a tiny manikin; but more often it was an invisible thing that wandered from the body in sleep, escaped in sneezes, and could be stolen by a clever sorcerer. Primitive men, trying to understand their dreams, called them the life of their soul and put more credit in them than in their waking life. Wizards, by incantations over some relic of a person—his clothes, nail parings, or hair—could extract the soul and hold it for their own evil purposes . . . or more likely, allow it to be ransomed for a profitable fee.

The sorcery, ritual and spells designed to kill a man were directed toward the pilfering of his soul, since with this valuable adjunct gone, the body would collapse like a sucked egg, withering and dying by rapid degrees.

I lay down on my couch and held some ice cubes in a rag on my forehead. The cold was intense; it seemed to stimulate the headache. I have it up and lay there, my body as relaxed as I could make it. Then the phone rang and abruptly my skin prickled with nervousness and my heart pounded insanely. I got to my feet shakily and answered the insistent ringing.

"Joe darling?"

It was Abbie. Evidently Morelle had reported back

and they were confused. I waited silently

"Golly, you're the queer one," she said lightly. I waited, telling myself again and again to be careful. She wasn't Morelle. She . . . she was magic or something. And I had to conceal everything from her. "Aren't you going to ask why?"

"Okay Why?"

"Well, I like that. Why don't you call me up, darling? It's damaging to a girl's morale to have to keep calling a man. I mean it degenerates into a chase."

"I hadn't noticed," I said.

"I'll bet you haven't. Look, darling, why won't you tell me what's the matter with us? That . . . that business last Saturday was frightful."

I laughed sheepishly. "I guess it was," I said, "but I've been badly overworked and . . . well, you know, man isn't made of wood."

There was a long pause on the other end of the line. Then I heard her laugh, a sort of liquid gurgling that sounded soft and delightful. Even from her mouth it sounded that way. The trained voice, no doubt. "That's really very good," she said, catching her breath, "coming from you."

I shouldn't know what she was talking about. "Huh," I said.

"Never mind." There was a quick change in her voice. "Tell me, Dr. Loomis, are you taken up with your practice this evening?"

Something coming, no way of knowing what. Invitation? To what, where? I couldn't refuse; this was what I had planned for when I concealed everything from Morelle. "I'm not doing a thing," I said casually.

"Feel up to a little sociability?"

What did she mean, feel up to? A veiled thrust again. I had to parry it. "Ready for anything," I responded in what I thought was a gay voice. "What's on your mind?"

"Cocktails," she said, "and conversation . . . at Jacques Khereniev's."

KHERENIEV settled us at one end of his huge living room, put martinis in our hands and left us to our own devices for a few moments. I believe I carried on some kind of conversation with Abbie but I can't remember the details. Small talk, chitchat, possibly about radio or something kindred. My mind was busy with other things. I was sizing up the people in that room.

There was one of those tremendously chic women curled up on one end of a long divan, a woman in her fifties with every outward, superficial manifestation of age or beauty carefully under control. Her vernicose hair was gray, or had been; it was now tinted a startling shade of violet. Her shoes were complicated arrangements of suede and gold, huge platform soles and cup-like backs that ended in extravagantly formed pennants or triangles or whatever *haute couture* called them. She was monopolizing three men, two of them her age and showing the effects of their years rather more openly in balding heads and swelling paunches. The third was much younger, perhaps barely of voting age, a slight, bony young man with stringy red hair, eyes so pale they verged on pinkness, and a nervous habit of snapping the fingers of his left hand to some offbeat rhythm all their own. When Kereniev finally saw fit to introduce them, the older men turned out to be faculty colleagues and the nervous young man a prize student of some kind named Foss. The elegant woman was simply a Mrs. Demester, nothing more. Across the room ensconced in two chairs much as Abbie and I, were two people who nodded politely to us, but failed to break the thread of their own conversation to say hello. One of them was Sam Olson . . . the other, Jason Flye.

So this was to be a board of inquiry then, a sort of kangaroo court that would pass on my condition. The initial report by Morelle had given them some worry, evidently. I showed no signs of the headache. I gave no hint of suspicion. Either I was bluffing, and they'd have nothing more to worry about, or else I was immune, and then . . . then they'd have trouble on their hands. I wondered how many of them were in on this inquisition. I was sure of Abbie, Olson, Flye and Khereniev. What of the others, the suave Mrs. Demester, the portly professors (if they *were* professors), and the ill-at-ease Foss? This thing was evidently wider than I had imagined. As soon as the business at hand got under way, as soon as the polite chitchat ebbed and died, I'd find out just who was who. For half an hour nothing much happened.

Then the doorbell rang. Khereniev scurried out of the other room and pressed a button on the entryway wall. "Late arrivals," he shot over his shoulder as he opened the door.

Into the room stepped a woman in her thirties, platinum blonde with hair roots of a darker shade and eyebrows to match that telltale color clad in a print dress of loud pattern, red patent leather high-heeled pumps and nail polish of the same hue. She smiled insipidly at Flye out of a heavily rouged mouth that seemed to have been deliberately painted into an arched pout. Her pale blue eyes were vapid, netted in fine wrinkles. A palpable double chin flabbed below her own rather weak one, yet her figure was fairly trim. She held her body, however, in a slumped position, her shoulders bowed forward, her breasts half pushed into her abdomen. Behind her entered my old friend, Mr. Morelle.

Sam Olson jumped to his feet. "Don," he said, "long time no see."

Morelle extended his finely modeled hand to Olson. It was immediately swallowed up from sight in the latter's massive paw. Jason Flye, one arm lost from sight behind the blonde's back, turned to the rest of us and made the necessary introductions.

"Mrs. Demester, Dr. Cranach, Dr. Yount, Mr. Floss, this is Mr. and Mrs. Morelle." He smiled in my direction. "I guess you know everyone else," he added.

"Not him," Mrs. Morelle said in a thin, hard voice.

"Dr. Loomis, darling," her husband supplied hastily. "Remember I was telling you about him?"

"Oh, sure," she said. By this time the two of them had found their way over to my side of the room. Morelle stood slightly behind his wife, smiling thinly. The blonde was eying me dispassionately as she talked. "You got Mr. Jones's place. Right?"

I nodded. "I understand you folks would like to find a place out there."

"Us?" She seemed surprised. "Why, I—"

"Not much chance of that," Morelle cut in quickly. "Flo, why don't you sit down and relax while I pay our respects to Khereniev."

"Flo," Abbie said, "I love that dress. Is it new?"

"Last month," she said by way of a reply. "I never get the chance to wear it. Seems Don's always out on business or something. I had to . . ." She lowered her voice to include only the three of us. ". . . I had to argue like crazy to get him to take me tonight."

"It's such a lovely night out," Abbie agreed heartily. "I hope the weather holds for weeks like this. I hate to think of summer."

"I get tired," Flo went on, "just sitting around the flat and reading. I like to get out. I told Don, I said: 'Don, I'll take roots if you don't get me out of this flat at least one night a week.' I guess I would, too."

"Well," I said entering the conversation as heavily as I could, "your husband's a very busy man. From what he tells me, he's on the go night and day."

"Maybe," Flo agreed, reluctantly. "But you're not married to him."

"I should say he isn't," Abbie put in, smiling.

Flo looked at her wonderingly for a minute, then laughed a tiny, silvery laugh and slitted her eyes at Abbie. "You didn't tell me you . . ." She made a terribly unsubtle gesture involving the two of us. "How long's this been going on?"

"I sometimes wonder," Abbie rejoined archly.

Flo sighed and looked wise. "Doctors," she said. That was the end of that.

My mind wandered a bit. Seeing Morelle had startled me and my headache suddenly increased in intensity until I could hardly keep my face smooth and blank. I tried to shut out the talk of the two women and concentrate on my own thoughts. Why had Morelle come here? He'd already made his report, otherwise I wouldn't be here for the official examination. Why had he brought his wife? Was it as she said, because she'd forced him to take her? When was the polite chatter going to take on meaning and purpose? I was one against so many. I knew I could rebuff a straight attack, but evidently they were working one or two removes from a straight attack, the way Abbie had worked that horrible night when, somehow, I'd let something slip. What about the four people on the divan? Were they part of it? My brain pulsed and throbbed. A knifing, thrusting sensation welled up from the base of my skull, shoving inward on my brain in a single vibrating rush. The more I tried to think the worse the agony grew. I had to talk or listen. I couldn't think anymore, the pain was too much. I felt my Jaw clamp down tight on itself. Could they see the bulging of my cheek muscles? I tried to relax them.

Khereniev entered the room and behind him I could see Morelle carrying a large tray of highly professional canapés and a tall shaker frosted with water vapor. "Anybody feel the need?" he asked the company at large. He held up the shaker and gave it a flourish.

"Me, Don" his wife announced.

Morelle seemed reluctant to take notice of her. "I'll pass around the canapés," he muttered.

"He always does that," Flo confided to Abbie and me. "He thinks I can't hold my liquor."

"But you can," I said more to use my tongue than for any other reason. "I can tell you can. And after all, I'm a doctor."

"You said it," she informed me. She got up and went across the room to the cocktail shaker, her hips flouncing back and forth as she walked. I saw her pour herself a brimming glass, taste it, murmur something unintelligible, drain the glass and pour it full again. "Did you mix these?" she asked Khereniev.

"Your husband," he said briefly, relieving her of the shaker. Flo returned to us, a slight pout on her lips that had nothing to do with the artificial one already there.

"*You* know I can, anyway," she whispered to me. She upped her glass in a salute, then emptied it with dispatch down her throat.

Khereniev's hands were hidden from me. He was pouring drinks for the rest of the group and the contents of the shaker, in the brief moments, when I caught sight of it, were slowly diminishing. There seemed to be no more than a single drink left in it. He turned away from me, then wheeled around. "One more," he announced genially. He poured it in the glass I held out to him.

"Lucky you," Flo murmured in my ear.

I sat there holding the slim-stemmed glass and trying to think. Why had my drink been the last? Khereniev had undoubtedly put something in it. I didn't know what and I wasn't in any condition to find out by experimental drinking. Not me. Not any- more. I smiled at Flo Morelle, swung my eyes to my full glass, then to her empty one, and winked. She winked back. We understood each other perfectly, Flo and I. I handed her my glass and received hers in return. Perfect.

"Flo," Abbie spoke up, "I don't know if—"

"Now, Abigail," Flo said. "Now, now, now. This is doctor's orders, Abigail. You wouldn't go against doctor's orders, would you?"

"But you've already had two and you know how—"

"Flo." It was Morelle's voice. Out of nowhere, apparently, he had materialized to stand before his wife, his hand outstretched for the full martini glass. "No fuss, now," he said quietly.

"No fuss," she agreed. She lifted the drink to her lips.

"Flo." The single word, nothing more. His body was shielding her from the people on the divan. If need be, he could take the glass from her by force but I knew if he did Flo would protest vociferously. It was a neat problem in calculation and depended on whether or not there was anything other than vermouth and gin in that cocktail. If there was, and if it were powerful stuff, then Flo mustn't drink it no matter what the cost in social embarrassment. I sat back and watched, patiently.

"Come, Flo," he muttered under his breath.

"Sure, darling." She grinned at him, tipped the glass to her mouth.

"Flo." The word had a keen edge of menace in it. "Give me the glass."

"Sure I will, honey," she replied. She emptied the cocktail into her mouth, gave a terrific swallow, and handed the empty glass to her husband. "Here's the glass, honey," she cooed. I promised myself to remember her in my will.

The next fifteen minutes were strangely quiet ones. On the divan Foss was trying to convince one of the professors that he was no more immature than the next person and the other professor, as the next person, was protesting wittily. Mrs. Demester was smiling impartially, the seeming arbiter for this repartee. Across the room, Olson and Flye were involved in some quiet sort of discussion which I couldn't hear. Khereniev's unevenly bloated body hovered before them, his eyes snapping back and forth between them and the people around me, his mouth pursing nervously as he spat out a brief response to Olson's queries. Morelle seemed to have no resting place. He stood for a moment beside Khereniev, then drifted to the divan group, listened, smiled baldly and wandered over to me. He gave Flo a hard look, then turned to Abbie and engaged her in a desultory conversation about some radio producer she knew who was interested in buying a large insurance policy from him.

I kept my eyes on Flo.

My pulse seemed to be fairly normal, a trifle fast, but nothing out of the ordinary. I could feel it beating in my throat,

in that hollow just below the Adam's apple. I tried not to stare at Flo, but my glance kept returning to her as though she were a firecracker with a long fuse. She seemed to have quieted down considerably. Once, when she caught me watching her, she gave me a soft little wink and rolled her eyes. She seemed like a nice, simple, slightly cheap girl. I wondered how far she was involved in this business. Being Morelle's wife entitled her to some understanding of the thing, but from what she had said I felt that he was hiding most of his affairs from her. The fact that he hardly ever took her any place pointed to that sort of situation. I sighed deeply. I didn't know how much longer it could take for whatever she'd had to react, if, indeed, there had been anything foreign in the martini. I wondered how long it would take me to use up my reserve supply of nerve. Whenever I was alone with my thoughts the torturous pain nauseated me, revolting my sensibilities like some loathsome intruder. I closed my eyes for a moment, then opened them quickly, not daring to be caught in such a pose.

I watched Flo. Something seemed to be building in her. Suddenly, I saw her heavily-rouged lips move, soften, grow slack. I thought I heard her say something but all that came out of those lips was a kind of puling noise, as of a tiny infant amusing itself. I saw Morelle straighten up and look at his watch.

"God, I didn't realize how late it was," he said. Nobody paid any attention to him.

I started to say something about it being scarcely ten o'clock, but thought better of the idea. Flo's mouth closed, tightened. When she opened it, it was to speak. "I hope it never gets to be summer," she said.

Abbie nodded gravely. "Summer in Chicago is simply frightful."

"Simply frightful," Flo echoed, and I couldn't tell whether it was straight agreement or the numbed miming of a person whose mind is out of control.

Nobody was listening to us. The divan group was entranced in their own discussion, whatever it might be. Olson and Flye still conversed in low tones. "Summer is terrible," Flo said then. "I can't stand summer all cooped up in that stinking little flat of ours."

Khereniev's bulbous head swiveled about on his shoulders. His little eyes examined Flo's face. "The heat," she went on softly, "all that lousy heat. But it isn't the heat," she giggled quietly, "it's the humidity."

"Ha," Abbie said dryly.

Khereniev glanced at Morelle, then came over to us. "If you're warm," he purred, "it's cool on my balcony. I get a strong breeze off the lake there."

"Not now," Flo said fuzzily. "It's wonderful now. I meant summer. Don leaves me alone in that stinking flat and I just boil. I dissolve, actually. Do you have another of those cool, cool martinis, honey?"

Morelle shook his head. "I was just talking," Khereniev said, "with Jason and Mr. Olson. They tell me someone has secured an option on the large dune. Is it so?"

"That's right." Morelle's voice was flat and committed him to nothing.

"Amazing," Khereniev breathed. "The man must be exceedingly wealthy to afford such a construction. The cost of transporting equipment and material alone must be tremendous. To say nothing of lifting them to the top of the dune." His eyes switched to me. "Do you know the dune I refer to?"

"I don't think so," I said. "On my way up I passed something of the sort but it's hard to tell which dune is higher than its neighbors."

"Oh, then this is the *high* dune?" Khereniev pounced. "Then you *do* know it."

Had I slipped? My mind refused to respond. I had to force it, crush down the punishing spasm of pain that racked my head.

"Mr. Morelle mentioned it this afternoon," I said finally. "He . . . wasn't it some auto magnate from South Bend?"

"That's right," Morelle said. Apparently he had decided to limit himself to those two words from henceforth.

"If it is the dune I have in mind," Khereniev continued smoothly, "it is quite close to your cabin, doctor."

I forced an expression of mild surprise. "I didn't know you were a Dune-Dweller too," I said. That was as safe as anything else.

"But of course," he assured me. "I am perhaps the founder of the group."

"Really." Was he? Or was this a trick? "I had the idea," I hazarded, "that the Olsons were the earliest settlers."

"Perhaps," he replied, "but the idea of the organization was mine. Mr. Olson . . ." his voice lowered, "is a very sincere man, perhaps more so than I."

Whatever that meant, he let it stand. "That's very strange," I heard myself say, meaninglessly. My mind didn't seem to have anything to do with the words coming from my mouth.

Khereniev smiled broadly at me. "There are times and places for everything," he said.

I nodded and the motion sickened me. My head throbbed and reeled as the pain pierced through my skull, gnawed and bit and wrung at the soft gray of my brain. How much of this could I take? The pressure from within was unbearable. Now the outside pressure was intensifying. "I see," I heard a strange voice say. It sounded like my own but I couldn't be sure. I felt consciousness begin to slip away from me, like the shore retreating from an outgoing ship. I tried to hold on to awareness. If I fainted, the secret would be lost. If I fainted, the—

"You and those crazy Dune-Dwellers of yours," Flo's voice said. It had a tinny ring to it, unreal, filtered through receding waves of palpitation inside my head.

"Now, Flo." Abbie's voice, low, muted, muffled, unearthly.

"I don't see what all the hush-hush is about." Flo. Loud, strident.

"Well, every organization has its petty secrets." Khereniev. Soothing, soft.

"That sounds crazy, too." Flo. Nasty, sharp.

"Look, Flo, you've had too much." Morelle. Warning, menacing.

"Too much, too much. I know when I've had enough, all right!"

"Please, Flo." Abbie. Consoling, calming.

"And I've had enough of all of you right now."

"Flo!" Morelle. The sharp thrust of his single word was like a jagged knife thrust into my brain, stabbing and slicing and ripping through in one convulsive wound that radiated a harrowing pang of intense pain.

"Flo. Flo," she mimicked. "I got a right to speak my mind. I hate the bunch of you."

"Look here, Flo . . ."

"Look here nothing. You and your crazy carryings-on. I know what's going on. I may not be as smart as you, Mr. Fancy Don, but I can see. Boy, you bet I can. I got eyes. And how I got eyes."

"Flo . . ."

"Think you can shut me up like you do at home?"

"You're not—"

"Hell you can. This is a free country, at least outside that rotten little flat of yours it is."

"You'd better—"

"And Miss Abigail, Miss Priss, Miss Demure. I know what's back of that just as much as the rest of them."

"I can't have you—" Khereniev's voice.

"What? Look, professor or whatever you call yourself, I drank your liquor but it don't give you a claim on me."

"You'll have to excuse—"

"Excuse my fanny, Don boy. I've got you where it hurts and you know it, you fancy little faker you."

". . . awfully sorry about—"

"About my fanny. All these people'd love to know what goes on, I'll bet they would. They'd get the surprise of the year."

A kind of repellent laughter filled my ears, billowing up over my head like the frothy scum of some festering, noisome broth. It was the giggle of a madwoman laced with the hysteria of fear. My eyes were open but across the pain-racked field of my vision nothing but odd spiraling shapes could be seen. They coalesced for a brief instant now and then, took on the vague shape of human figures, but disintegrated into bizarre wheeling patterns of sheer eyestrain. I held my lids open by some kind of ultra-human force. I listened, I waited. I would remember that girl in my will, all right. She was saving me. If only she'd hurry . . .

". . . and I hope you'll all—" Morelle started to apologize.

"All my fanny. Go on, take me away. You're not strong enough, lacy-pants. You gotta have your boys along. They're here, aren't they? Why don't they help you, lacy-pants?"

". . . good night, and—"

"And my fanny. I'm not drunk. I'm sober like mad. I could tell you things that'd make your eyes bug down to the floor. You see that pretty-pretty Abigail? She looks so sweet, but did you ever see her when the moon's—"

Door slam. Hard. It shook the pain patterns out of my retina. I would remember Flo in my will. She was a darling, that kid. Sorry about switching the drink, all fair love and war. The second battle mine. War wasn't over, but this battle mine. If I played it right. Had to play it right.

THAT WAS YESTERDAY. Today was wonderfully quiet, the simple monotony of a regular day, menopause, spastic colitis, a particularly virulent case of eczema. The blessed monotony of the common-place. I felt grateful. I even let myself feel hopeful.

At four-thirty this afternoon my last caller was not a patient. He was a burly man of my age, his brown hair clipped close, his suit faintly baggy at the knees, a cigar in his mouth. I remember thinking that it was strange to see a young man with all the appearance of a confirmed cigar-smoker. He showed me a nickel-plated star fastened to the inner flap of his wallet.

"You were at the home of a Dr. Jacques Khereniev last night?"

"That's right. Why?"

"I'd like some information from you."

"Certainly. Why?"

"There was a Mr. and Mrs. Donald Morelle there?"

"Yes. Can't you tell me why?"

"She's dead. He killed her."

8 «◊» Flye, By Night

WE WERE ALL IN A SMALLISH ROOM, a sort of locked chamber whose walls were curved. There seemed to be no corners, as though the room were the inside of a ball, and all these cats were chasing themselves around inside, slipping and clawing at the walls for a foothold on the slimy surface.

Globules of some fluid sweated out of the pores of the walls, which made the footing even more treacherous, until this one cat smiled at me and said: "If you have any sand . . ?" Such a pleading expression, but I had no sand, only a little emery paper I had once used, when in high school, to file the ignition points of a sparkplug. "No sand?" they chorused, a kind of *a capella* chord on the last word, swelling and holding like the final syllable of a Gregorian chant, and I shook my head as I smoothed my fingernails with the emery paper. Little fragments of some shiny metal were imbedded in its black, grainy surface and when I had finished, my fingernails were ringed with glittering crescents.

"No sand?" they chanted again. I tried to stuff the emery paper in my pocket but I had no pockets, no clothes. I folded it quickly and tucked it behind my ear.

"No sand?" The room was getting smaller and I took the emery paper from behind my ear and tried to stuff it in my pocket. I had no pockets, no clothes.

"No *sand?*" The room had dwindled to the size of a beach ball and the cats were pressing in on me, yowling and spitting, their eyes green, their tongues red, their teeth sharp and bony, their whiskers tickling me. I tried to put the emery paper in my pocket.

"No SAND?" The words rose like a crescendo on ill-tuned cellos, wavering and squalling and shrieking in dissonant chords, and finally I found a pocket. I tried to stuff the emery paper in it but instead it was a glass ampoule. It crumbled in my fingers with a tearing noise and a hundred million tons of sand spilled out in a prolonged rush, hissing and tearing out until the whole room was filled with sand and the cats and myself, we inhabited the sand like worms, like bugs, drilling channels and pawing at all the sand and trying to get air or light or water, anything but all this sand.

"He said no *sand!*" they yelled, muffled now by all the sand and I tried to smile at them but my mouth was filled with all this sand. It trickled slowly, then more quickly, back along my tongue, hot and grainy, down into my windpipe, and then it filled me like some fleshy children's toy, filled my stomach and lungs and the cats cavorted in the sand, their eyes glowing in pockets of it like live green coals from a beach fire.

I could feel the sand begin to course through my

blood-stream tearing at the inner walls of the delicate arteries and veins. "When it reaches the cranial capillaries," a cat explained carefully, "he will suffer cerebral thrombosis, which, in his attenuated condition, will undoubtedly prove fatal."

I could feel an advance column of sand grains marching slowly upwards through both venous and arterial systems climbing higher, along my cheeks, my temples, upward into my brain where they would meet at last in a final embolism, sudden, lightning-like, instant—and there would be a blinding flare of light, as I knew, struck by the impact of their opposing columns, and I would die in the sudden moment with a grinding, moldering, simultaneous decay as of some ancient edifice, its underpinnings honeycombed with explosive. And I waited, breathing hard, the sand blowing in and out of my mouth and nose, my eyes pressed shut, the cat smell huge and compelling, a musky, fleshy smell, rancid and gamy, and the twin columns of sand crawled higher, upward, skyward to the recesses of my brain. "No *sand,* he *said,*" the cats chorused. I woke up.

An intense spasm of pain exploded behind my skull, blasting my head forward off the pillow. I was completely conscious, my neck craning forward, my eyes gritty and raw in the darkened room, the immense shuddering roar of my wristwatch coming to me in unbearable pulsations of noise. I looked at it. Midnight. I had been asleep for two hours and thirty-seven minutes. Now I was wide-awake, trembling, the pain in my head filling me with an appalling nausea. I got out of bed, stumbled through the darkened apartment to the kitchen, and drank a glass of cold water. It tasted revolting.

I lay down on the living room couch and closed my eyes, not to sleep, but to think. I had plans to make and since I couldn't sleep, this was as good a time as any to make them. I got up and put a piece of paper in the typewriter.

I might as well add this to the narrative as keep it locked in my mind. The important thing now is to get my thoughts down on paper where they make some kind of coherent sense. There are three things to think about. I'll write them as a kind of agenda. "(1). Flo's Murder. (2). The Dune-Dwellers analyzed. (3). Action."

(1). Flo's Murder. This is cut-and-dried stuff, easily analyzed. She was killed, obviously, because she was dangerous, just as Colin and Profit were killed—and now me—because we knew too much and were not to be trusted with our knowledge. There remains then the begging question: why didn't they kill her in their own demoniac fashion, as they are trying to kill me? They have a perfect weapon, whatever it is, that leaves no evidence and kills as surely as a bullet. Yet they *used* bullets, two of them, .22 caliber copper-nosed slugs fired from a Colt Woodsman's Special at close range, almost point-blank (powder burns on her dress), that neatly punctured her heart and brought almost instantaneous death.

The detective-sergeant who interviewed me yester-day explained only a little of the murder. The rest I got from newspaper accounts. There seems to be general agreement among all the newspapers as to the main outlines of a crime the *Herald-American* calls, "Sex-Crazed Slayer Defies Police," and which the *Sun-Times* sees fit to headline: "Passion Killer Snared in Own Alibi." The events of the murder run something like this:

Morelle called the police early yesterday morning to report his wife's death. They found the gun on the floor beside the bed on which her body lay. Morelle sat in another room of the apartment, evidently fairly calm and coherent. His story was that he'd returned a few minutes before from a business trip into Michigan and Indiana, arriving to find Flo dead. He professed no knowledge of the gun, claiming he'd never seen it before and that neither he nor his wife had ever bought it. He'd seen a man, he claimed, escaping by the back stairway. The serial number inside the gun had been filed off and the metal hammered down in such a way that the police were unable to bring the numbers up by their usual methods. There were a variety of fingerprints on the gun, but the checked-wood stock offered poor material for accurate impresssions. The only identifiable prints were those of Morelle, a few on the barrel, one lapping over the grip from the wood to the surrounding metal.

The coroner decided that Flo had evidently been dead only a few minutes before Morelle called the police. The elevator operator reported that Morelle had left the apartment about one A.M., hardly the usual hour to begin a business trip, and had returned more than half an hour before the officially-set time of the murder. Morelle had refuted the elevator man's story by offering the name of a witness at whose Dunes cabin he'd spent the night. The witness, one Maida Teufler, explained to the police that she didn't know what Morelle was talking about, that she'd never seen him before in her life. Morelle countered by claiming the gun didn't belong to him; why didn't they find the gun's official owner, the murderer? The police were holding him for the inquest on suspicion of murder when the final bit of evidence showed up, a policy for $15 thousand on Flo's life, naming as beneficiary Don Morelle. They booked him for murder, and the district attorney's office was preparing for an early trial. Morelle's attitude in jail was sullen but not despondent. He was quoted by the *Sun-Times* reporter as saying: "I'll never die for her murder."

I was inclined to agree with him. He probably never would, if I knew my Dune-Dwellers. He'd probably be stricken, while in jail, with a malignant headache, ending in his eventual death. It seemed certain that he'd be found guilty. No one had seen anyone but him enter or leave the murder apartment. That was circumstantial evidence, but coupled with the phony alibi, the juxtaposition of death and discovery and the powerful motive, he seemed a cinch for conviction. There remained only the mysteriously anonymous gun, the .22 Colt with the obliterated serial number. He wouldn't say where he'd gotten it or to whom it belonged. Only seven or eight knew the answer: Khereniev, Flye, the Olsons, Maida, Kelk,

Abbie and myself. And, of course, Don Morelle. We all knew it was Colin's gun, now mine, stolen a few hours before the murder from my unlocked cabin. What Morelle had overlooked was the filed serial number, an easy thing to overlook. Why Colin had obliterated the number I couldn't guess. But he'd done it so carefully that even the police lab couldn't bring it back. And Morelle, faced with this embarrassing surprise, had to remain silent or further incriminate himself by confessing burglary.

So much for the crazy-quilt background of Flo's murder. As I sit here now, it seems fairly obvious to me why Morelle did it. After that disastrous switching of drinks at Khereniev's party, Morelle knew that his wife was not only untrustworthy but downright dangerous. She had to be removed. My feeling was that the group blamed both husband and wife for the fiasco; Morelle for entrusting what secrets he knew to her, Flo for blabbing out even a slim hint of them. They held both of them equally guilty and my hunch was that they planned a double retribution in their own good time unless they could bring the Morelles around to a more satisfactory arrangement.

But Don was frightened. He knew the lingering agony of their accursed retribution would fall on him somehow . . . and soon. He was probably in a state of hysteria and his mind worked inefficiently. He had to get rid of Flo, thus clearing himself. What better plan than to kill her with my gun, thus removing her and incriminating me? I seemed to be immune to their retribution; could I escape the legal penalties of murder? To his fear-crazed mind the logic was perfectly sound. Two birds with one stone. During the short time he waited, the plan must have assumed real and foolproof proportions to him. He filled in the details, fixed what he thought was a watertight alibi with Maida bought some cartridges, probably in an out-of-the-way Indiana hamlet, stole the gun and killed his wife. Still imbued with the success of his scheme, he called the police and sat back waiting for them to trace the gun to me.

Thinking it over now, I realize that Morelle was not as fear-crazed as it might seem. The plan had definite possibilities, hinging on the serial number and Maida's alibi. True it wasn't an alibi for the actual murder time, but it successfully contradicted the evidence of the elevator man (and later of a garage attendant), thus giving some credence to his fairy-tale business trip. The mysterious man escaping by a rear stairway could, upon the tracing of the gun, become me. Yes, the plan had possibilities. But Cohn, from the grave, had foiled it. And Maida had tied the last strap of the electric chair around Morelle's body.

This proves, to me at least, that the Dune-Dwellers have washed their hands of Morelle. At one stroke, the simple switching of a drink, I've effectively removed an opponent. I didn't plan it this way, but it's happened and I'm in no position to ignore the fact of its success.

(2). The Dune-Dwellers analyzed. This will be a bit rougher to follow than the straight deduction of the previous. I feel that the time is now at hand for a rather more detailed analysis of both the group and its individual members, an analysis based on observation and intuition. Perhaps it would be more fitting to begin with the one member who is no longer a menace to me, the effete and dapper Mr. Morelle.

Morelle: This man, for all his vaunted ambition, is, or rather was, an exceedingly weak link in the hidden organization of the group, which, for lack of a better name, I must call the Dune-Dwellers. I have the definite feeling that he was not particularly welcome at that cocktail party of Khereniev's, that he more or less invited himself there to be in on the kill, so to speak. But yet he *had* come. Flo, out of curiosity or boredom, had wormed her way in too. Morelle had to be there to gloat perhaps, or to partake of the possible success. This smacked not merely of insubordination but of greediness . . . for prestige, for acclaim, for possible advancement.

This, then, was the basis of Morelle's bungling, the reason he'd shown his hand, the reason he'd whipped up that flimsy confection of a frame-up, because he was an underling and he didn't want to remain in that lowly position.

The Olsons: I must confess that I can't understand either of them. Dora seems harmless. Sam, by the very fact of his retiring, taciturn nature, seems to hold potentialities I can't picture. There is a haunted, empty quality about him. He lives out there, which puts him on a par with the rest of that bloody crew, but he wasn't part of the ceremony I witnessed. If he is one of them, his affiliation could be only one of two things:

either he is a rank subordinate, as Morelle was, or else he is at the top level of their mysteries, and his laconic manner covers up the authority he holds. If only he would talk more, do more, I could tell more about him. As things stand now, he remains an enigma.

Maida Teufler: I know almost as little of her as of Sam Olson. To begin with, what is her basic urge? To answer that, I have to know the purpose of the group, and even now, at this late date, I haven't the slightest intimation of its nature. What is she like, aside from this central urge? I remember my characterization of her as a small, sturdy elephant, the beast of memory, the animal of tradition. Objectively speaking, there is very little more to add. She seems to be the kind of European product one sometimes associates with the Old World, the product of centuries of tradition, steeped in mores, memories. Her approach to matters is factual, direct, the approach of a peasant woman on whose shoulders ride dead generations of forebears who ate and worked and lived as she does locked in the cyclic rut of tradition, resisting change, fearing the new, fighting progress.

If my estimate is, correct, she is a key member of the Dune-Dwellers, a link with the Old World, a bridge to the ancient, hidden fears of man, to the dead yet deathless supernatural dreads that lie in the blood of all men. She is a repository of this mysterious lore, an authority, a steadying influence. As I think about it, it seems possible that she might even be the leader of this band of demon-possessed souls, giving them direction and purpose. It's possible. With these people anything is possible.

Sebastian Kelk: Here is easy ground, ripe for analysis. Kelk, in all his vulgar, gross, brutish horror, is a thing out of the animal past of mankind, a kind of loathsome throwback to an age when the human animal had but recently risen off its four limbs to walk like a man. Simple things satisfy him, the simplest, most bestial things of all . . . food and sex. His approach to food is purely physical. He worships the oily feel of it on his labial nerves, the sickening palp of his tongue violating each morsel, the unclean slobber of his red wet lips ravishing each mouthful with a lascivious, indecent adoration.

And in the lewd bulk of his body, the blubbering flab of fat and gristle, there are hints of stranger loves, a feculent, corrupt desire for blood and pain and the hideous scream of outraged flesh tormented beyond human endurance. Here is sadism and, I feel positive, masochism, twin vices such as few men are degraded and polluted enough to enjoy. The simple sadism of modern civilization, the besting of competitors, the subjection of lovers and wives, this is not enough for him. He craves more. He craves a foul and whispered life a delicious submersion in it, a wallowing in the forbidden, flesh-remembered debauchery of that time on earth when animal-man walked erect and yet ape-like, when man, the beast, was supreme and the human brute reveled in outrageous passions that a million years have not yet wiped from his blood.

Khereniev: I have here a different specimen by far, a man as complex and involved as Kelk is simple and direct. Here is a twentieth-century man far removed from the primitive lusts of Sebastian Kelk, in whose body and mind no vestige seems to remain of the age-less and infinite character of man. Yet there are certain lines that might prove helpful.

Of his appetite for food and sex there is little indication. I know only that such hungers seem to have no importance for him. His relations with Abbie are strangely ambivalent. At one point, if you will remember, he showed positive mastery and control, and then, the next second, he seemed to retract his domineering attitude and become almost cringingly subservient.

Yet throughout his actions I see a kind of central thread, hard to define, yet existing. I shall call this thing the superiority of self-love. It seems to me that Khereniev is obsessed with his own intelligence. In the very way he holds himself, a mockery of the human posture, he seems to be saying: "I am the most important thing under the sun. My own needs are the most important of the human race. Anything that helps me is right. Anything that thwarts me is wrong."

Abbie: I'm still very confused about her. Either she's a tremendous actress of compelling talents, or else I've been taken into camp like the greenest schoolboy who ever stood outside a stage door, autograph book in hand.

Consider: I've seen Abbie do things no sane person would even think of doing. I've seen her soil herself in the most brutal manner, subject herself to a man like Kelk, pervert her mind and her wonderful body to something so revolting that the memory of that night is still a gnawing torment to me. I've seen her lie, entreat, seduce, cajole, scheme. She has been a party to the death of two men, an attempt on me, and the murder of Flo Morelle.

Yet I cannot hate her.

If the shape of her personality refuses to focus into something with form and mass, then it must be because the personality simply doesn't have form and mass. By the time a woman reaches Abbie's age— which I peg at thirty—and makes a successful career in a tough business and acquires the poise she has, it seems highly unlikely that behind all this façade is nothing but a nebulous thing without direction or desire. But that's my decision and I'll have to stick with it, whether it's likely or not.

For every evil act she has committed, for her lies, her trickery, her support of the evil of others, for all this I can find what the lawyers would call extenuating circumstances. I can say, as I have in the past, that she does these evil things purposefully, with a full knowledge of their meaning and her part in them. But I can also say, and I have time and again, that she is innocent, that she does not understand the nature of her actions, that she is under the baleful influence of the rest of her group.

One thing seems to support this view. I refer to her actions on that night when I crouched on a neighboring dune and watched, spying on unclean horrors. There was something in her stance, in the expression of her face and the movement of her body that I was too repulsed to account for at the time. As I recall it now—and it returns with a piercing clarity—there was a kind of dreamlike quality to her actions that night, the waxy inflexibility of a person in some catatonic state. She seemed almost to be sleepwalking, sunken in the flowing yet curiously restrained frame of reference peculiar to the somnambulist. Had she been drugged . . . hypnotized? But would either of these account for the relish, the abandon of her actions? Neither hypnosis nor drugs can dredge up out of the mind what is not there. It is puzzling. And yet above all thought, beyond my analysis and planning, one fact looms like a thunderhead that blots out the sky. The fact is, I cannot find it in me to hate Abbie as I hate the others in this foul conspiracy. I cannot.

The appalling dimness of Abbie's past must bother her greatly. What a terrifying thing it must be to have no childhood, no memories, to hope so pitifully for "good and important things" to fill one's life. I know that feeling. The heartbreaking thing is that it is an emotion of adolescence, not maturity. Young people have it always. "When I grow up," they dream, "what important things I will do."

But Abbie is an adult. I feel an immense, absorbing pity for her, for her lost childhood, the wondrous sunny days when all life is dreams. It hurts to see her now, eaten by the great cravings of childhood that pile in on her only now, only at this all-too-late time. What has blanked out her past, stunted her dreams?

Jason Flye: I've left Flye to the very end of this because, as I've been writing, an idea has formed at the back of my mind, a new plan based on the accomplished fact of Morelle's imprisonment and eventual execution.

Though possessing more power than Morelle, Flye is just as vulnerable because he is, to put it as succinctly as possible, a sycophant. His basic urge is thus more dangerous to his own welfare than those that spur the others on. He needs an object of adoration, something to flatter and abase himself before, something to toady to and serve. He languishes for a kindness from Abbie. *He* tends the sacrificial fire, does the menial work; yet when the time comes for the supreme act, it is Kelk who is chosen.

Time after time, as my glance has flicked about the room, waiting, tensed for the next attack, I've intercepted Flye's nervous gaze, fixed unsteadily on one member of his group, Abbie. He never watches me because he doesn't know what to watch for until someone tells him.

I can remember only twice when he seemed to express original thoughts, expressions of his own, not echoes of others. Both times they concerned Abbie.

The first was in her cottage when she stood in the firelight fondling the kitten. And as she stood there, I caught an expression of sheer adoration in Flye's face, as though he had never seen anything quite so wonderful, so desirable in his life. The second time was atop the high dune in that taut pause before she chose Kelk. All the pleading and desire of the spurned male was in his face as he entreated her with his eyes to choose him.

That was Flye, a sycophant, but especially a slave to Abbie. I could hardly blame him, yet I realized that in this special attraction there was fuel for my plans.

(3). Action. It seems plain to me that alone I am powerless against these people, if indeed they are people at all. I may be hiding this headache from them and, in so doing, giving them cause for confusion. But I can't be sure. There is only one thing to date that I consider reliable and that is what happened to Morelle. I did this to him, but I was merely the trigger that set off an explosive situation. At the time I did it I understood nothing. I switched my drink out of sheer terror determined to elude their trap, determined to keep hidden the agony of my racking headache. But nevertheless I did it, with the help of Colin and whatever mysterious reason he had for removing the serial number. In this affair there is a certain direction I cannot ignore.

I am too weak to fight them alone, but isn't it possible that I can put them against each other? It calls for the finest sort of calculation. I must determine the correct combination of character, bring it into being, and trigger it into explosion to do this, I must have fairly accurate information about their actions. If they choose to ignore me now, to sit back and wait, I am lost. If I fail, I suppose I can expect nothing more than the fate of Cohn and little Mr. Profit—incredible though it sounds. Above all I need a clear head. I *must* have a clear head.

THIS IS THREE DAYS LATER. I wonder if something greater than me is guiding my efforts? I have been floundering about so badly, grasping, at such intangibles, that I've neglected the one line of exploration I should have followed at the very beginning. It was undoubtedly the failure of the codeine and morphine that stopped me, but I hadn't attempted any other method of allaying the pain.

Now, when a clear head is so essential to me, I have finally turned back to that original line of inquiry. And when I wonder whether a greater force is guiding me, I refer to a series of coincidences that took place the day before yesterday. The last of my patients had left and I was seated before my desk in an attitude of extreme exhaustion. I think that perhaps my face was contorted, with pain. I can't remember too clearly, but it was at that moment that my receptionist entered.

"What's wrong?" Her voice sounded shocked.

"My head," I let slip. "It hurts like blazes." I looked up at her and we remained that way for the longest moment I can remember, our glances locked, her eyes probing mine. I wasn't going to say another thing. She'd never believe me anyway.

"And you've tried codeine?" she asked suddenly.

I was startled. "What makes you say that?"

"The bottle's half empty." Her eyes were calculating. "I think you've tried morphine, too. There're a couple of ampoules missing." She stopped talking. It was like a game, neither of us willing to make the next move. How much did she suspect? She stood there, watching me with a kind of clinical fascination. Then, after a long moment, she wet her lips and broke the silence.

"You really are the limit," she said slowly. "How did you ever get mixed up in . . ."

She let her voice fade away. She didn't have to say any more.

"Never mind that," I managed to get out. "Just leave mealone, okay?"

"God," she burst out, "what's the use of having friends if you're going to ignore them? All I want to do is help you, but you won't even let—"

"I know," I cut in painfully. "Just stay clear. You'll be happier that way."

I watched her face. For a while it was blank and then a smile emerged, the old smile, the bantering, slightly cocky smile. "By the way," she said, "do you do much professional reading nowadays?"

I shook my head. "Why?"

"On your desk," she said, motioning with her head. "This month's copy of the Society's magazine. Page thirty-two."

"Hunh?"

"Well, see you tomorrow." She grinned and closed the door behind her.

Page thirty-two. I picked up the magazine and began leafing through the ads in the front, all the glittering new machinery, the very artistic layouts concerning new commercial drugs, four-color things full of dashing abstract design. What an overwhelming variety of drugs, new ones coming on the market all the time. Page thirty-two.

"Nerve-Block Anesthetic Proves Helpful in Herpes Zoster Treatment."

Two researchers in an eastern hospital had achieved some success in allaying the horribly itching pain of herpes zoster, or shingles. The technique—not new—involved the blocking off of certain nerves in the afflicted area by the injection of common anesthetics of the cocaine-derivative group. They had used Novocain with fair results, but the really effective anesthetic, they clarified, was a new product called "*Intracaine*," a recent derivative especially designed for the nerve-block technique. It had, they reported, a powerful intra-muscular penetration, but it tended to build immunity against its effects if used to excess. The next morning I bought twelve ampoules of *Intracaine*.

Last night I set up the experiment. It lacked quite a lot of the essential attributes of a true experiment. I had no control object, no other unfortunate who was suffering my own pain. Too bad. If *Intracaine* would help, I'd know it soon enough, control or no control.

Before I describe the experiment, a little background is necessary to understand the effect of an anesthetic on the neural system of man. In brief, I was concerned with a cerebral pain. If it had been located in any other portion of the body, the solution would have been simple; straight anesthesia of the afflicted area would suffice or, failing that, the deadening of the afferent nerves bearing impulses from area receptors through the dorsal portion of the spinal column to the somaesthetic (body feeling) cortex of the brain. This is the normal path of pain outside the cerebral hemispheres. Experimental surgery has determined that actual brain areas do not experience pain in and of themselves. What I was experiencing was a special manifestation of cerebral sensitivity. Any unduly harsh or unexpected stimulus wreaked havoc inside my head. I couldn't hope to deaden the brain's sensitivity, therefore I must block off or subdue outside impulses traveling to it from my dermal, optic, aural, and olfactory receptors.

The pain was *not* a result of neural stimuli outside the cerebral areas. It was merely intensified by such impulses. My plan, then, was to block off these stimuli, stop them from passing through the *thalamus* (the brain's central switchboard) and reaching the parietal lobe (*somaesthesis*), the occipital lobe (optic sensation), the temporal lobe (aural sensation), and the olfactory bulbs that underlie the frontal lobe.

The problem, stated so clearly, was a bit more complex when resolved into direct action. It would be a simple matter, for example, to anesthetize the *thalamus*, thus, in effect, shutting down the brain's switchboard and preventing sensations from reaching their appropriate cerebral areas. But in the process I would render myself mute, deaf, blind and paralyzed. If I traced the path of afferent or incoming impulses farther down from the *thalamus*, past the *hypothalamus* and *midbrain* to the *pons* and *medulla*, I reached the intersection of the pyramidal tract where the so-called "brain stem" connects with the spinal column. At no point along this complex path could I risk anesthesia without similarly disastrous results.

Was there, however, a point just below this juncture of the spinal cord with the brain stem where a judicious amount of *Intracaine*, injected into the gray matter of the cord, could affect the associational neurons enough to deaden afferent impulses? The technique was not new. Spinal blocks have been a matter of medical fact for years, their use restricted to highly specialized instances. But spinal anesthesia is a far different matter from local anesthesia, requiring a technique as expert and as accurate as the hand of man can achieve. Short of using a mirror system, I would have to be double-jointed to inject my own spinal cord with *Intracaine*.

So then what?

I sat there mulling over the data on *Intracaine*, tracing aimless lines on my brain charts. Supposing, just supposing I could perfect an auto-anesthesia technique. Could I use it in an emergency? Clearly not. At its very best it would require special mirrors and extensions, careful sterilization and absolute calm. What I wanted was a drug to deaden my pain whenever I needed it, no matter what conditions I was experiencing at the moment. I put away the charts and papers. The twelve ampoules of *Intracaine* leered up at me with a nasty, knowing air.

They were about as useful as mouthwash or brilliantine. I sat there morosely, rubbing away at the patch of bristly hair on the back of my head, that area of hair that seems to cover a kind of hollow formed by the upward surge of the spinal cord at the back of the neck and the downward thrust of the cerebellum just above it. That was the core of my troubles. One needle, expertly inserted, could put me out of my misery. It also might kill me.

And then I had an idea. As I said before, it almost seems now as if something were guiding my actions. The idea was crazy, a reversal of everything logical and scientific. Well, wasn't I dealing with just that, the reverse of reason? *Intracaine* had powerful intramuscular penetration. I would shave my head at precisely that spot. I would *rub Intracaine* on the newly bared skin.

I dashed downstairs, hopped in the car and raced over to 71st Street. If only the barber were still open. This was Saturday evening. Chicago barbers have little business on Saturdays because they charge more then than on weekdays. But my barber, thank God, was still open.

"Crew cut," I ordered, sliding into the chair. "Not too close, but shave the back of my neck right here. Down to the skin, mind you."

I never spent a dollar and a quarter more wisely. I stopped off at a Walgreen's drug store on the way back, bought a piece of pumice stone and drove home fast. Once upstairs I locked the door and took the phone off the hook. I didn't want to be disturbed by anything. In the bathroom I gaped at my face in the mirror. I looked weird in the crew haircut, but it had to be. I couldn't risk showing that telltale bald spot to any of the Dune-Dwellers. They might guess its purpose all too accurately. But this way the shaven neck seemed natural. I wet the pumice stone and began rubbing at the bare skin there.

Finally, when I could feel each stroke of the abrasive like a file across my spinal cord, I stopped, dried the area, swabbed on alcohol and let it evaporate. The skin felt raw; it burned furiously. With quick motions, holding my fingers tight to stop their trembling, I snapped the neck of an ampoule and their trembling, I snapped the neck of an ampoule and turned it upside down over a wad of cotton. Could it possibly work? *Intracaine* was a new thing, its possibilities as yet only half suspected. This extravenous technique was also crazy. Yet the skin that shielded that conjunctive area of the neural system couldn't be too thick. There were muscles there, but they were imbedded in skin. And skin was, after all, only cells. And cells had intercellular spaces. And *Intracaine* could penetrate the . . . What the hell. I had to stop thinking and start acting.

First the conditions. Were they proper? My head throbbed dully, an aftermath of the abrasive pumice. But I wanted real shooting pangs, the kind I'd experienced so often before. The wet cotton was dripping through my fingers, precious *Intracaine* dropping off into the bathroom bowl. Quick now. I tensed my hand and hit myself hard on the temple. The ache was abruptly stinging, hot, intense. It ricocheted and thundered in my head. Perfect. I could hardly see through the waves of pain across my brain but the conditions were perfect. Trembling, hardly knowing exactly what I was doing, I brought the soaking bit of cotton to the back of my neck. The *Intracaine* smarted and stung. It felt cool, then hot, electric, flashing.

I stood there before the mirror, looking blankly into my own eyes, waiting.

And then, slowly, my face came into focus. Every line of strain stood out as I watched, and suddenly each separate indentation smoothed out as though a giant eraser had rubbed my face clean of the outward symbols of pain. And my head?

A dull throbbing pulsed at the back. But the huge sheets of agony were gone. Were they? With a quick, maddened gesture, I lifted my leg and rammed my shin hard into the side of the bathtub. A shooting pain surged upwards, vibrated. But inside my head only a muffled throbbing. Nothing more? I stood on tiptoe and shoved my face within inches of the electric bulb. The sudden increase of light blinded me for an instant and I felt my irises contract with a harsh pain. Yet inside my head only the dull thrum, the same as before, the original pain, nothing new, nothing increased.

I stood back from the sink and smiled at myself in the mirror. Crazy, was it? My eyes were like brilliant pinpoints, glittering with an almost insane light. My face was flushed. My neck seemed to end before it reached my head. And I seemed to have no head, nothing but a muted quivering somewhere in the immense reaches of space above my neck. Perfect. Absolutely perfect. Only I must be careful to use it sparingly. I mustn't build an immunity to it.

And now, I thought, standing there and grinning back at myself with an awful, fixed leer, now for that action I'd been promising myself.

CRICKETS were cramming the late evening with a sibilant cacophony that played against the rustle of leaves, a busy treble against a steady surging bass. The lights were on in Abbie's cabin. I tiptoed up the steps and opened the door quietly. Surprise was important. I closed the door behind me and surveyed the room.

She was reading a book, lying on a couch drawn up before the fireplace. The evening was cool but hardly chilly enough to warrant a fire, yet one blazed in the hearth. She was dressed in a cotton summer dress of yellow and rust in alternating stripes. I stood there for a long moment, orienting myself. Then I spoke, quickly, loudly, for an effect of surprise.

"Abbie!"

She reacted slowly, her body uncoiling, her eyes lifting leisurely to me. Then they focused sharply and the irises seemed to contract with startling rapidity. "You," she breathed. "What are—?"

"Social visit," I said, giving her no time to recover. "I have a lot of important things to discuss . . . about the Dune-Dwellers." I emphasized the words. They seemed to rebound about the four walls of the room.

She stood up and tried to smile. "You sound angry," she said. "Why didn't you tell us you were coming out this weekend . . . with your brand new haircut?"

"Don't play any more games, Abbie. I know all about it."

"I don't understand," she said quietly. She sat down on the couch again and gestured to me to join her. "What do you know all about?"

I hadn't realized how tense I was. The mere action of taking the few steps to the couch sent stinging pangs up my spine and into my head. But this was only a prelude to the night. I wouldn't need *Intracaine* until later. The heat from the fire hit me full as I came into range. It nipped at my brain, squeezing, fretting at the hypersensitive fibers inside my head. I took a deep breath and sat down. This was Abbie. She was smart, smarter than I'd been. I had to be careful.

I found myself wondering for a moment what I'd say in her position. She was treating this as a joke. Perhaps it was. But I couldn't stop to enjoy the humor of it. "First," I began briskly, "I know about

Colin." I held up my hand to stop the words that formed on her lips. "I know how he died, how you people killed him . . . how you killed Mr. Profit. How you *tried* to kill me."

I had expected a camouflaging reaction from her, mockery, a smile. I wasn't prepared for what actually followed. She stood up from the couch in one swift movement, her arms tense at her sides, her face contorted in a fierce grimace, the muscles of her legs bunched and knotted, her fingers working convulsively and her eyes . . .! In the flicker of the firelight, demons seemed to dance in the sharp recesses of her eyes. Her mouth curled in a hateful gesture, grim, repellent. "You *fool!*" she whispered harshly.

The violence of her reaction shot a cutting anguish through my head, as though someone had felled me with an ax. I blinked and held my eyes open by sheer will power. "You accursed *fool!*" she spat at me, her neck a mass of tight cords that seemed to twang with the effort of her speech.

I tried to keep my face immobile. The pain was intense, punishing. Why hadn't I used the *Intracaine?* The pain was forcing an answering grimace on my face and it took all my effort to turn that agonized grin into a smile. "I overestimated you," I said at last. "You aren't angry . . . you're *scared.*"

"Am I?" she snapped. The words seemed to relax her and she turned away from me with a sudden whirling motion. "If anyone should be frightened," she muttered, "it's not I. It's you, you stupid fool." Her lips were quivering strangely.

"But you see," I said, attempting an easiness that came hard, "I'm not frightened. In fact, I'm a little contemptuous of you people. I know exactly what you tried to do. You've failed."

"I doubt that," she said indistinctly, her face turned from me. "For your own sake, Joe, I doubt it very much."

"For *my* own sake," I echoed in amazement.

"Yes," she said. I thought I heard her sob, but it might have been a quick intake of breath. She turned around to me and her face was calm again except for lines of strain around her mouth. Even so, even after the face I had seen just a moment before, she still looked beautiful. "For your own sake," she said slowly. "If you had any idea of what has happened, you'd never speak of it. You'd . . . you'd run away, you'd hide."

"That's where the others made their mistake," I retorted. "But you see, it hasn't worked on me. None of you are strong enough to make it work on me."

Then she did an amazing thing. She put her hands over her ears and pressed them tightly. Her knuckles were white with the effort. "I don't want to hear anymore," she whispered. "You don't know what you're saying, Joe."

"I don't? It doesn't take much sense to separate a sheep from a goat, or a dupe from her masters."

"A dupe?"

"Look" Abbie, I wouldn't waste my time with you if I didn't know that. I wouldn't be trying to . . . to . . ." I couldn't find the proper word.

"To help me?" she finished scornfully. *"You* help *me?"*

I didn't know what word I wanted, but "help" wasn't quite it. "No," I began and then stopped.

"Some people, Joe," she said, "don't take well to help. Some don't want it and some . . ." she faltered slightly, ". . . are beyond it." She stopped, sighed once, and looked boldly at me. "Anyway, Joe, you don't know what you're talking about."

"I don't think *you* know," I persisted angrily. "But perhaps Khereniev will know. Or Maida. Or even your pal, Kelk, he might know."

Her eyes closed tight in a tremendous spasm, as though she were trying to shut out all sight and sound of me. "Don't say that" she moaned. "Please, Joe!"

"After all you've been to each other, you and Kelk?"

"God," she cried, "can't you stop talking?"

"Why should I?"

"Why?" She opened her eyes and an insane gurgling laugh filled her mouth. "Listen to me, Joe," she said, leaning over me with a kind of tense earnestness. "I know what you know. You . . . you talk too much. I knew that night you were drunk. You told me. And I had to tell them." She searched my face for some sign of recognition. "Don't you remember, Joe? You said . . ." She turned away from me and again I heard that harsh, racking sound of a sob that seemed to retch up from her guts. Her body shook with the effort.

"I said . . . ?"

"I can't forget it," she moaned. "The sound of it rings in my head. I was asking you, begging you, for something I . . . the most important . . ." She seemed to give up trying to put it in words. "And you laughed at me, drunkenly. You said you didn't want to f-follow in—" Sobs broke off her words.

"Follow in what?"

"I-in Kelk's . . . in Kelk's footsteps."

I watched her body go limp. It took a long time for the muscles to let go, and when they did her body seemed to crumble in on itself like a tired concertina, to fold up and condense until all that remained, after a long moment, was a kind of puddle of her, spread out on the floor. She was like a lump of some gelatinous substance, her body shaking and quivering with the fury of those sobs.

So that was how I'd let it slip. And all this now was an act to make me think she was sorry. She'd set about deliberately to get this very bit of information from me, the tip-off. Then why should she be sorry? I started to reach out a hand to her body, a comforting gesture. I stopped myself, bewildered by what I'd almost done. And this unconscious tenderness was the most infuriating thing of all.

"You do that crying thing well," I said then. "Just the way you did the sex business in your apartment."

Out of the shivering mass of her body, her head seemed to emerge and lift into view. Her eyes were red, moist with tears. Somehow she'd smeared her lipstick awry and it reminded me sickeningly, of that night on the high place, when the smear had been something else. Her eyes were huge, luminous, searching. She seemed to be drawing at me with her eyes, as though they were the tentacles of some monster. "Joe," she said softly "you're so goddamned cruel!"

A snort of angry laughter escaped me. *"I'm* cruel," I repeated sarcastically.

"You hate me. You make it so . . . so hard for me."

That did it. I stood up abruptly and my foot jarred against her body. "Goodbye, Abbie," I said curtly.

"No!" I felt her hands clutch at my ankle with a convulsive grasp. "Where are you going?"

"To see people," I replied. "I want to find out if . . . well, if Khereniev's so little impressed with me."

"Oh, you fool," she sobbed. The grasp of her fingers tightened in a kind of spastic paroxysm that jarred my head and made it throb. "Can't you leave it alone, Joe? Can't you enjoy what's left, at least for a little while?"

"Enjoy? I'm enjoying it all." I tried to shake her fingers loose.

"It's not for you. I'm begging," she whispered harshly, "for *us,* Joe. We can have a little happiness. Just a little, Joe."

"Let go," I snapped. I kicked at her and felt the toe of my shoe sink into her soft flesh. "Get your hands off me!" Her fingers were like decaying snakes.

"No, please!"

"Let go, you goddamned witch!" I shouted. "Get your filthy hands off me!"

I saw her body buckle and slump. There was a

loud thump as her head hit the floor. Her chin smacked against the boards and then her head rolled sideways, inert. I stared at her. She seemed to be unconscious. As I watched, a thin rill of blood oozed up and out of her mouth and trickled down her chin. It was only a faint line of red and it didn't seem to be flowing fast. Did witches have real blood? I didn't have any time to argue the point with myself. I had work to do.

JASON FLYE was asleep. His cabin was a small affair, hardly more than a lean-to with one window, now dark as I approached. The back of my neck smarted where the fresh *Intracaine* was sinking in. After a minute of pounding on the door, a light went on inside and I could hear bare feet on the floor. The door opened a crack and an eye peered out at me. I couldn't recognize Flye in the dim light but I knew it must be him. In the twilight, when I'd skulked about the woods for an hour or so, I'd made sure he was here. Kelk wasn't, nor Khereniev. But Flye and Abbie, the Olsons, and Maida were. I made sure of that. It was important to my plan.

"Jesus," he said. "What d'you want, Loomis?"

"You," I said tersely. I gave the door a shove and strode in. Flye had been knocked off balance. He almost fell to the floor but recovered quickly.

"What's the idea?" he asked wonderingly.

"Just that you're not going to get Abbie away from me."

"What?" The word was a gasp in his mouth.

"I know about you and her. I've been watching it for weeks but she doesn't give a good damn for you. We're getting married." The whole business was a pack of lies, but I had to shake him up fast.

"You're crazy!" he exclaimed. His frame shook as he giggled uncontrollably.

"Maybe, but you're just dull, Jason. You can't see what's going on under your nose. You thought you'd have to take her from Kelk, didn't you? You thought I was out of the way because you'd—" What did they call their ceremony? I couldn't afford to make even a small mistake. But I didn't have to remember. The idea had sunk into Jason with just my bare suggestion to give it momentum.

"You . . . you didn't—?"

"That's right. It didn't work on me, of course, because I'm stronger than any of you. So I get Abbie. And you can't do a thing about it."

"You can't be," he said dully. "You can't be."

"Listen, Jason. As the rejected suitor you'll be interested. I think we'll have our honeymoon right here, right in her cabin."

"You can't. You're dead."

"Jason, we'll honeymoon in her cabin. And do you know what? *You* can watch!"

That shook him. He seemed to draw back from

me as though I had become a hateful, repulsive object. A horrible gagging sound bubbled up out of his throat and for a moment I thought he was going to be sick. "You can't," he giggled wildly. "I won't."

"You won't? All right, you've had your invitation. I'm going back to Abbie. She's waiting for me."

Sudden action gripped his frame. A thin hand shot out and managed to grab a fold of the jacket I Was wearing. "Don't do that!" he yelped. "Don't even say that!"

"The hell with you," I said harshly. I shook free of him and went out the door, purposely leaving it open behind me. I could see his thin body stagger to the doorway. He peered out into the darkness after me. If he followed, and I was banking my life that he would follow, I wanted him to be far enough behind me so that I would have time to rig my plan. I turned and shouted back to him, "Come on along!"

He slumped back out of sight and the door closed in front of him. That would slow him up, but I knew it wouldn't dissuade him entirely. I started running through the woods, my feet slipping in the sand, every jog of my forward motion muted, deadened, as though I were running on somebody else's legs. A branch slashed at my face as I ran and I hardly felt it. I jogged on through the woods. If the *Intracaine* would only keep a tight rein on the torture inside my head . . . I dashed up the steps and threw open Abbie's door. The room was exactly the same. The fire was low, almost down to its last dying flames. As I slammed the door behind me and shot the bolt to, I saw

Abbie's body on the hearth, almost where I'd left it. She stirred and again her head seemed to lift upward out of the looseness of her body.

"I've been thinking about us," I said softly. "I've been thinking about what you said."

A wild whiteness sprang into her eyes, as though someone had ignited a roaring fire there. "What do you want?"

I was beside her now, kneeling beside her, my arms under her shoulders lifting up hard. "Abbie," I said softly, "you were right."

She slumped back against the tension of my hands and her mouth opened to speak. The line of blood had dried on her chin to a black smear. In that instant fear seemed to slide off her face like a shade rolling up out of sight. "Joe, listen," she whispered. "Did I tell you I loved you?"

"No."

"I do," she breathed. "I love you with my whole body, with my blood, Joe. It's like a fire inside me."

I could imagine it was. She was a campfire girl from way, way back. "I know," I said, trying to sound like I meant it. "It's that way with me."

Was it? Was it the same with me? Could I let myself love this . . . this woman or whatever she was?

"I'm glad it is, Joe darling," she responded.

The whole thing sounded too pat. How could she be sincere? But then, why not? If she could only exorcise the foulness around her, burn it and rise from it with her own mind and body like some bird of fable, then why couldn't she know her own soul and speak it out, free, controlled by herself alone, the ultimate freedom of all?

"Is this . . ." I didn't know how to say it. "Is what you're saying . . . ? I mean—"

"It's my own, darling," she cut through. "All my very own. I don't understand it or even . . ." she seemed to falter, then go on much stronger, ". . . or even trust it. But it's all my own feeling. Believe that."

I wanted to. I wanted it to be so and yet I felt like a fraud. Outside the cabin, even now, there might be the one I had planned to bring here. This wasn't the way for love. This was a rotten, lousy fraud, and I . . . I was even worse.

"And we won't worry about anything else," she murmured then. "I won't tell them and neither will you and we'll have a little happiness of our own before. . . ." The words died away. They didn't have to go on anyway; we both knew what they were.

I could feel her body hot and moving under mine. She seemed to be boiling inside, as though a flame were driving her in many directions, licking at her insides, pulsing, heaving. "Yes, I love you," she said harshly. "I won't tell them. They won't get it from me."

"Sure," I said softly. "Sure." I didn't understand everything she was saying, but it sounded good. She made everything sound good, this girl. The strain of holding her up was gone. It was like holding air. If only it hadn't come like this. If only I hadn't deliberately set this up, like a chess player. I felt ashamed and sick of myself.

"Darling," she murmured. "It'll be all right for a while. That's all we want, just a little while."

"Sure," I said. I listened to other sounds, outside sounds . . . a rustling, leaves or perhaps sand under someone's feet. This was all wrong, all rotten.

"You needn't be afraid," she told me urgently. "I can shield us."

"I know."

"And it'll be so wonderful," she said. The words were welling up out of her mouth like . . . like the licking, burning tongues of some hidden fire, flaring and soaring like live things. Her eyes were closed, those huge staring eyes, hooded by lids of the warmest white. "We'll love," she whispered. "For as long and as long as we' can . . . we'll love."

"Sure," I said. I was watching a window to one side, hoping all of a sudden that he wouldn't use that one, hoping there was no way for him to see us. I was watching the window and all the while her body was thrusting and searing against me with the driving fury of her words. I was a cheat, a liar, a fraud. My head began to ache with a hot agony.

Suddenly her arms shot up around my neck, her muscles tense, hard, pulling herself into me with a jarring rush. Her breath was warm . . . hot . . . like flame. "Now!" she whispered.

Her body seemed to go limp, all but her arms locked vise-like around my neck. The weight of her was pulling me down. Great shooting spasms of pain lanced through my head, shooting spasms of pain lanced through my head like white-hot swords. She was pulling me down. I didn't want to, but I glanced at the window in time to see Jason Flye's face at the window, stark white and trembling in the firelight. Then, together, we sank to the floor, my mouth on hers. I could taste a musky saltiness as we kissed and then I remembered . . . the blood. I closed my eyes and let pain wipe my mind blank. A sham, a cheat, a filthy, conniving fraud . . .

AS I WRITE THIS NOW, it is the next evening and I'm back in town. I wish I could report that the basic headache has lessened. Originally I had some secret idea that perhaps as the members of the Dune-Dwellers dwindled one by one, the agony of the curse they had laid on me would diminish. But, although it's grown no more violent, it still bothers me. I avoid using the *Intracaine* too frequently, but with its help I managed a few hours of sleep during the afternoon. They gave me sufficient energy to write the account of what happened last night.

The end of the episode is brief, pallid by comparison. A lifeguard from the Indiana State Dunes Park found Jason's body the next morning. It had evidently drifted fifteen or twenty miles along the shore and been brought in on the waves caused by the early morning breeze. The authorities blame it on a midnight swim, unfortunately too far from shore, and a cramp caused by the excessive coldness of the lake in spring. At least, the Michigan City paper puts it that way. Abbie is probably back in the city by now, wondering why I left so hurriedly, and waiting for my call. She may not know about Jason and neither may the others of the group. The event has caused little stir . . . the first fatality of the season, but hardly an important news item. They may not know until to-morrow, Monday, when the morning papers will probably carry a line or two about it.

I would give a pretty penny to see their faces when they read that squib.

9 «◊» A Midsummer Madness

THERE ARE SOME DAYS, even in the most well-regulated of existences, when nothing works. You wake up feeling like the man in the laxative ads, dull and logy, whatever that means, and you look forward to your morning coffee. And when you drink it, it tastes like hot water in which some bitter, oily herb has been stewed . . . not at all the bracing beverage you expected. With that as an inauspicious beginning, the day falls into a pattern of suspended desolation. Appointments are missed, people shove you in elevators, the newsboy gives you the wrong change, some imbecile cuts in front of you in heavy traffic and narrowly misses your fender, there is the taste on the floor of your mouth that was immortalized by some brilliant copy writer a few years back in one poignant phrase: "Bird-cage mouth." The world is suspended, insipid, bleak.

The people in it are all ill-tempered idiots. You begin to believe the pathological drivel of the magazine ads. In addition to the traditional dull and logy feeling, your stomach needs "sweetening," you are suffering from "borderline anemia" you must "pull the trigger on lazy bowels," you're only half safe, you can't pass the fingernail test, your friends whisper behind your back, your toothbrush shows a disturbing shade of pink, you have halitosis, lordosis, gaposis, dandruff, ear wax, tattle-tale gray, cigarette hack, coffee nerves, systemic poisoning, body odor, five o'clock shadow, dishpan hands and secretary spread. All you need is the snap, crackle, pop of this amazing new all-purpose, quick-acting, economy-sized, handy container with its patented improved formula, easy-to-use, double-strength, locked-in secret ingredient that medical science knows as—

This is Friday. The weather report reads: "Cloudy, scattered showers increasing to heavy rain tomorrow." And for once the weatherman is dead right. It has been more than cloudy; it has been murky, the air like dense broth. The scattered showers are an infuriatingly fickle form of late spring rain, the kind that waits until the sun peeps fuzzily through a bank of low-flying scud before unleashing great torrents of sharp droplets that collect instantly to clog the sewers and make walking an obstacle race. The intervals between these scattered showers have grown increasingly smaller. By Saturday morning they will have merged their individual might into a single, monotonous downpour of rain that always reminds me, except for its temperature, of a tropic monsoon season. This is the kind of rain, I feel sure, that Noah watched with an eager eye as his sons herded the animals up the ramp. It's the kind that drove the Reverend Davidson to certain famed excesses with Miss Thompson. I have only to sit tight in my apartment and cock a sharp ear. By midnight it will coalesce into an entity of water. Tomorrow, when I navigate myself to the office, my receptionist will greet me with one of her gems of meteorological wit. "Think the rain'll hurt the rhubarb?" I have my answer all prepared. "Not if it's in cans."

I'm sure she'll laugh. That's the bad thing about it. Of late she's been laughing at everything she says. On Tuesday I asked her if she'd seen a container of *sodium perborate* I had at the back of one of the cabinets. "Is that the stuff that's effervescent?" she wanted to know.

"My," I responded acidulously, "aren't you the observant character."

"Did you effer see me ven I effervescent?" she asked. It slew her.

On Thursday, quite an ordinary day as far as most things went, I made the mistake of telling her to order more formaldehyde. "Knock, knock," she retorted promptly.

I sighed. "Who's there?"

"Formaldehyde."

"Okay," I gave up. "Formaldehyde who?"

"Formaldehyding places come the Indians. *Ahoo-woo-woo!*"

A thing like that can only go so far. I know why she does it, of course, and I should be very grateful. But I'm in no condition to be anything, much less appreciative or thankful. My headache has become a partner in the affairs of my life, much as a persistent ulcer giving continuous notice of its presence. My receptionist knows what's happening to me; in fact, she knew it almost before she jimmied the secret out of me. She doesn't seem impressed. Her idea is that I need cheering up. My idea is simpler, and, in the long run, less wearing. I need guillotining.

It hasn't helped matters much that Abbie calls me regularly at least once a day. That's right, she calls me. I don't understand it, but there it is. When I get through talking to her my head feels like a grape some vintner is trampling on. The pressure squeezes it, kneads it, it has to burst and spew forth its juices, yet it can't and the pressure continues, irregular but constant . . . always constant. Wearily, I reach for the *Intracaine*. How long before I build an immunity to it?

"*Why* can't you come over?"

"*I told* you, Abbie. I'm too busy."

"You were too busy Monday and Tuesday and yesterday. Don't you think I can tell, darling? If you don't want to see me, just say so. But tell me why. I've got to know why."

I try my best to smooth things over but these days my best is far below par. Aside from that, aside from the pain and the knowledge that soon it will become too intense for the intracaine to stifle, aside from all that, I can't make up my mind about Abbie. Why doesn't she hate me? Things were said that night that echo inside my aching head, tones of voice and expressions return with a vivid immediacy that only increases my confusion. I wonder: perhaps she's never connected Flye's suicide with that night?

Is she still honest with me? Can you trust anything an actress says? Aren't they capable, the good ones, of making their voices, faces, and bodies mimic any emotion, any thought? I've often wondered about that, especially about Abbie. What about the husbands the lovers, the friends of actresses? I wonder if they ever really know what the actress is thinking. There must be some norm of behavior for her, some level at which one can say with confidence: "This is the real thing."

I suppose another woman might pierce the façade of her character. They say that a liar usually succeeds with the opposite sex but that someone of his own sex can see through him in an instant. I wonder if my receptionist could see through Abbie? I've thought of asking Abbie down to the office, but I'm afraid to. I'm afraid to see her any more than is absolutely necessary.

I know she can be sincere. I know that once— maybe still she loved me, or thought she did. It must be hard for a woman like that confused, maneuvered, with no will, to know her own mind—even in that bright flash of recognition when it speaks out free and unafraid. I wish I could go to her and tell her everything and . . . and help her. That isn't really love, is it? The desire to help, the pity, the compassion— that isn't enough. Is it?

Dora Olson called me earlier this evening to tell me they were holding an emergency meeting Saturday night, matter of extreme importance. "If the rain stops," she explained, "we'll have it at our cottage. Otherwise I guess we'll have it in town, although it seems such a shame to stay in the city when the summer's beginning and everything's so nice out at the dunes."

"I wouldn't say that," I replied sternly.

"You wouldn't?" She seemed to be collecting her thoughts, shooing them back into the henhouse again. "Oh, I suppose you're referring to poor Mr. Flye. They say he looked so pale and nice when they found him, just like a statue, you know. I don't know what's happening to us, first Mr. Jones, then that *terrible* business with the Morelles, and now Jason Flye. It looks like Providence is striking once too often, doesn't it to you?"

"Providence" I agreed, "or something else."

"I tell you what," she went on, switching subjects without giving it a second thought, "you call me up Saturday morning and we'll know then whether we can have the meeting in the country. It's about this house the new people want to build on that high dune. Sam says it's important and everybody seems to be stewed up about it so I guess that's why we're having such a rush-rush meeting although if it were up to *me* I'd say live and let live. They've got as much right to build as we did. And if they have the money to *cart* everything all the way up the side of—" Eventually we said goodbye.

From the looks of the weather, this meeting will have to be held in Chicago. It ought to prove enlightening, if not to me, then to the Dune-Dwellers as a group. I intend to spring a surprise on them. I feel sure it will be a surprise because when I sprang it on Abbie, her reactions were spectacular, to say the least. I intend to lay all our cards on the table. Unless Abbie's tipped them off, the result should prove important.

I have some confidence in the direction my plans are taking. The idea of playing one off against the other has already worked twice, the last time through my deliberate instigation, much as I hated it. It proves that the idea is good and that I can handle it. I had serious doubts about people like Morelle and Flye, simply because it hadn't been proved yet whether they could actually die. Morelle comes to trial within the month, but I have my answer already: these people are mortal. There remains one more question. Does death stop their power?

That awful power must reside in one or, at the most, three of them. This person, or this combination, must be considered the absolute authority. If I can determine where the authority lies, I can plan to remove it.

Oddly enough, I have the feeling that the storehouse of this satanic power could be Maida Teufler. There is something quiet and somber about the woman, yet something very businesslike that makes me think she knows infinitely more than she shows. Yet it is Khereniev who gives the greatest *outward* impression of authority. Also there is the power Kelk showed that night of the sacrificial rite. And if I count him in, I must add Sam Olson, the president of the Dune-Dwellers, remote, taciturn, impossible to fathom.

It is precisely this kind of dead-end floundering

that excites my headache to higher levels of pain. I was incautious enough to let the pain overcome me on Wednesday night. It came on like the whine of a fast-moving buzz saw, shrill, harsh, rising in pitch until it seemed to slash its teeth through the soft matter of my brain. The power of sight left me and, although my eyes were open, I could see nothing. I remember feeling blindly for the ampoule, breaking it into my hand and smearing the fluid on my neck. Then, after a moment, everything faded in again, like a dissolving cinema scene, and I was all right. The whole business must have taken less than a minute. It worried me because I had never noticed, for all his agonizing pain, that Colin had ever blacked-out. It made me wonder if perhaps they'd done something different to me. How many accursed schemes have they at their command?

THE MEETING was held in town at Abbie's apartment. This was my first opportunity to inspect the place fully. It's a four-room affair, with a number of windows and a very comfortable decor. The living room, which I finally got time to look at, is huge and airy, furnished with an amazing number of chairs, ottomans and couches that nevertheless seem to disappear until needed. Abbie has hung one wall with a series of twelve Hieronymus Bosch prints framed in scarlet-painted wood. Another wall boasts a Fuselli and two di Chiricos, evidently reproductions. The third wall is windows and the fourth is mostly fireplace—Abbie being a campfire girl from way, way back—but the amazing thing is that the fireplace wall has been covered almost entirely with colored prints I've never seen before, faintly old-fashioned in treatment, the technique being a kind of cross between Currier and Ives and the *Godey's Lady's Book* illustrations. The pictures themselves are of rural or bucolic scenes. I recall a snowscape with a farmhouse sending out cheery warmth, two cows cropping grass, a boy fishing on the bank of a winding brook, farmers piling hay.

The curious thing about the living room is the odd mixture of tastes. The Bosch and Fuselli works are bizarre, nightmarish filled with demons and monsters. The di Chiricos are similarly less than cheery, being distorted, dream-like, filled with monumental symbols and infinite-reaching perspectives. And if I didn't know whose room this was I'd be inclined to call those rural prints downright corny. Yet I can conceive of certain persons enjoying such pictures for their simplicity and warmth, for their uncluttered look and the cleanness of the execution. That is precisely where the situation becomes strange. Would the same person also, and in the same room, enjoy the imp-tormented fancies of Hieronymus Bosch?

This is a strange room, mirroring a strange person. It is a room I could be very relaxed in a room that, for all its oddly-assorted components, still has a unity that makes itself felt by its occupants. There are *good* things about Abbie.

Sitting in Abbie's room, I picture my own rather bleak, thrown-together apartment. It isn't right for a man to live in such a hodge-podge. Everyone deserves a background honest to his own personality and yet I'm not happy with the drab, colorless things around me. They're like the quick charcoal under-drawing, the fast sketch that is soon demolished and reborn in glowing oils. If a woman like Abbie could fill in that bare outline . . . But I'm tricking myself. Marriage isn't that. Yet I feel incomplete before the masterly evocation of herself that Abbie has put into this room. Could she . . . ?

I had plenty of time to inspect the apartment because I was one of the first to arrive. Khereniev was already there, lying on the couch and seemingly asleep.

"He's had a hard day," Abbie whispered.

"Looks like it." I felt sudden relief. She didn't suspect, didn't hate me.

"Come in the kitchen," she said. We walked halfway back and turned off the central corridor into the kitchen, a large room done in white, and red. Abbie closed the door behind us. Then she put her arms around me and pulled me to her. "Quick," she whispered.

"Now?"

"Yes, now, darling."

We kissed. I don't believe I've mentioned before the

qualitative change that has taken place in her kisses. Or rather, I should say, in my reaction to them. The hypnotic, almost swooning response is gone and in its place is a feeling not unlike my reactions to any of the other kissing I've done in my time. It's pleasurable, but hardly the dark, tempestuous thing it once was. I can't really account for this change. It may have to do with my better understanding of Abbie or it may stem from some change in her. Whatever it is, it no longer puzzles or frightens me. We parted after a long moment and I saw her eyes were wet.

"Why the tears?"

She slipped out of my arms and began puttering with some bottles stacked up on the sink. "Women love a good cry," she said in a lighter voice. "I'm glad you could come tonight, Joe. But does it take a meeting to bring you to me?"

"Looks that way." Did I have to be nasty? I saw her face darken and I hurriedly tried to take the sting out of my callousness. "It just worked out, that's all. I had no late calls, so I came over." What was the matter with me? Why couldn't I say what I meant?

She turned away so that her face was hidden. "You don't have to lie to me, darling," she said in a low, trembling voice. Could she read my mind, this woman? Did she see through all my ruses? But she couldn't. Hadn't one of them worked already? If she'd seen through it, would she welcome me this way? "Too bad about Jason," I mumbled, trying to focus the talk.

"Don't say things you don't mean."

"What?" I felt a sharp pang of fear shoot forward from the base of my skull. "What are you talking about?"

"You're not sorry about Jason." She turned toward me and her black eyes were big and full. "You don't have to hide anything from me, my darling. I love you, remember?"

"I remember." I couldn't forget. I didn't want to forget.

She laughed and made a tiny gesture with her long fingers, a kind of coin-tossing gesture as if to say: It doesn't make any difference. "There are so many things you don't know about me," she said softly, "and so few things I don't know about you."

"Thanks for not mincing words."

"But it's true. What do you know about me? That I'm . . . that night on the dune . . . and," she smiled, "that I'm from North Dakota with an unhappy childhood."

"And that you're beautiful," I heard myself say, not knowing where the words came from, "the most beautiful woman I've ever known."

She closed her eyes for a moment and then opened them slowly, as though wanting to imprison my words in the dark caverns of her eyes. "Joe," she began, begging with those huge eyes of hers, "you trust me now, don't you, darling?"

"Yes, I—"

"And believe in me?" she hurried on. "That's all I really want, to be believed in. Just one man to believe in me. And I can live in that belief." She paused and looked away. "The rest," she added quietly, "can come later."

I felt suddenly cold. "What rest?"

"You think I'm going too fast?" she interpreted. "Joe, dear, I can't go fast enough. Not with you."

"Never mind," I said. Again the words were welling up of their own volition and I couldn't stop them. "I don't even care to know," I said, approaching her. "All I care to—"

She stopped me by pushing back hard on my chest. I recoiled, off balance, amazed. Then I heard the kitchen door swing open behind me.

"Ah, Herr Doktor." A stabbing ache went through my head.

I turned to watch Khereniev. His little eyes seemed puffy with sleep. "Good evening," I said.

"Tell me, Abbie," he said, "when is this triple-damned meeting to begin? I arrive in advance of the rest of these people and I must be kept waiting like a second footman."

"The rain must have slowed them," Abbie said. "Maida's coming with the Olsons and I imagine it's bad driving in this weather."

"What interests me," I said, "is which you are, Khereniev, a leader or a second footman?"

I grinned at him.

"You'd like an answer?" Khereniev replied sweetly. "I say only this: Let my actions classify me. I assure you, Dr. Loomis, they are much more accurate indices than words."

"A cagey answer to a cagey question."

"One less cagey than the other," he remarked.

"Time," Abbie called. "Why don't you please let me finish this in peace?" She indicated a bowl of what looked like fruit punch, which she was slowly building up out of assorted cans and bottles. "Go into the living room and play host for me, will you?"

Khereniev bowed in a mockery of the minuet, turned and left. I was about to follow when I felt her hand on my arm. "Please," she murmured, so softly I could hardly hear her. "Be careful with him."

I made a surprised face at her. "What difference does it make?"

She shushed me and nodded silently to the living room. "Please."

I ducked into the bathroom, locked the door behind me. Things were moving too fast. I hadn't counted on needing the *Intracaine* until much later, when all of them would begin to bear down on me. But I needed it now, quickly.

I smashed the ampoule, swabbed up its precious fluid in a cotton ball and sponged at the back of my neck. The stuff would last, I knew, for slightly more than an hour. Then I'd need it again. What to do?

I opened the medicine cabinet and rummaged through it till I found an aspirin tin. Three tablets inside. Out they went, in went the soggy cotton. If the intracaine didn't evaporate, I could use the swab once more that night. If. I hurried back to the living room.

Khereniev had resumed his favored position on the couch, this time in a semi-erect attitude. He looked like a snotty little urchin somehow, a smart-aleck kid perched atop some convenient spot, daring all comers. "You know," he said as I sat down in a chair, "you impress me as having a very high opinion of ratiocinative powers."

"I know a hawk from a handsaw," I cracked. "And a leader from a footman."

"Remarkable."

For some reason or other I felt that this was the time to begin my little speech. Perhaps it was the warning Abbie had given me. It seemed to act as a dare and Khereniev's cocky, sneering attitude only spurred me on. He had to know some time, why not now? Quick, while the *Intracaine* was working. "Khereniev," I began heavily, "it strikes me that you're not tooobservant yourself."

"I am, after all, only a lowly political scientist."

"It seems to me that if I were in your position, I mean in the position of *all* of you, I'd stop to consider a few facts. There is such a thing as being confident and such a thing as being foolhardy."

His bulbous head, huge on a ridiculously thin neck, snapped forward. "Speak to me not in riddles," he barked. "If a thing is worth saying, it is worth saying understandably!"

"We understand each other," I murmured politely. "I only want to point out three things. The murder of Flo Morelle, the imprisonment and eventual execution of her husband, and the suicide of Jason Flye."

His eyes narrowed until they were grayish slits of trembling flesh behind which something glittered. "Life is a series of unexpected accidents," he said slowly, with emphasis. "One learns to take them as they come."

"A man I know," I said heavily, "once told me that in everything there is a plan. Only the ignorant worship the irrational."

"I see." He sucked at a carious canine tooth with evident relish. "But we digress. You were saying . . . ?"

"I was saying," I picked up, "that in everything there is a plan. So, too, in the series of what you term unexpected accidents. The Morelle business and Flye's suicide . . . there's a plan behind them, too."

"Extremely interesting," he replied, and I was amazed to find that he really meant it. And why shouldn't he? This could turn out to be a life-or-death matter to him. I decided to leave the gambit to him. We sat there for a long, silent moment, eying each other speculatively. My head felt marvelously clear, insulated from all but its own internal pain.

"I wonder," he said at last, "if you know what you're talking about, Dr. Loomis."

"I thought *you* might know."

"I? I know nothing. I worship the irrational." Half-jesting, half-heckling, the perfect podium attitude of a superior instructor.

"Well, then." I tried to organize my thoughts, pushing them around through my hollow-feeling head. "Let's say that it's *my* plan," I said finally. "Let's say that these unexpected accidents are neither unexpected nor accidental. I planned them."

"You? Surely you don't expect me to believe that you planned Mrs. Morelle's unfortunate murder? Did you, perhaps, throw Jason Flye into the waters of Lake Michigan?"

"Nothing that crude," I retorted. "As a matter of fact, I'm legally innocent of all these things. But they had to begin some place. Something had to set them in motion. Their source, as I said, is in my planning."

Khereniev opened his mouth and threw back his head. What came forth was less a laugh than a kind of pinched cackle, as though he were laughing politely at a joke that he had heard many times before. "Capital!" he exclaimed. "Leaving aside for a moment the sheer idiocy of your statement, let me ask: Why? What motive? Surely a man, even one with delusions of grandeur, must have reasons for such lethal strategy."

"Let's put it this way. When I see something that shouldn't be, something evil that must not be allowed to continue, I take pains to stamp it out."

"Highly commendable. And what is this something evil?"

He seemed bent on pumping the last bit of information out of me. But, thanks to the *Intracaine*, I could still think clearly. Precisely because he was concentrating on this tactic, I decided to say nothing more. "It isn't so much what it *is*," I parried, "but rather that it can be eradicated. And since I have the power to eradicate it, I am."

He made a mocking gesture of alarm. "Aren't you afraid?"

"Not at all. It can't harm me, but I have the power to destroy it. If you'll simply look about you, you'll see I'm succeeding." He looked sharply at me, paused, then seemed to retreat within himself, his body sinking back on the sofa, his neck pulling in, his head seemingly balanced without support on his thin, birdlike chest. He looked down at his hands, then off to one side, his mouth working slowly as though worrying a bit of meat off a bone, the kind of motion children make when they work a piece of bubblegum into its proper consistency. After a while, after his mouth slowed to a halt and he seemed to have reached some conclusion, he made his move.

"I'm inclined," he said, "to disbelieve everything you've said."

"Good," I enthused. "I could ask nothing—"

"But," he went on heavily, "I'm not such a fool as to follow initial inclinations. The thought has occurred to me that even such an obvious lunatic as you must have some reason for making public his unbalanced thinking. And with this in mind, Herr Doktor, I want to know why you've told me all this."

"Then I'll have to explain." I assumed a look of casual interest. "My plans affect *you*," I said. "I have no respect for the rest of your group, but I consider you an intelligent man. It is part of my plan to acquaint you with its very existence in the hope that you may . . . well, let's say, you may realize its power and submit peacefully."

Again Khereniev threw his head back and for a moment I thought he was going to peal forth his harsh cackle. But instead he merely closed his eyes and rocked back and forth for a long moment. At last, opening his eyes to focus vaguely on the ceiling above him, he spoke. "If I thought you were serious," he said slowly, "I would consider this whole warped business an opening bid. You have my attention and so you proceed to sell your wares. What they are I can only guess, since you are taking great pains to conceal them. But, as you say, I am an intelligent man. Tell me," he said, breaking off and snapping his head down to gaze closely at me, "do you want to join us? Is that your game?"

"*Join* you?" I burst out. "Are you crazy?"

"I know a hawk from a handsaw," he rejoined, smiling archly. "And a denunciation from a proposition. I wonder," he continued quickly, "if you realize what one wrong move can cost you?"

Realize it? I lived it, every moment of my life. But *he* mustn't

know. "There is no penalty," I retorted hotly. Then, abruptly, I checked myself. I mustn't get excited. It would disclose my anxiety. I had to be assured, calm. "You must know by now," I went on more quietly, "that no penalty affects me. I'm not Mr. Profit," I added in what I thought was a cool, well-tempered voice. "Nor Colin Jones."

"I agree," he said in a curiously flat voice. It admitted nothing, it conceded nothing. It was a dull, level statement of what he evidently took to be fact. "Perhaps," he went on, "you have been underestimated."

"There is no perhaps," I assured him.

"Quite possibly." He seemed to consider his words carefully. "Then let us say, speaking hypothetically, that what might have satisfied those gentlemen would not satisfy you."

"Exactly."

"And again hypothetically, that a proposition remains a proposition?"

"That's entirely up to you," I said in an offhand manner. "I've made my plans. If you'd care to change them, that's your business." I thought my words had a sufficiently careless, disinterested ring to them. I hoped they did.

"Yes?" he asked curiously.

"And if you'd like to check matters with Maida or Sam Olson, you'll—"

"With Sam Olson?" His whole expression had changed in an instant. He was suddenly alert, watchful.

"That's what I said."

A smile flicked across his face, his expression almost triumphant. "Dr. Loomis, you've overreached yourself. Congratulations."

The door buzzer rasped into life, two brisk bursts that shattered the tension about us. I felt something in my head twitch twice in sympathetic vibration with the buzzing. What had been wrong in mentioning Olson's name? I had no time to think. Now the real fireworks would begin.

If they were fireworks, I soon found out they were tame ones. The Olsons arrived with Maida Teufler and the meeting got under way without the elusive Kelk. Everything went smoothly, it seemed, and yet there were strange snags to the progress of the discussion.

"I've seen the blueprints," Sam Olson remarked. "They're planning a big thing, ten rooms, power plant, water pump, butane gas. It's unheard of."

"They must be very wealthy," Abbie observed.

"Too wealthy," Maida snapped coldly. "Such people should not be allowed to desecrate the landscape."

"Well, really, Maida," Khereniev said smoothly, "who are we to call it a desecration?"

Maida's pale blue eyes flared like Bengal lights, brilliant, chill. Then they dimmed to a pale reflection of their former intensity.

"Who are *we?*" she asked meaningfully.

"We're really lucky," Dora Olson chimed in, "I mean, nobody was around when *we* built to say yes or no and we just went ahead the way we *felt* like, without having everything picked apart the way we're picking these *new* people apart." She paused for a quick breath, then plunged paused for a quick breath, then plunged on. "What I say is that if nobody stopped *us,* who are we to stop somebody new? I mean, they've *paid* for the land and they've *hired* an architect and if they want to build—"

"They've bought the land?" I cut in. "I thought they only had an option."

"No," Sam assured me. "They've bought it. The contractors will be there Monday morning to lay the foundation."

"Then what's all this discussion?" I asked. "We're closing the barn door after the horse has run off."

"I suppose you're right," Sam agreed.

"Of course he's right," Abbie seconded.

Maida's squat head revolved slowly on her neck until she was facing Abbie head-on. She was in profile to me, but I could see the hard line of her mouth quirk up at one corner. "It is never too late," she said, putting a metallic kind of emphasis on each word.

"Perhaps it is," Khereniev surprised me by saying. "It appears that we have no recourse except to talk with these new people and in some way influence them."

Maida's laugh was brief and guttural. "Influence them not to build?" she asked. "They lay the foundation Monday."

"Maida, my dear," Khereniev said in a thin but courtly tone of voice. "It should be obvious to you that we can no longer control the existence of the house. They have *purchased* the land, Maida. Do you understand that?"

She shot him a lightning-like flash of a glance, sharp and crackling, out of those cerulean eyes. "It is never too late," she said slowly.

It went on that way for the better part of an hour. Even when Abbie sought to adjourn the discussion by producing cookies and punch, even then the interplay between Maida and the rest of the group was a taut, flicking thing. Maida seemed bent on holding that plot of ground with an almost physical grip, as though she could grasp it in her two hands, press it to her breast and shield it from the encroaching advance of these new settlers. I knew why . . . we all must have known why. This dune the South Bend automobile magnate had purchased was the sacred place of their demoniac ceremonies, the high place, the altar, the consecrated ground. And only Maida seemed to feel the loss of the high place so keenly. It fitted her character, this love of the *status quo*. She was the elephant who never forgot, the lover of tradition. To her there could never be another high place. This one had been consecrated in blood and worse than blood, in wild orgies, in the satanic saturnalia of people obsessed by something inhuman and dark, something not of the earth, something out of the deep, out of the nocturnal past of the race.

I felt I knew the fears in her simple mind: the fear of leaving a sacred place, of offending the dark powers that had conferred on that oval of sand, that circle of stones, the hidden mysteries of the tomb of mankind, the night secrets, the fierce, lusting secrets of blood and evil. And more . . . I knew she feared to rebuild that hideous place in another spot. Would such sacrilege anger the impulsive minds of her carnal deities? Did they have the right to change or the power to do so?

"I know nothing of options and deeds," Maida said angrily. "All I understand is *that—this—dune— is—used.*" She spaced out the words like individual bursts of some powerful explosive. I had to admire her single-mindedness. She called the dune The Dune, which no one else had the temerity to do.

"What matter?" Khereniev asked for the twentieth time. "Can't you comprehend, Maida, that one dune is as any other?"

"It's just a hill," I said lightly, "lots of sand and

grass. There are a hundred like it, maybe not as *high*, but so what?"

She eyed me for a moment and then, deliberately, turned away to face Khereniev. "Well, Jacques?" she asked in a challenging voice.

"Well?" He shrugged his shoulders.

"Am I to understand that no one agrees with me in this?" Maida asked.

"Oh, goodness," Dora put in hastily, "it isn't that we don't agree with you, it's just a matter of being practical. They've bought the land and they're going to build. It's up to us to make sure they don't build an eyesore up there, but I don't see that we can do anything else. I was thinking that we might get up a delegation next weekend and run over to South Bend. We might *talk* to the people."

"Quite so," Khereniev said. "I second the motion."

It was such an obvious method of shifting attention from Maida that I saw her blink as though she'd been slapped. "One moment," she said, her neck corded and tight. "We must not think of letting them build. Not at all. We must prevent them."

"But how?" Dora asked mildly. "I mean, they've bought the land and the—"

"There are ways," Maida interrupted flatly. "And if none of you have the will to do them, I must act alone."

"Maida," Khereniev said. His voice was a command, a warning.

"What do you mean, alone?" Sam Olson asked suddenly.

"There are things," she said stubbornly, "that can be done."

"But, darling," Abbie demurred. "Anything we do must be done in a group. You just can't simply—"

"If it must be alone," Maida stopped her, "it will be alone."

There wasn't much point in discussing the matter after that. The six of us sat around for a little while, talking disjointedly about a variety of things. Or rather I should say the five of us. Maida took no part in our conversation. She sat stiffly in her, chair, her chunky body inflexibly erect, as though she intended to remain rooted there till Judgment Day, defying whatever might come.

At last the evening petered out, the last trickle of water from a turned-off faucet. The Olsons excused themselves early and Maida, mumbling something about spending the night with Abbie, declined their offer of a ride home. They left immediately, in the wake of Dora's insipidly cheerful: "Well then, it's all settled? We'll go to see them next weekend in South Bend?"

"Of course," Khereniev replied, his brownish teeth bared in a nasty smile.

The four of us were alone. We sat listlessly, every-one undoubtedly waiting for me to say my goodbye and leave. I sat tight. I would either force their hand right now, or, at any rate, prevent them from acting. I waited.

"Well," Khereniev said, "I have work at home." He glanced briefly at his watch. "I must say that this has been a singularly unfruitful evening." He looked at Maida. "I trust no further discussion is necessary?"

"With you," she replied, "none."

"Obviously," he retorted. He got up from his chair and disappeared into the back of the apartment.

This was not too promising, but I didn't know quite what else to expect. I decided to throw as many monkey wrenches into their mechanism as I could conveniently do in the time allotted to me. "What sort of plans have you made?" I asked Maida.

"None that would interest you."

I was about to reply when I caught Abbie's glance. She seemed to be pleading with me to stop talking. A mute, pained expression was in her eyes and I saw her head move very slightly from side to side. "Everything about you interests me," I said lightly.

"*Ja!*" Maida burst out unexpectedly. "I know of you, Dr. Loomis!"

"That's very flattering." Abbie's eyebrows contracted in a frown and she shook her head again. "I didn't realize I was such a source of interest."

"Since you, everything has gone wrong!" Maida exclaimed harshly. "Since you, everything is breaking up, is going away. I tell you, I—"

"*Maida!*" Khereniev stood in the doorway, topcoat over. His arm his head shoved forward in a challenging attitude, his beady eyes glaring at the stocky little woman. "You have a quick tongue . . . too quick."

"*Teufelsdreck!*" she spat. "You tell *me* what to—"

"Shut up," Khereniev cut in sharply. The words were low-pitched, yet had a kind of direct, swift thrust to them, as though he had knifed her with a tiny blade. All masks were off in that instant and yet his face went bland as he looked at me. "Dr. Loomis, would you be kind enough to drive me home? The rain still falls and I am improvident enough to own no umbrella."

"Take a cab," I said softly, coldly.

"Really, is that any way to treat a possible confrere?"

"Take a cab," I repeated.

It is now five hours since I left Abbie's apartment. As I sit here, I can glance past the typewriter and see my trench coat lying on the couch where I threw it. The light fabric is dark with water, the bottom hem mired with smears of sandy mud. I can see my wet-weather hat beside it, the brim like a mass of sodden newspaper, the crown black with water, as though someone had poured bucketfuls on my head. Such is the intensity of the rain, a full, steady downpour of water. And yet you might wonder that a man could get so wet inside his car, driving the scant ten blocks from Abbie's apartment to mine. It's a short story, much too short to warrant more intracaine, and although my head is splitting itself and my skull seems ready to disintegrate into a welter of bony shards, yet I have enough strength to repeat the story without drugs. I must have. What happened in the past five hours is a warning to me far more ominous than any other, than even this accursed ache they have put upon my head.

It began shortly after I returned from the meeting.

I had hung up my hat and coat and was lying down on the couch trying to blank out my mind, trying to soothe the fevered aching inside my brain. Khereniev hadn't believed me. What went wrong? The tension of the evening had accumulated inside me until I was like a vessel from which something tremendous and potent is trying to escape. It had almost succeeded when the telephone rang and sent a sharp spasm along the crest of my skull, a twinge of nauseating agony that pulled me up off the couch in a single stabbing pang of action. I stumbled to the phone and picked it up.

"The high dune," a voice whispered.

"What?"

There was a confused grating sound at the other end. I couldn't place the voice. It sounded like Abbie, but I couldn't be sure. "Hello?"

"The high dune, now, tonight!" There was a click and the wire went dead. I wonder now whether I wouldn't have been wiser to ignore the whole matter. But after that veiled message, I couldn't rest . . . I reached the side road leading off the lake highway in a matter of less than two hours. I had the roads to myself that night. The back of my neck smarted from intracaine; I was using it much too often. The rain slanted down across the double beams of my head-lights, constant, changing, yet identical through every mile. Towns were deserted as I shot through, the car tires singing a high note as they sucked through the surface rain. Neon lights were dimmed and hazy in the heavy downpour. I raced along the lake road, past the beer baron's place, along the inland road that led upwards in the rain-misted night to the high dune. I wanted to shut off my lights, but it was suicide to drive without them. I dimmed them and drove on, peering past the rhythmic flick-swish of the wind-shield wiper that pulsed and slowed with the speed of the engine.

The car twisted and rumbled under me, jostled from side to side in the slick ruts beneath its wheels. The rain cut down my headlight beams to mere mushrooms of light that faded off a few feet from the lenses, devoured by the gallons of needle-sharp water lancing past. The wipers stopped as I jammed down the gas, then started their endless arcs again, *chick-whoolsh*, *chock-whoolsh*, *chick-whoolsh*, squeegeeing off the film of water for a brief instant before the rain blotted it out again. I pushed the car onward, higher.

Suddenly, as the road began to level out and the whining of the gears was muffled to a steady thrum, I caught sight of the gears was muffled to a steady thrum, I caught sight of something white in the road ahead. In the quick moment before the rain washed down the glass again, I thought it looked like the body of a human being, stretched in an odd, sack-of-laundry position across the muddy ruts.

I slammed hard on the brake pedal, pushing it down, standing on it with all my weight. *Whoolsh*. The glass was clear, the road through it weaving and shift-ing crazily.

The wheels stuttered, dropped, the steel frame of the car rising up and slithering sideways through the slimy roadbed, skidding and slipping, the rear of the car wheeling slowly, spinning me around, end for end in a circling sideways sliding rush.

It came to a halt abruptly, almost as though it had come to rest against some huge soft obstacle. I jumped out. Rain slashed down on me with a vicious fury, drumming on the brim of my hat, spotting my glasses with drops that soon merged into a full, screening film. I stumbled about in the mud, feeling it gurgle and slosh around my shoes. Suddenly, my shoe-tip sank into something that was not mud. I reached down in the rain and picked blindly about me.

It was a small body in a white raincoat, the legs doubled up sideways under it, the arms flung out wide, the hands palms down, fingers buried in the yielding mud as though they were clutching at it for strength. I shoved my arms under the body and lifted it up. It was heavy for all its smallness. It was Maida.

After I got her in the car and jockeyed my way out of that oozing, treacherous spot, I finally thought to test her pulse and found signs of life. Her frame was inert as I moved her, yet there were no signs of violence visible. I clutched in, let the car slither down the hill in the direction I'd come, rocketing from side to side as it plummeted downward to the beach road. Once on concrete, it seemed to shake itself, like a wet dog, and take to the highway eagerly. I drove a few miles, then pulled over to one side of the road and stopped.

As I did so, I heard a soft moaning sound from Maida. Her iron-gray hair was streaked with mud, dark with rain. Her chubby face, so bland, so immobile before, was old now, the facial fat flabbing in loose sacs under her eyes, at her jawline. She seemed to have no muscles in her face, no will to use them if they'd been there. I lifted her head and as I did so a thin trickle of muddy water gushed out of her lax mouth. She blinked her eyes and moaned again.

"Maida, what happened?"

"Was?"

"This is Dr. Loomis. What happened to you?"

"Ich . . . Ich verstehes nicht."

"Maida! Speak English, Maida."

Her eyes opened wide and seemed to loll about in their sagging cups of flesh. *"Was?"* she asked weakly.

"I'm Dr. Loomis. Tell me what happened."

The words seemed to have no effect on her. She looked at me for a moment without interest, then looked away. When she spoke it was in a high, breathless croon; she was singing something to a light, lilting kind of melody. *"Ein strumpf an, und ein strumpf auf . . . ja, ja, ja-ja-ja . . ."* The tune died away.

"Do you know who I am?" I asked vainly.

Her eyes flicked back at me, the wide, open stare of a sleepwalker. *"Ein strumpf an,"* she crooned, waving her pudgy finger in time to the melody, *"und ein strumpf auf, ja, ja . . .*

Again the tune died away without warning.

I picked up her arms and shook them violently. "Maida?" I said loudly.

"Ja?"

"Do you know me?"

"Ich verstehes nicht."

What kind of trick was this? What was she trying to get me to do? I decided not to bother finding out. "We're going back to Chicago," I said firmly.

She gave me another empty look and then began picking her nose, shoving her thick finger upwards until it was almost hidden in her nostril. "Don't do that," I said, slapping her hand away. "What's the matter with you?"

She giggled queerly and hid her hand behind her back. I started the car and pulled onto the road again. We began to pick up speed. A curious lisping sound came from her mouth and I took my eyes off the road long enough to glance at her. She was opening and closing her mouth, meanwhile pushing out spittle and air through her teeth. Little bubbles of saliva welled up on her lips, broke, were replaced. I shoved hershoulder hard. "Cut that out," I said sharply.

She giggled again and looked down at her hands. "And don't pick your nose," I added. She was beginning to get under my skin. If this was some kind of gag, it was working too well. I decided to stop in Michigan City and have it out with her where the presence of some townspeople might give me a little moral backing. We were silent. The car shot along the road with a high, whispering hiss, the tires sending a spray of water up under the fenders. The road was empty, no cars, certainly no people. It wound along past signboards, deserted stores. *You Are Leaving Morton Groves, a Restricted Suburban Community. No Peddlers Allowed.*

Michigan City was equally unpopulated. The heavy rain splashed on the wide streets and a fine mist hovered just above the pavement. Inside the car the air was oppressive, damp. I was sweating and I could see Maida struggling with the buttons on her white raincoat, as though she had not yet learned how to use them. I pulled the car to the curb and turned to face her.

"All right," I said brusquely. "Now what's this all about?"

She giggled mildly and kept on picking at the coat buttons. I reached over, slapped her hands aside and finished the unbuttoning for her. She looked up at me with empty blue eyes like milky marbles. *"Bitte,"* she murmured.

"Come off it," I snapped back. "What's the idea of all this?"

"Ja." She began pawing aimlessly at the door handle, working it back and forth as though it were a toy. The effort of her actions set the fatty sacs of her face to trembling. It was a sickening sight, this squat little robot of a woman, always so precise, so mechanically exact, her hard mouth a tight steely line . . . now every inch of her flesh like gelatin, her stumpy fingers loose and boneless, fumbling with the door handle and the window crank, her mouth damp with drooling slobber. It was almost as if she had been softened up in some powerful solvent so that the muscle and sinew of her tightly-knit frame were converted to a fantastically flexible rubber. The idea of what she had been and the sight of what she was now appalled me.

I felt the corner of my mouth pull sideways in a grimace of disgust.

"Jetz!" she giggled. She had finally mastered the secret of the door handle, pushed it down and felt the door swing open into the rain. Past her I could see a torrent of water sluicing down, rapping sharply on the open door, turning the mohair upholstery black. "Shut that!" I yelled.

As though my shout had been an order to do so, she slipped off the seat and bounced out of the car. She stood there for a moment in the rain. Then, still giggling, she grabbed the door and swung it back awkwardly, her whole face a mass of blobbing bulbs. The door slammed to and caught. I could see her standing there outside the window and then she took a few steps along the street, a curious kind of gait, half-skip, half-slide. I watched her through the windshield.

She skipped on and then, with the perverse kind of luck that sometimes happens to drunks, she stopped in front of a tavern, its windows filled with bright neon tubing that must have attracted her wandering gaze. She stopped short, felt the glass, then drew back and slapped the windowpane hard. I had a sudden impulse to get out of the car and stop her, but before I could do anything, a man stuck his head out of the tavern door and peered through the rain.

Maida took this moment to step forward and hit the glass again. Then, finding it impervious, she kicked at it. The man yelled something I couldn't hear and immediately three other men materialized around him, their heads bent toward Maida, their mouths shouting something I couldn't distinguish. They were almost halfway down the block from me; I could see everything through the water-swept windshield, all movements sliding and glassy. One of them stepped out into the rain and tried to grab Maida's arm. He succeeded in catching hold of the white raincoat, which was flapping loosely around her. With a sudden, colt-like movement, she spun around and the man was left holding the coat. Then she flew into action.

She tugged at the skirt around her chubby hips, pulling hard at it, and finally she must have torn the fabric because it gave way with a rush and she was standing there in the street, her heavy, veined legs naked in the rain, her mottled buttocks bulging loosely, already slicked with a shiny film of water. The men drew back hastily and as they did so, Maida yanked at her blouse and it came free in a single tearing motion. She was now naked except for her shoes. She kicked them off and began a kind of jigging dance there on the sidewalk, her stocky body white and revoltingly shiny in the rain, tinted strange hues of red by the neon sign, her blubbery breasts bobbing up and down with the exertion of her movements, her legs flabbing heavily as she pranced and ducked and minced about. The four men stood there, their eyes wide, their mouths open. Eight O's above four ovals. I shifted into low gear, my eyes on Maida. She began to dance jumpingly, dashing toward the men, her pendulous breasts pink and red and glittering in the rain, then ducking back with a violent motion that made her flesh ripple and shiver in repulsive waves that raced up and down her flabby buttocks.

I let out the clutch and started past her. As I drove by I could hear her voice, high and crooning through the heavy rain.

"Ein strumpf an, und ein strumpf auf . . . ja, ja, ja-ja-ja-!"

I AM SITTING HERE NOW, having written all that happened, and trying to understand. I know what happened but somehow I cannot push myself to realize what lies beneath the events of this night.

What took place on the high dune tonight? There is something in the sight of a fat forty-year-old woman's nude and jellying body, bright scarlet and sensuous pink, glazed like a roasted suckling with the slickness of driving rain, performing like a wanton madwoman before the astonished eyes of four by-standers . . . something in that scene that grabs the pit of my gut and gives it a hard squeezing jolt that almost overpowers me.

She has been driven mad. There is no doubt of that. The Maida Teufler I knew would never in her life have done those things. They have taken her mind away. The Maida I knew was a hard, purposeful woman, full of brutal cunning. But this was a lisping, drooling idiot girl, flapping her bulbous breasts into the faces of strangers as she footed that insane, nauseatingly lascivious dance. Her mind has been stolen and her body set wandering.

Yes, they could steal her mind. For a whim, almost. At least it seemed that way. In reality, for her stupid obstinacy. And with her mind went her power over the darkness they commanded.

Maida has been reduced to babbling infancy, to a time in her life when she knew nothing of the satanic power she later controlled. Innocent of it then, she has been forcibly returned to that previous state of innocence where, I am sure, she will remain until she dies one day in the charity ward of some public mental institution.

They have removed her from their hellish clan as effectively as if they had killed her and—the sheer brilliance of it! There is nothing the law of man can do to punish them. What they did to Maida they can do again. As I sit here now, the rain drumming endlessly against my apartment windows, I wonder when they will do it again. And to whom?

10 «◊» Just a Little Love, a Little Kiss

I DON'T KNOW HOW MUCH LONGER I can continue writing this thing. The days are so long now, so intolerably dragged out. Time has become a different thing for me than for other men.

The minutes and hours men use to mark off their lives have become bloated, elephantine moments for me. The simple act of shaving myself each morning is now an act encompassing days of time, huge empty hogsheads of hours while I stand, swaying, before my mirror, daubing soap on my face, scraping the razor's secret blade across the stubble that grows there. Each hair has an intimate, crepitating sound as it submits to the blued steel, each hair snaps and whispers as it surrenders a fraction of itself to the edge of the razor. One side of my face seems to take hours. I start off under the side burn and work down, everything insanely detailed, as though my cheek were the slope of a heavily treed mountain and I, shriveled to mite size, were riding the sharp prow of the blade like a tobogganist. I am old, weary, before I come to rest at the point of my chin. There is a slight pockmark, relic of childhood, halfway down that immense slope, a tremendous indentation a man could drown in, and I take hours to round its ovoid circumference, careful lest I trip and plunge headlong into the creamy ocean of lather that bubbles and boils in its depths.

And the washing off, what an eternity of time there! I am old; ancient generations have issued from my loins. It is a new century. Time has left me behind. I am of the next century, and my prolonged life has been spent in the overwhelming activity of a morning shave. Then I look at my watch, taking it up, cold and clammy, from the vast marble plateau of the medicine chest shelf. The ticking is like a leisurely pile driver hammering an eternity of underpinnings deep within the soil of my wrist. I look at the dial.

I have taken eight minutes to shave.

I don't know how much longer I can continue this writing. As I sit before the typewriter now, the colossal billboard of each key blinding me with the single intensity of its message, I feel something burr-like, multi-pointed, like a grapnel, imbedded in the soft grayness of my cranium, something sharp in each direction, an armored thing that throbs and lances out at the yielding matter of its bed in tempo with the monstrous yammer of the typewriter. I feel that death is a matter of weeks now, unless one measures time by my personal standard. By the seven-day, 168-hour, 10,080-minute week of ordinary men, I have only a few more to live.

But perhaps the greatest agony of all is a purely mental one. All this noise, this horrendous clatter, can be muffledeasily; the merest touch of *Intracaine*-soaked cotton will give relief. The temptation is monstrous. It lives with me through every hour of each twenty-four, beckoning, coaxing. "Just once more," it urges. "Once more won't spoil anything."

Above all things, I cling stubbornly to the idea that action alone will extricate me from my danger. And my chance to act may come at any moment. I must know, beyond all doubt or insecurity, that when I need the *Intracaine* it will work.

Although I haven't seen the need to mention it before, I've been doing a certain amount of research on my own particular condition. I've attacked it from both the logical and illogical approaches, delving into pagan lore and primitive magic, checking against the findings of modern science and especially psychopathology. My research has been interesting but—the temptation to value it is great—not very conclusive.

In all my books and learned treatises, the practice of dark knowledge is an accepted fact. Whole books are devoted to the role of sorceresses in the Dark Ages, carefully outlining the correspondences with political and social developments. Tomes are dedicated to describing, in all their nauseous detail, such rituals as the black mass, the Witches' Sabbath, the detection of satanic possession, the signing of covenants with the Devil. Yet none of them seek to question their premises. And as I read the wonder grows: Was all this true? In volume after volume, such matters are taken for granted, stated as fact, set down as thoroughly as Einstein outlined his theory of relativity, as Mendelyeev his periodic tables of elements. Was Satanism equally true?

I put away the histories. There was something un-explained here that mere recital of past events would never clear up. Of the gross aspects of black magic I knew much. The witches and sorcerers had tremens-dous knowledge of primitive medicine. They knew the value of herbs and simples, and further, they kept their knowledge so secret that the founder of modern medicine, Paracelsus, had to learn everything he knew about pharmacopoeia from *sub rosa* sources. At the risk of being burned or flayed alive, these ancient practitioners gathered their strange plants, brewed their potent draughts, and prescribed their odd, nox-ious philters out of one-third ignorance, one-third charlatanry, and one-third sound medical science. But I wasn't interested in this aspect of the supernatural, so-called. It was the rest of the body of history that baffled me. I understood how they put people in trances; their drugs did the work. I knew how they induced what Mother Church called that arch conception of Satan, abortion; we still use their time-tested preparations. Their miraculous cures were all laid bare; the same cures are run-of-the-mill today. I was interested in something else, something closer to home, as close as the racking pain in my head. How, without contact, could they reach across miles and oceans to maim and cripple, wither and lay waste?

The gist of the problem lay in one word . . . hypno-sis. By this I do not mean the more theatrical aspects of the idea, the mesmeric passes, the mumbo jumbo of the carnival sideshow. That was all part of it, but by hypnosis I refer to the broadest possible meaning of the word, the influencing of one person by another, the induction in one mind of the will of another.

There is, after all, nothing strange or unfamiliar about hypnosis. In its many forms we see it daily, experience it, use it. It blankets human intercourse as few other ideas have the power to do. It ranges from the contrived campaigns of advertising and the spellbinding speeches of politicians to the protestations of lovers and the arguing of a traffic cop out of a ticket. Wherever one man seeks to impose his will upon another, some facet of hypnosis lives.

When we watch a stage practitioner stiffen his subject's body to board-like rigidity, immure the neural system to pain, electrify the musculature to superhuman strength, affect the respiration, pulse, body temperature and perspiration, take the subject back to his childhood, summon up forgotten events, metamorphose him into a hundred states of being . . . then we begin to catch the deeper meanings of hypnosis. We begin to see how truly secondary the body is to the mind, how much a tool it is, controlled and evoked by the mind to feats our normal lives would never encompass, catalyzed into the extraordinary or debased into the most menial subjection, all through the will and direction of the mind.

And from this simple, almost clinical demonstration of hypnotic power, go one step further into the area of mass hypnosis. Recall the Nazi mass meetings, summon up the camp-meeting atmosphere of the old revivalists, remember the ancient Saturnalia, the feasts and orgies of our primitive progenitors, rituals of, fire and frenzy that whipped their participants into high ecstasies of passion, negating the body, immolating it, sacrificing the living flesh in a wild whirl of drumbeat and chanting. Mass hypnosis, whether invoked by one man or whipped up by the willful cooperation of the mass itself, is a symbol of the mind's supremacy over its body. Or rather . . . the supremacy of the blood, the beating, throbbing course of red that overwhelms the body and drives it on, that hammers down the caution of the mind as it spills and swirls and beats itself higher and higher in a mounting tempo of passion.

And then, finally, take one step more into the primeval past of man, into an area of hypnosis that, for sheer incredulity, makes the Saturnalia and revival meetings pale to a pink blush. There was once in this world—as there still is under other names—a formalized system of what we now call taboos. Primitive men hedged round their lives with commandments that prescribed their actions down to the merest breath of air sucked into their lungs. All morality, all intercourse was thus classified, codified, enforced. It was death to touch the person of a king, death to look upon a bit of his fingernail, leprosy and death to wear his castoff clothes. Pregnant women were reservoirs of unclean evil, fit only for banishment and isolation during their nine months, and who touched them then would surely break out in festering sores and die within the month. Twins were the work of Satan, to be isolated from other men as terrifying objects of evil. Strangers were to be avoided, blue-eyed children shunned, certain animals, certain plants, certain times of the year, certain clouds, hills, rivers, fields, all *taboo*.

And that was long ago, you say. That was ages past. Yet until this decade the Japanese feared death if they chanced to look on the Emperor. Some hotels now, this minute, have no thirteenth floor. Are the old taboos gone? When you say so, knock on wood. Just for a laugh, of course, but don't forget to knock on wood.

But the core of taboo is not the mere prescribing of it. It is its *enforcement*. What happened to the savage Australian bushman when he chanced to pick up a stick that someone later told him was thrown away by a chief? He sickened and died. What happened in 1947 in a small Guatemalan town when the members of a secret religious society put a curse on one of their members? He sickened and died. The volumes I read are glutted with such data. The reading of them became a kind of antiphonal chant. They sickened and died. They sickened and died. Down through the ages, through the mists of antiquity, the blackness of the Middle Ages, the ascendancy of the nineteenth century, they sickened and died.

There is no trickery in this enforcement. No drugs are surreptitiously introduced into the victim's food. When the Haitian voodoo *mamalois* pierce their little wax dolls, they do not curse already diseased men and women. The only link between the curse and the accursed, between the violated taboo and the punished violator, is a thin, steel-pliant thread of what, for a better name, I must call hypnosis.

The victim, reared in his faith, knows the penalty awaiting him. He hears the ritual drums beating for him. And it is this faith, this acceptance, this submission, that caps hypnosis with success. He knows the law, the punishment. He hears it pronounced. And suddenly all will is gone from him. With the flight of will, the body lies powerless. The mind has surrendered; how can the body live?

I SEE ABBIE QUITE REGULARLY. Is that surprising? For one thing, I am no longer capable of sustaining any prolonged semblance of normal behavior. If left to myself, I would certainly remain locked in my apartment, never leaving it to carryon my practice, breathe fresh air or buy a newspaper. I would crouch and wait and hoard my *Intracaine* against a day of action. Since food is no longer important, I would not even have to shop for my needs. I'd be perfectly satisfied to sit in some corner, my eyes closed, my ears plugged, and wait like Colin for the inevitable death that must come within a matter of weeks.

That is the natural inclination, but my superego, my mental police force, derides the idea as cowardly and selfish. From somewhere in my past, this part of me has become obsessed with the concept of responsibility. What folklore calls conscience, and what psychology calls the superego drives me out of myself to continue my work, to treat patients dependent on me, to maintain my practice. And I cannot uphold my responsibilities alone. So I see Abbie almost every night. Sometimes she comes here, often we meet at a restaurant or at her apartment. But every afternoon at five, when the last of my patients has left and my receptionist has gone home for the day and I sit at my desk trying to summon up the will power to take my body home without recourse to *Intracaine*, at that moment my phone rings and Abbie talks to me.

She always has something interesting to suggest. In my present condition it's hard to find anything that will interest me. Plays and movies I cannot watch. I can't bear the idea of sports and parties. But Abbie always manages to come up with something I can do, something interesting enough to take my mind off the more incisive aspects of this thing that is killing me. She takes me out of myself for a few hours each night and gives me the strength to go on each day. Our relations are strange. I think no two people have ever meant such odd things to each other. Our conversations are bizarre.

"The water is so cool," she murmurs. She has driven me in my car to a deserted beach on the North Shore, a private beach belonging to some Winnetka people she knows. "It's like the sound of a viola," she tells me.

"That's my favorite instrument."

"It's a girl's name," she says, "and it has the sound of a woman."

In the twilight, we watch the waves surging in, lapping at the crust of sandy shore. "I'd like to swim," I say.

"Would you?" She takes my hand and leads me out into the cool water. "Just float," she says. "Relax and let the water bear you."

The lake is like a cradle, rocking me in a soundless sleep. It is almost like the blessed peace of *Intracaine*. I watch her long slim body in a white bathing suit cleave the water some way off. She swims well, her long black hair swirling behind her like the filmy, gauzy fins of some rare tropical fish. She disappears from sight and I am alone, rocking in the firm yet gentle embrace of the water. The sky is dark above me, the stars like cracks through which some tremensdous light breaks out. There is a sudden rushing sound and she comes up beside me, the water falling down her face and hair as though it were part of her, slipping off in a shining cascade.

"It's night down there," she says. She doesn't seem to be winded. Her breath comes naturally, easily, as she speaks. "It's the darkest night below there."

"Darker than anything else?"

"Much darker. The womb."

Saturdays, when my visiting hours end at noon, she calls up with a suggestion that we drive to the dunes for the weekend. The very word "dunes" shudders inside me like a spear that pierces my body, its shaft twanging and shivering.

"Not there," I manage to say.

"It's cooler than the city, darling, so much cooler."

"There are things out there," I say.

"No," she assures me. "They won't be there."

"You don't know."

I refuse. I cannot make myself accept; the words simply will not leave my mouth and take to the air. For two weekends now I've refused and I will continue, with the obstinate power of a dying man. I know those dunes. The city's concrete jungle is of man, for man. But the wild sweep of those dunes is of something darker than man, something out of his dreams, a stage for unnamed deeds of the night and the earth and the blood of man. I will not go there.

Yet tomorrow is Saturday again and in the inexorable swing of the clock, through its eons of minutes, through each tick that lasts a day, the swing of time will bring me to noon again. And as surely as the earth revolves, the telephone will burst into clangorous life and Abbie will be calling me. And I know what she will ask. I know that as surely as I know that I am going to die.

THIS IS SUNDAY NIGHT. I am writing this in pencil and I hope whoever has the task of deciphering this narrative will not find the job too difficult. It must be deciphered. I know that now. It must be told.

Saturday, a hundred years of my time ago, Abbie's call came through as the minute hand inched its way to the top of my watch dial. I let it ring. Each sharp blast of the bell set my teeth on edge. I winced, tightened my jaw. The vibration of the telephone set up a buzzing at the back of my teeth, as though I were being shaken and buffeted. It stopped and I gathered my strength, stood up, reached for my coat. I had to get out of the office before it rang again. My hand was on the doorknob, my fingers tensing. I turned the knob and the phone rang again, once, twice, a third time . . .

"It's me, darling."

"Yes."

"I know what you're going to say, but please, please, can't we drive out there?"

"I . . ."

"Please darling, it'll . . . it could be important tonight. I have the feeling it could be very important to us."

We made it to Michigan City in three hours, driving at a leisurely pace that minimized the bumps in the road. Abbie drove well, carefully avoiding sharp turns and sudden bursts of speed. She pulled my car into the parking ground next to the Michigan City bus depot. "Why here?" I asked.

"We'll take the bus."

"Don't you want them to see my car?"

"It'll be dark in a few hours," she said by way of an answer. It was all I got from her.

We waited in the depot, the long benches hard and unyielding, the noise of children and dogs and buses driving my brain from one corner of its skull to another as it tried to recoil out of the path of these monstrous sensations. If only I could slip away and use my *Intracaine*. But by eight o'clock the sky was dark and the depot was fairly deserted. I had a few ampoules of *Intracaine*. Should I use one now, or wait until action seemed imminent? Before I had a chance to make up my mind, it was time to go. We boarded a bus, got off at the last stop, ducked into the brush along the road and slid down the steep sandy incline to the beach. "Why?" I asked, the pain in my head almost unbearable.

"We can't take the road."

"I know, but why?" The sand, heated to an incredible pitch by the day's sun, was still hot under-foot. I felt its prickling intensity through my shoes and once, when I tripped over something and fell forward full-length, it burned at my skin like a bed of hot spikes. Abbie's cool hand slipped under my arm and helped me to my feet. I couldn't see where we were going. All I could feel in the darkness was the guiding support of her hand.

"Wait here." Her words were a quiet whisper in the silent darkness.

I heard her footsteps on something hard and reverberating, not sand, but wooden steps. Was there a stairway behind her cottage? I'd never had the chance to know. I still didn't know. Was there going to be action now, right now? I waited there, alone and tense, like a granule of sand in the immense vacuum of eternity. Hours passed. I reached in my pocket, found an ampoule. The year wheeled and was lost to sight. I wrapped my handkerchief around the glass tube. The century loomed old and dying. I started to crack the ampoule.

There was a soft, caressing sound, falling slowly, approaching. I opened my eyes and saw a whitish shape swimming down the side of the dune toward me. Abbie, barefoot on the steps. Quickly, I stuffed the unbroken ampoule back in my pocket. She hurried across the sand to me.

"All clear," she whispered.

I felt her hand guiding me upwards, the coarse wooden steps under my feet, the splintery shift of a hand-railing under my clutching fingers. After a while we reached level ground. The cottage was dark. She led me inside, closed the door and bolted it. Then she produced a small white candle, lit it quickly and propped it up inside the fireplace.

"They won't see the light," she murmured. "Now lie down here, darling." She eased my body onto the couch and I felt the gaping weave of its covers press into my flesh like a hot waffle grid. After a moment I let my muscles relax. The room was dark. Only the barest of essentials, the floor, a wall or two, were picked out by the tiny candle flame. I noticed the windows were shuttered and curtained. Whatever she was hiding me from, she was neglecting no precaution.

"Something will happen tonight," she said softly. "I don't know what, but it will be important."

"You keep saying that," I groaned. "If you don't know what it is, how——?"

She watched me distractedly for a moment, as though she were a nurse with a capricious child. "All right," she said at last. "I'll tell you what I know. It won't be much, but you'll have to believe it's all I know. Then will you try to sleep?"

"Talk."

"Yes. Well, it's the house, the new house on top of the dune. They laid the foundation two weeks ago and all the rafters are up now. Khereniev's nervous."

"Fine time to be nervous," I snapped viciously.

"Why?"

"The time was back when Maida warned you. God, you people don't even know your own business. You're just a——"

"*Shh.*" She laid her fingers across my mouth, cool fingers across the tortured flesh of my lips. "That was something else," she murmured. "The important thing is to preserve a strong front. If one of them acts like Maida, they have to——"

"They?" The word rocketed out of my mouth like a hot rivet. "Why do you say 'they'? It's *you!* You're in it, too."

"*I'm not!*" She almost shrieked the denial. "How many times must I tell you I'm not!"

"I saw you," I retorted.

"Oh, darling, you . . . you're confused." She stroked her hand across my forehead. "You're all mixed up. And I am too," she rushed on. "I admit that. I don't know what I am except confused and mixed-up. Don't you see that?"

I grunted painfully. "Tell me about tonight," I asked.

"Tonight they're up there, in the, new house. Something important will happen, they say. I . . . I think they mean to blow up the foundation."

"That'll get you nowhere."

"But it's more than the explosion. Khereniev says it's the— what did he call it?—the ultimate ritual."

"What the hell is that?"

"Darling, I don't *know.*"

I grunted again, meaningfully.

"Joe, my dearest, haven't you trusted me? All these weeks, haven't I been right for you? Why can't you trust me now?"

I gazed up into her dark eyes that seemed to have unplumbable depths, like ancient wells, shafts sunk to the very core of the earth. "I trust you," I heard my voice say. "What the hell difference does it make what I do?"

"It makes all the difference," she said then. "Just to have you *with* me is all the difference. Just to know you believe in me."

"I don't know what I believe any more," I sighed.

"You know I love you."

"I know you say that."

"Joe!" Her face went apart as though I'd slapped

it. "I don't say things that aren't true. Why should I lie to you? You're my only hope."

"For what?"

"For . . ." she faltered. "For everything, for a new life. I . . . I need only one thing, darling. Other women might need so many things, but all I need is someone who knows, *knows* I'm right. Knows that whatever I've done, I can still come right in the end. It's the truth, Joe. Believe me."

I watched her face for a long moment. What did I know? What did anybody know? Truth, beauty, justice, how could I . . . I looked away, the sight of her face, that haunted, beautiful face, was too much. "I know," I said finally. "I know."

She bent over me. I could see her face grow huge, like a gigantic movie close-up, her mouth opening over mine, the lovely warmth of her breath spreading over my face. Then her lips touched me and I felt a ring of pain spring up to meet them and then the whole day piled up on me in a quick rush. What did I know? The weeks, the centuries of agony and sleeplessness poured out in a furious stream of agonizing hours and for the first time in too long, so terribly long, I slept.

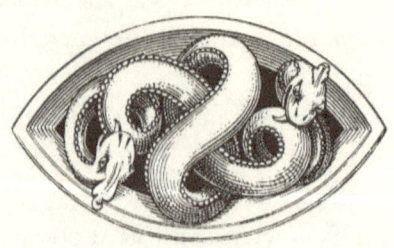

THE DREAM IS HARD TO REMEMBER. Sitting here now, my writing hand tight with fatigue, I can only recall vague episodes from it. I remember Khereniev or someone like him hunched over the rostrum of a huge podium, a bobbing sea of human faces upturned to listen. He spoke at great length about things I can't remember and his words were punctuated with shrill cheers and rhythmic chanting. It was like a scene out of the newsreels of Hitler, everyone pitched to a high frenzy, reacting like automatons to each searing phrase, leaping to their feet to scream their response like a congregation of fanatics. The only difference was that each face, each distorted, wildly gleaming face of that multitude, was Khereniev's face. I remember that.

There was more to the dream, but I recall fully only one incident—a scene filled with strange monumental shapes, weird towers and obelisks set in distorted rows on a flat plane that receded toward an eternal horizon, a perspective not of this world. It was like one of the di Chiricos in Abbie's apartment, the perspective wild and dizzying, the monuments ruined and massive. I walked among them, wondering at the masonry. Then I looked closer and saw each brick was a human head. The cobblestoned plain was millions of heads, mortared together like paving blocks. It gave the scene a kind of oneness, a basic unit, a module that lent unity to the disparate parts. Everything—monuments, streets—was constructed of human heads. And as I watched, their eyes opened and their mouths broke the quiet. They were alive.

I awoke feeling better than I had for weeks. The sleep, tortured by nightmare, was still a sleep, and it helped me more than anything else could have. I got up from the couch and took a step. The candle in the fireplace was guttering out. It had been only a few inches high and now it was little more than a wick flickering in a pool of tallow. I looked at my watch. Midnight. "Abbie?"

No answer. I was afraid to shout her name, afraid to light a lamp. I stumbled through the rooms of the cottage calling her in a whisper. The place was deserted.

Quickly my hand shot into my pocket. I pulled out my handkerchief, wadded into a wrinkled mass, felt the hard outline of an ampoule within its folds. Tensing my fingers, I pressed the thin tube. The ampoule snapped with a dry sound and instantly the handkerchief was wet. I swabbed it on the back of my neck, felt the liquid cold and stinging. I shoved the wet rag into my pocket. And suddenly my brain was cavernous again, empty, hollow, only that muted throb of the central pain still vibrating. I left the cabin quickly.

The high dune was easy enough to find. I had no binoculars this time, but I could see the outlines of the unfinished house atop the upthrust of sand. Moonlight shone through the studs and rafters, the gaping window openings.

Then, as I watched, I saw something move, something white, the size and clearly the shape of a human figure. I remembered then. It was Abbie. She was wearing white tonight. Didn't a priestess always wear white?

There was a kind of singing, thrumming sensation in me, a kind of keen excitement as one word repeated itself in my mind. *"Action."* It drew me on, the word, the thought, the concept of action. I had had enough of sitting, enough of waiting, enough of the fear that robs a man of every decent thing.

It wasn't easy. The high dune was steep, the sand piled at an angle one would almost believe impossible. The neighboring dune, from which I'd watched that other night, had been simple to ascend. But this huge thing was as close to the perpendicular as mere sand could ever get. I circled the base of it, peering upward into the night. A slight sound, a low grunting sound that started and stopped almost immediately, came down to me on the cool air. How was I to mount the dune? How had they climbed it? That was obvious. Men—and women—in good condition could climb it easily. For me it was impossible. My mind was insulated from pain but my body had taken cruel punishment. This was the crowning irony, then, that I should be drawn to this dune, thirsting for action, and fall short of fulfilling my desire. I stood there for a moment, then walked a few more yards around the base. My shin barked against something hard.

It was a small platform hastily knocked together of old lumber. Looking at it more closely, I saw that two thick wire cables swung upward from it and disappeared over the crest of the dune, their length upheld by stout posts at intervals of a yard or two. This was a pulley system the workmen had rigged to lift their materials. Perfect. I waded as far up the slope as I could, then grabbed the cable in my hands and started the actual ascent.

I reached the crest of the dune, swung clear of the cable, and dropped to my knees a few feet from the concrete foundation of the house. I found myself wondering, like a starving man thinking of the multiplication table, how they'd managed to sink a concrete base in this sand. They sank piles, I told myself gravely.

They sank piles.

Sweat was icy on my forehead. The night air was turning each stream of perspiration into a chill river. I passed my hand across my brow and wiped it clean. Now my hand was sopping wet. It looked dark in the uncertain light. I brought it to my eyes. There was a kind of diagonal blaze or stain across my palm, across both palms. The hands of a doctor have none of the protective callouses of more fortunate men. My numb palms were stained with blood. I crawled forward through the rubble of discarded lumber, concrete chips and rusty nails, inching my way toward an open window space in the bare foundation. As I closed in I could distinguish a faint flickering light from somewhere inside the half-finished house. So they'd started already. I hunched my way to the window and fell prone before it, my arms supporting my upper trunk as I peered over the sill.

There they were, all four of them. From somewhere they'd hauled up those precious ceremonial stones again, laid them with fanatic precision in a circle on the concrete basement floor. Branches burned within the charmed circumference of the boulders. The ceremony was under way. I could distinguish Khereniev's scrawny neck and pinched face beneath a hood of some nubby white material. A small black box lay on the concrete beside him. Next to him sat Sam Olson, looking dull and not quite aware of anything. Across the circle from him, his massive bulk bulging the folds of his robe, sat Kelk, his profile a series of soft, bulbous protrusions. Across from Khereniev, her back to me, sat Abbie. I knew it was Abbie even though her hair was hidden by the hood. I knew her back the way I knew the—

She stood up. I couldn't see her face but I had a good idea how it looked. It was probably as blank and as impassive as Olson's, robot-like, devoid of expression. Khereniev's beady eyes followed her as she rose, then fell slowly to the fire before him. He seemed to be watching something in the fire, his eyes half-lidded and thoughtful. Kelk's face was shining with sweat and he pursed his flabby lips for a moment, then watched the fire with a patient eagerness. I found myself wondering where the kitten was. There had to be a sacrificial animal of some kind. Was it in the black box at Khereniev's side? Abbie's hands were almost hidden in the folds of the robe, yet I knew that one of them held a knife, a metal blade of something that had looked like gold. I couldn't see it, but it had to be there. Her other hand held an object I hadn't seen before, a large object, concave and irregularly shaped, like a pottery bowl, deep, wide-brimmed. She couldn't sacrifice that, could she?

The silence of the scene was underscored by a sound that was so quiet and muffled that at first I overlooked it. But as I became accustomed to the tableau before me, my drug-muffled nerves sensed it more clearly. It was a kind of shuffling sound, a scraping or chafing of something being rubbed in steady rhythm. I tried to localize its source and then I noticed Kelk's huge, hairy hands. He had two flat bits of wood that he was rubbing slowly across each other in a kind of rotary motion. The sound was small but insistent, and as I watched I saw Khereniev's body begin to sway slowly to its tempo.

Abbie's body stiffened to rigidity. She began to speak in slow cadence, timed to the beat of Kelk's rubbing, the words long and strangely sonorous. I couldn't make sense of them; they seemed to be another language. They had the sound of English—almost—but there were too many gutturals and an insistent pattern of clicking, throaty stops that punctuated the slow rolling progression like castanet snaps. She seemed to be speaking from the very pit of her throat, a new voice I had never heard before. The tempo of Kelk's rubbing increased slowly and Abbie's words followed the beat, an obbligato to his bass.

Her voice had a compelling, hypnotic quality to it, the words an endless, periodic cadence, rolling and ebbing and rolling on again higher and higher, faster and faster, spinning upwards in a long, steady chanting that seemed to soar skyward like the powerful

thrusting flight of some great bird, higher, higher, the
tempo beating faster, the cadence whipping itself
upward in a contained frenzy of limitless passions,
higher, faster, now faster, now soaring and rising and
scaling and beating and—

She broke off on a note that was almost a scream.
Her hand, hidden all the while, rose upward into the
light of the fire and I saw what it held. The golden
knife. But where was the sacrificial animal?

Khereniev's hand delved behind him and brought
forth a bundle of twigs. He reached across the fire,
seeming to ignore the fierce heat that pulsed upward
from it, reached across the charmed circle of the
flames and brought the twigs sharply across Olson's
face in a hard, slashing motion. Olson blinked; his
mouth moved convulsively. His hands twitched momentarily and then he got to his feet in a slow, single
movement, rising to his full height like an extension
ladder pushing upwards. He blinked again and his
eyes swung in their sockets to look at Abbie . . . or
rather, at the golden knife in her hand.

Abbie thrust the knife across the rising smoke of
the fire in Khereniev's direction and slowly, with a
kind of intense thoughtfulness, he brought the twigs
down on the gleaming blade three times. The folds of
Abbie's robe stirred and then I saw the round white
heel of her bare foot thrust back under the hem. She
stepped back, turned slightly and took a long step
forward. The action brought her face to face with
Sam Olson. I saw that he was dressed in a pair of
white flannel slacks and a tan khaki shirt, the sleeves

rolled up past his elbows. Why wasn't he wearing a robe? What was he doing here if he had no robe?

As I watched, Abbie's hand came up, the blade of the knife held flat to Olson's chest. With a deft, quick movement, she brought it down along the front of his shirt. The buttons came away in that instant, sliced clear. They fell with a soft clatter to the concrete floor beneath, and the shirt gaped open.

A pause came over them and they froze into a tableau that seemed mobile as the changing light from the fire cast dancing shadows on them. Abbie broke the spell. Her arm came up high above her head and the golden blade flashed out a tawny gleam of reflected fire. I couldn't see her face, but I could see Olson's. For the first time it held something besides emptiness. As he stood there his glance flickered, shifted from the knife to Abbie's face, to the knife, then to Khereniev, then Kelk. He seemed to be aware for the first time of where he was and what he was doing. With a start, he stepped back hastily and his hands came up in front of him, trying to guard himself. I heard Kelk's brutish voice grunt. The insistent rubbing noise stopped. He came to his feet quickly, a cup clutched in one heavy paw. With soft, rapid strides he circled the fire and came up behind Olson. Now there was emotion in Olson's gaunt face, now there was real emotion for the first time. The emotion was fear.

His face contorted and his mouth went out of focus, twitching, deep lines bitten in his face, his eyes flicking back and forth madly. Kelk had some kind, of hold on one of his arms and seemed to be twisting it with a mighty pressure. Slowly, unwillingly, Olson quieted and stood there, hunched over from the pain in his arm. Kelk brought the cup to his trembling mouth and pushed it past his fear-convulsed lips.

I heard the grating sound of Olson's teeth dancing on the cup's rim. Then Kelk tilted the cup and a whitish, foaming fluid poured out, most of it into Olson's mouth, twin streams of the overflow coursing down either side of his face like the mustache of a gray-haired mandarin. I heard Olson choke and gasp. Kelk shoved the cup harder against his lips. After a moment he withdrew it, empty. Kelk returned to his appointed place at the circle of flames, set the cup gently on the ground and squatted again, watchful, intent, waiting. A long rill of perspiration had coursed down his face and was running into his soft, flabby mouth. He licked at it with a thick, red tongue. Then he picked up the two bits of wood and resumed his rubbing.

Now Olson stood more erect. All fear was wiped from his face. It seemed almost as though the whitish bubbling of the liquid he had drunk was mirrored on his face, as though the foam were breaking out through his pores in a thousand sparkling bubbles. He seemed to froth and boil as he stood there, his face like the surface of some heated fluid, fired by an inner warmth. He drew his sparse body erect, and the thin furze of hairs on his chest arched over the ribs that showed through the wrinkled skin. His eyes were bright now, fixed on the knife that seemed to hover

over him as though sustaining itself in mid-air.

I saw Abbie's fingers tighten around the handle of the blade, her knuckles bulge and pale with the tension. And then I came to my senses.

There was no sacrificial animal. I should have seen that the instant she shaved the buttons from his shirt, the instant she bared his chest for the plunging thrust of the golden knife. He was the sacrifice. No kitten, no mute beast, but a living human being, a man.

I had made a fatal mistake in assuming that Olson was a member. He was an outsider, and would always be, to the last moment when his blood should be spilled for their obscene purposes.

I tried to summon my body to action. I had to stop the knife before it flashed in that last lethal arc. And the bowl in her hand . . . I knew about that now, too. It was the receptacle for Olson's lifeblood. I had to stop this, I had to get the use of my body, spring forward and wipe this thing out of existence. But as I sprawled there, the harsh concrete gnawing at my chin, I couldn't make my body respond. I had to get up, call a halt and blast this infernal ritual into the blazing embers of its sacred fire. But I couldn't move. Great shocking spasms of pain shrilled along my limbs and speared into the base of my brain. The *Intracaine!* I had to move but I couldn't. Treacherously, the *Intracaine* had worn off. I called to my muscles, willed them, urged them, prayed to them. They were limp, imprisoned in a fiery web of pain.

But she couldn't do this. Abbie couldn't kill a man. She must realize that, no matter what kind of spell there was on her. Of all this accursed assemblage of murderers and worse, she was least tainted by the dark magic of their worship. I believed in her. She couldn't betray my trust. Even if she'd been a part of their masses and rituals, had helped to suck out the life of Profit and Colin and then of me, even so she couldn't take that gleaming blade now clutched in her hand and cut down the living man before her, catch the hot smoking blood that would gush out from his plundered breast and then . . . I didn't know what then. But I knew I loved her. I believed in her and she *couldn't* do it.

I was wrong. It appeared, as I crouched there in an agony of paralysis, that she could. Olson's eyes bulged bright and mad in the light of the flames, his pupils contracted to flecks of black as he stared with awful concentration on the glittering knife that would tap his life from him in a sudden, slashing plunge. As I watched, the knife seemed to waver and tense, the last fatal moment of preparation before its downward thrust. Abbie, I thought, *Abbie!*

The knife seemed to have a life of its own, an animate, living evil that possessed it. Please, Abbie! It trembled again and cords of tension surged in Abbie's long white arm. Then, with a sudden, shuddering movement, as though throwing her mind and her soul into the hellfire of that nightmare blaze, her body shook, convulsed. The knife clattered noisily to the concrete floor.

Khereniev's mouth flared open and his brownish teeth were glittering fangs. *"The knife!"* A fine spray of spittle fizzed out from his lips.

Kelk stirred and his pig-eyes blinked in amaze-ment. An animal grunt of fear surged up out of the unclean depths of him and he seemed to tense his blubbering body for action.

"The knife!" Khereniev screamed. He jumped to his feet and the hood that shielded his bulbous head fell back to reveal oily ridges of balding scalp and the powerful backward slope of his huge brow. He dashed behind Olson, snatched up the knife and turned to Abbie.

Her body was sinking slowly, folding in on itself. Khereniev's predatory face twitched once and he kicked at her with a movement so powerful I could hardly believe that it came from his oddly bloated body. Abbie fell sideways, her hand trailing across an outlying branch of the fire. Her eyes were open. She had not fainted. She was watching Khereniev.

His small frame seemed all sinew as he crouched in a boxer's stance before the mute, waiting form of Sam Olson. At his feet lay the small black box. The golden knife slashed upwards, clutched tightly in both his hands. He poised for the down-stroke and suddenly, in that instant, my body returned to me.

I felt it tense and gather itself. My voice was the scream of a demented man. *"Khereniev!"*

I felt the concrete floor slam up under my feet. I had jumped down onto the concrete and was poised in a crouch, my eyes smarting from the smoke and heat.

Khereniev whirled, saw me, recoiled. Abbie's body

stirred and she pulled herself half-erect to watch me. But none of this registered in my mind. All that filled it was the monstrous, quaking shriek of terror that howled and surged from Kelk's wet lips.

He jumped up as though exploded, threw his hairy arms into the air, his face flabbing and pulsing with the sheer terror of his screams. I had frightened this beast of a man the way a wild animal of the forest is frightened. He screamed and the sound filled the low-ceilinged room with a rebounding reverberation. Then, his eyes stark-mad, he whirled and ran. His bulk crashed brutally through the flimsy doorway, bits of temporary two-by-four lumber snapping like toothpicks in his wake. I heard him scream again, and the sound had a dwindling, dying quality. I knew what had happened. In his insane flight, he had blundered over the edge of the dune. His gross hulk was rolling and tumbling head over heels down the steep incline. I glanced back at Khereniev.

"Drop the knife!" I shouted.

"Damn you," he said in a dull, mechanical way, "damn you." He seemed to be repeating a lesson by rote. "Damn you," he cursed slowly, without emotion, automatically.

Abbie got to her feet swiftly and came to me. "Joe, get out!"

I felt Abbie's arms pinning mine down to my sides but my eyes were on Khereniev. He raised the knife again, clutched with an interlocking grip in his two hands, and brought it high over his head again, the point aimed at Olson's unmoving breast.

Abruptly, I stooped and snatched a huge branch from the fire, a long branch, coated with a flickering sheet of flame that crackled and sparked as I lifted it. With a quick, underhand motion I lobbed it at Khereniev. I saw it hit and break into smaller embers on his body. They skittered and danced over the floor and the black box. A shower of sparks enveloped him and he cried out in pain.

"Drop it!" I yelled.

Abbie was pulling at my arms, dragging me across the floor to the doorway Kelk had burst through a moment before. "Get away from here!" I heard her repeating. "Please get away from here."

All strength had left me. I could feel her dragging me away. The doorway jolted my body as she pulled me through it. Khereniev stood there, his robe charred and smoldering in places. The knife was poised above his head, the black box at his feet. The floor of the basement was a litter of smoking embers. I had failed. The scene was framed by the doorway, growing smaller as I retreated, diminishing in size as Abbie pulled me further and further from it. Khereniev's arms bulged with motion and the knife started into instant movement, downward like the swoop of a hawk, downward in a golden arc as it flashed toward Olson's bared breast.

Then the scene seemed to grow larger. It expanded suddenly in size and light and I could see the main outlines of it begin to crack and break. A mighty roaring sound filled the night, a huge, enveloping surge of noise that swelled into an unbearable crescendo. The house seemed to lift before my eyes, the wooden superstructure lifted in jagged pieces off the crumbling concrete foundation. Noise filled my head and a hot blast slammed against my face. There was the sound of an explosion bigger than any m the world, a sound to erase the world, huge, overwhelming. A wave seemed to wash me backwards. All that I felt was the clutch of Abbie's hand in mine. Then we were sinking, falling. Then we were unconscious.

AS I SIT here now, writing this, the rest of the night seems to dwindle to nothingness before the gigantic fact of the explosion. Yet what happened afterwards is by all standards even more important, if not to the authorities who flocked to the scene, then to me, and, ultimately, to you who read this.

When I came to at the base of the dune, the house was burning like a funeral pyre. Flaming fragments of lumber were all around me, and Abbie's hand was still in mine. Trembling, I felt in my pocket and found the handkerchief. It was still damp in spots. Wringing it feebly, I sponged in on my neck. I was too groggy to notice any effect. Somehow I pulled Abbie up and managed to shove my shoulder into her midriff. I don't know where I got the strength to do it. Maybe the tiny bit of *Intracaine* helped, but I imagine it was the instinct of self-preservation that really accounted for my actions. I carried Abbie, fireman fashion, to my cabin.

The door was unlocked, and I managed to shove my way in and dump her body on the cot. I found the lantern, lit it and examined her. She was alive. A feeble, unrhythmic pulse flickered in her wrist. After a while her eyelids twitched and she lifted her head before she was fully conscious. When she opened her eyes and saw me, she seemed to smile. We said nothing to each other.

There was a feeling inside me of everything spinning out, unwinding, as though the thread of this whole ghastly affair was reeling rapidly off the spool and the final strand was in sight. Khereniev could not have survived that immense blasting explosion. Evidently he had had some powerful explosive in that black box. No one inside that house could have remained alive. Then there was a chance for me. The thought was new blood in my veins. If I could destroy the last of them the brutish Kelk I could make a bid for my life. If it came down, in the final moment, to Abbie—my beloved dupe—I knew my headache and the monstrous death before me were ended. She had nothing to do with them. She was not the leader; she was the led. I could see that. If she had been the leader she would never have hesitated when the knife was poised for Olson's lifeblood. She would have plunged it straight and deep into his heart. I had to remove Kelk, the last one, and I would be free.

I smiled back at Abbie and her mouth curved in an

answering expression. Her face was sooted and stained in spots but her eyes were alive and joyous. Then, as I watched, her glance swept up, past me, over my shoulder, to the door behind me. All emotion wiped clean from her face. There was someone there, someone in the doorway. I swung about and jumped to my feet. There, his hands loose and ready, his body heaving and panting, stood Kelk.

The abysmal futility of everything was suddenly apparent. I was no match for this monster even in my normal condition. He was taller, heavier, much stronger. And now, after a month of slow death, of no sleep, after the exertions of the night, after being blown off the top of a dune, after carrying Abbie half a mile to the cabin, I was in no condition to battle a spaniel pup. And worst of all, there was no time to use more *Intracaine*.

I had to get him away from the door, decoy him to one side and then dash through. I could do only one thing better than him—run. And I had to escape his simian clutch. I darted sideways in the cabin and a gurgling chuckle escaped his flabby wet lips. He recognized the maneuver.

Grinning lewdly at me, he reached behind him and slammed the door shut, then shot the bolt in place.

Abbie lay on the bed, her eyes wide-stretched as she followed Kelk's massive progress into the room. He maneuvered me into a corner. I had no alternative but to retreat. The angle of the wall behind me had an almost heated feel to it and I could sense its oncoming pressure before I touched it. It spelled death for me, a brutal death. I felt the rough boards grate on my back and I slid along them, seeking an escape I knew was impossible.

Kelk's huge body came on, his hands swinging free and ready before him, his bulging, coarse-grained face a grinning, slobbering horror. He passed the thick pink bulk of his tongue across his sensual lips and they grew redder with the laving spittle. He was only a yard from me.

I could smell him, a rank, festering smell as of an open sore decaying in the moist darkness of some sweat-filled cavity. He was a foot from me. Inches separated us.

His hand came up to bar any movement of mine, pinning me to the wall by grasping the front of my jacket. I felt the cloth tense and pull up under my armpits. He was lifting me up to pound my body to a pulp against something hard and unyielding.

I felt my toes leave the floor. He lifted me higher, higher, then he swung me, still with one arm, and threw me across the room. The floor slammed into my body with a sickening crunch. I felt a black wave of nausea ripple outward from the pit of my gut and surge upwards. The heavy tread of his huge feet shook the floor as he marched across the room to me. I prayed for unconsciousness. The nausea rose like an elevator along my windpipe and then, abruptly, something sharp and many-pointed slapped me. I reached blindly at it. My hands closed over a thin sprig of something and my eyes opened. I was holding a branch of mistletoe. The impact of my body had jarred it off the wall.

A kind of thrilling anguish pulsed through my hands, as though the mistletoe were charged with volts of energy. It seemed to give me a strange kind of strength and I felt my back grating over the wall boards as I pushed upward, erect.

Tension filled my legs. I was standing on them. Kelk's immense bulk seemed to waver and unfocus in my eyes. Had he stopped? I couldn't see his obscene face. The mistletoe branch was burning my fingers but I clutched it tightly.

What was Kelk doing? I could only see the huge outline of his body, nothing more. And then something happened that I never thought would happen again. I took a step forward.

The mistletoe was supporting me. I held it as a man grasps a life-hold, dangling in infinite space. It was moving, dragging me with it. The gross hulk that was Kelk wavered and shifted across the blurred retina of my eyes. What was he doing?

I had to destroy him. I had to wipe him out. His death was my life. I had to kill him to live and I was going to kill him. The mistletoe pulled me on, forward, its burning length like a torch. I was going to kill Kelk. I was going to live.

There was a tremendous clatter of sound, deafening. I closed my eyes against it and it thundered past me with a splintering crash. Where was Kelk? Was he behind me?

Trembling, shaken with a dry retch that throbbed and jerked in my throat, I wheeled around. Where the door had been, only a few shards of wood remained, hanging from the hinges like torn bits of paper. The rest of the door was flat, shattered in a hundred pieces. My eyes tightened and I saw Kelk's immense body dwindling, condensing before me as he ran along the path to the road. A blinding light silhouetted him against the trees and I heard the high screaming honk of an auto horn. There was a shrill screech and a hard, crunching thud. Kelk's body seemed to merge with the oncoming radiator of a truck, his legs to fold and caress the steel bumpers. The bulk of him faded in that instant to a bundle of clothing, a robe of flesh draped oddly across the truck's grille, as though thrown there to keep the engine warm.

Voices sounded. Two figures jumped down from the truck cabin, one pulling at Kelk's lifeless body, the other running down the path to me. A man—boots, leather jacket, some kind of insignia on his breast, a wide-brimmed campaign hat on his head.

"Hey," his mouth opened and closed. "What's going on here?"

His boots thudded along the path, all his actions slowed to an underwater tempo. "Who set off that explosion?" his voice pounded at me.

I felt the mistletoe drop from my hands . . . Kelk was dead. The last of them was dead. I turned to face Abbie and the motion of my neck sent a piercing, furious jolt of pain through every channel of my brain. Kelk was dead. But my head . . . my aching head was not free of this satanic curse. Kelk was dead.

And so was I.

I looked at Abbie. Her face was white, soot-smeared, her eyes huge and dark. So the last of them *wasn't* dead. The power was live, rampant, fierce. And it resided not in Khereniev with his air of mastery, not in the boneless sack of flesh that was Kelk. The power was alive. The power lay within Abbie. And I was doomed.

As I watched her, the sound of the fire ranger's boots in my ears, she looked at me with her great dark eyes and she smiled.

She smiled.

11 «◊» Last Chance

Excerpt, Page 1, *Column 4,*
Michigan City News-Argus.

TWO DIE AS
FIRE RAZES
DUNE HOUSE
Auto Magnate's Mansion
Wrecked in Explosion;
Third Killed by Truck

A series of accidental deaths was touched off last night in a mystery blast that baffled Dunes State police and fire officials. The dead are Jacques Khereniev, 55, Samuel L. C. Olson, 49, and Sebastian Kelk, 38, all of Chicago. An explosion and fire that destroyed the dunes home of Arthur N. Pauley, automobile company official of South Bend, was the cause of two deaths. Kelk was killed in a head-on collision with a State Park fire truck investigating the blaze.

Firefighting authorities put forward the theory that a tank of butane household gas had been left unshielded in the basement of the unfinished dwelling, but placed little faith in the idea. A nearby resident, Dr. J. B. Loomis, was quoted as saying: "I saw lights there and went to investigate. The explosion came before I could reach the house." Loomis and a friend were slightly injured in the blast.

Commissioner August R. Mantho of this city said that in his opinion carelessness was to blame for the tragedy. "People will not take proper fire-prevention precautions," he stated. "Open flames and butane gas do not mix. This is the first serious fatality of the summer season but experience tells us it will not be the last as long as people treat fire without proper caution." Inquest is set for Friday.

Excerpt from Obituary Column,
The Chicago Tribune.

Colleagues and associates at the University of Chicago today mourned the untimely death in a vacation accident of Dr. Jacques Khereniev, Ph.D., LL.D., 55, formerly of the Bucharest Institute of Political Affairs and erstwhile political commentator for *Morton's Magazine.* A world-renowned figure in political science, Dr. Khereniev's passing brings to a close a brilliant career in many fields of endeavor. (See foto, col. 3.)

Driven out of his native Russia after the Bolshevik terror of 1917, Khereniev fled to Paris and later to Bucharest. In 1938, he was brought to this country at the behest of Daniel Morton, prominent periodical publisher, to carry on his work in relative freedom.

Khereniev led an active political life in Europe as adviser to the ruling houses of Romania and Italy, and as Romanian delegate to the now-defunct League of Nations. He is survived by no living relatives.

Excerpt from "Chicago Chatter"
The Chicago Sun-Times
Radio busybodies are wondering what's happened to charming Abbie Cowper, star of the Bridget Flynn daytime soaper. The wise money is on a secret elope- ment and her agency is but frantic. This pillar opines that there's no man in Abbie's life and here's hoping she's back soon, or, in the words of a certain canine movie serial: "Abbie, come home!"

Memorandum to Star Telephone
Answering Service
Inform all callers to REgent 9-1202 (Dr. J. B. Loomis) that until further notice patients may use services of Dr. Gordon Bernstein, Ext. 993, Billings Hospital.

I am sitting on a folding chair and using as a desk a packing crate I found near the ruins of the house on the high dune. I hope the pencil comes through plainly enough on this rough surface but I have my doubts. Abbie is lying on the cot sleeping, the result of being blown off the dune top. Aside from my headache, I am as always . . . dying.

If I had that .22 caliber Colt here, I think I might put a bullet between her eyes as she sleeps. I had been clinging to the hope that she was not the receptacle of these satanic powers. As long as Morelle remained alive in prison, I had one last hope that his death might release me. But, to save myself from writing, let me add still another clipping to settle that matter, this from the Chicago *Herald-American:*

WIFE-KILLER CHEATS
CHAIR IN CELL SUICIDE
—By Helen Horgan

Curly-haired Don Morelle, awaiting trial for the recent passion slaying of his attractive blonde wife, last night cheated society and the County of Cook by opening a vein in his left wrist and bleeding slowly, painfully to death as the wee hours of early morning marched through his lonely cell.

County officials, as is their standard practice, had removed all possible tools of suicide from Morelle, taking away his tie, belt and all sharp instruments. But the handsome lady-killer apparently had cracked a sharp flake of enamel from one of the dishes in which food was brought to him.

Authorities believe he used the flake as a blade to lacerate his vein until a lethal opening was made. "This is the first time in 23 years," Sheriff J. C. Kowalski stated "that one of our prisoners has . . ."

It is only today that I have had the energy to leave the cabin's stifling heat for a short walk outside in the fresh air. I never venture more than a few yards away for fear Abbie may escape.

"But I don't *want* to leave you," she insists.

"I don't believe you."

"But I love you, Joe. I couldn't leave if I wanted to."

"Damned right you couldn't. And don't try anything while I'm gone."

At the inquest I held her arm tightly, afraid she might break away in the courtroom and I would be unable to follow her. But evidently she's sincere when she says she doesn't want to leave. If she knew the way I feel about her she might not like staying with me. I've been careful to conceal my thoughts from her—if anybody can conceal anything from her—and she seems to take matters quietly.

"Think back," I ask her regularly, whenever I can summon enough patience to resume my inquisition. "What was the ceremony like? Did you say a black mass for me or what?"

"I can't remember. I want to, darling, but I can't."

"Why? Did they drug you? Do you remember drinking or eating anything, or getting a hypo?"

"No, I—"

"Was it hypnosis? Did anybody hypnotize you?"

"I don't remember."

Of course she wouldn't remember hypnosis. It can be done in so many ways, so many veiled, seemingly innocent ways that the subject can be completely unaware of the process. Then, too, there is post-hypnotic suggestion. She might have been ordered to forget and now, no matter how hard she tries, she cannot remember. That is, if she really *wants* to remember.

"But I *do!* I want to help you, Joe."

"Then try to think. Remember anything at all, little things, unimportant things. Maybe we can break it down that way."

I think she tries. I watch her efforts and they seem genuine. But she's an actress. How can I be sure she's sincere when she can so expertly counterfeit almost any emotion?

"When did it all start?"

"I don't know. A long time ago."

"When did you first meet Khereniev and the rest of them?"

"In . . ." She makes a tremendous effort. "It was when I came to Chicago."

"When did you first decide to go to Chicago?"

"When my parents died. I had no money or relatives and I'd always dreamed of running away. And now I had the chance. So I . . . I just left."

"How old were you?"

"Oh . . . fifteen, something like that."

"You just came here and went to work?"

"Yes I . . . well, I worked in Woolworth's for a year, selling. Then I said I was eighteen and got a job at Field's as a stock girl in the dress department. When I was really eighteen they thought I was twenty and they made me a salesgirl. I was talking to a customer one day and she said she was a radio producer's wife and I had a nice voice. She got me an audition. I've been doing radio ever since."

"What year was that, when you got into radio, I mean?"

"1940. February 23."

"Now look, you can remember all that, even the date, but you can't remember what I really want to know."

"But it was the day after Washington's birthday."

"That's immaterial. What gets me is that you can—"

"Please, darling, don't be angry with me. I'm really trying."

I suppose she is. I have to suppose that or else there's really very little sense to all this questioning. If she's lying to me, if she's deliberately trying to throw me off the track, then I'm wasting my time. And since I don't have too much left, it's all precious to me. Or conversely, worthless, since it's forfeit already. I keep at her, probing, needling, asking the same questions again and again. And whether it's important or useless, I keep writing this account. I may have nothing more to add before I die, but I intend to keep writing up to the very end.

My ties with the outside world have dwindled away. My receptionist doesn't know where I am; nobody does. She would understand something of my condition but I'm sure she wouldn't believe it. Nerves, would be her diagnosis. Overwork, a psychosomatic irritation. I only *think* I'm cursed, the old business about Freudian accidents, etc., etc., etc. I know what she thinks.

The area around here is deserted, what with the sudden series of disasters that ate away the membership of the Dune-Dwellers. Dora Olson, I assume, remains in town, evidently still mourning her husband. An occasional holiday group passes by on the road outside, laughing or singing, but always on their way somewhere else.

This enforced isolation has turned my thoughts into fierce introspection. I spend my time mulling over the events of the affair, enacting them over and over again, as though they were a reel of film I project again and again on the glistening blank screen of my mind. I try to view them from different angles, to catch some detail that originally went unnoticed, rework each conversation, reanalyze each tone of voice, expression of face. I find myself getting nowhere.

But one aspect of the situation has always eluded me. It has always seemed central to the problem, and I find myself returning to it like a dog to a buried bone. I have given up trying to solve it through Abbie. She cannot—or will not—help me.

"Why?" she repeats dully. "I don't know why."

"But there must be some reason for the whole thing. What were they after? What did they want to get?"

"Please, I don't know." Her eyes start to fill.

"But this is basic," I hammer away. "This is the one thing you should remember. The goal . . . the goal. Try to remember."

"Darling, I can't." She is crying now.

"Can't or won't?"

I don't mean to be deliberately cruel but my uncertainty drives me to all manner of nastiness. She cries, not with vehemence, but silently, her face turned away. I really should use another ampoule. It might clear my head for this constant examining. The primary fact of my life is all-important, yet I have the feeling at such times that we are both caught in a mutual trap, that both of us are doomed in some obscure way, fated to torture each other until death steps in with merciful intervention. But I know otherwise. In weeks, just a few weeks, I will be dead and she will live. Before I die I want to learn her secret and set it down in this narrative. The chance seems slim, but to a dying man any chance is worth taking.

I have been thinking, as I said before, about the goal of this group. It must have a purpose. It is well known that devil-worship still exists in many parts of the world, that occult groups, bands of supernaturalists and sorcerers, still hold their strange rituals, still invoke their bloody, satanic gods.

There lies the clue, there in the word "satanic." At least, as I sit here chewing and re-chewing the arid events of the affair, it seems to be the one thin clue to the core of the matter.

In every culture and in every land, myths are constructed out of the fears and introspection of men. Even casual study of such folklore shows startling correspondences of episode and idea. One of the most compelling similarities is the concept of Satan.

In every mythology and every religion there is a figure like Satan, a fallen angel. He may be a god, a demigod or simply a hero, but the pattern is almost identical, from the bush mysteries of Australia to the complex hierarchy of good and evil in modern religions. He is a figure who enjoyed great power, partook of the highest of the All-High, yet somewhere, somehow, lost it all. He may, like Prometheus, have presumed on the authority and found his undoing in too much love of man. He may be the Norse Loki, whose fickle nature and self-love brought him disaster and defeat. Or he may be Lucifer himself. The principle remains the same. In all cultures and in all lands there is the myth of a man or god who took matters into his own hands . . . in defiance of a higher authority.

What is there, then, in all men that goads them to create out of their essential humanity the story of a man rebelling against authority? It is obviously the innate desire of all men to do just that, to take matters into their own hands. And this wish-myth discloses something still more basic: a dissatisfaction with the authority that guides the life of man. Life is a series of bearable or unbearable frustrations, plans gone wrong, thwarted desires, capricious disasters. Above them all is the man-created figure of an agency that controls this series of defeats, ending them in the final frustration of death. Man worships this agency because of its power, yet his devotion is the trembling adoration of fear.

ABBIE IS BEGINNING to grow restless. I caught her just now lying on the cot, her eyes wide open, watching me when she thought I wasn't looking.

"If you want to leave," I tell her, "you can. Just tell me about this and I'll let you go."

She looks at me and then glances away. I can't tell whether it's hatred or shame that makes her avoid my eyes. "No," she murmurs, "I'll stay. Only . . ."

"Only what?"

"Only I don't see where this is getting us, darling."

"It may get us something if we keep at it."

"How can I help?" she asks.

"By telling the truth." It slips out before I can stop it, so strong is my uncertainty.

Tears well up in her eyes and she looks at me like a wounded animal. "Joe," she says very slowly, "did it ever occur to you that I could escape any time I felt like it?"

"What!"

"You're so weak, darling, that I could hit you over the head with something and . . . escape before you came to."

It's never occurred to me before. This whole business is a farce. But why has she played along? The sudden surprise of it makes my head ring with pain, like a bell that echoes and booms with violent vibration. I have to rest again. I shake my head groggily and close my eyes. "Don't try it," I mumble weakly.

The sun on the roof is hot and penetrating; it feels as though the ceiling were lined with the endless coils of some electric heating element, as though this cabin were a toaster. I have a sudden image of myself spread-eagled, pinioned down, being burnt and charred by the seething heat, the pattern of the glowing element branded into my skin as on a piece of bread. I glance at Abbie. She is either asleep or faking. A fine spatter of perspiration beads her face. Her skin looks shiny and wet. There are great purple hollows under her huge eyes.

Sometimes I see everything quite clearly. At other moments, unexpectedly, things cloud up and odd patterns of strain blanket everything. At these moments, the actual physical objects in the cabin seem to glow from within. The whole thing is very strange. I can be looking at the cot and suddenly the Spartan lines of its steel tubing are like neon. It swims up larger and larger and even when I close my eyes or turn away, there is an after-image, painful and burning, that persists for quite a long time, blanking out everything else. I've found that if I press my eyeballs, the resulting spirals of retinal pressure manage to dissipate the original after-image. But the process is too painful and, I feel, injurious to the attenuated nerves of my optic system. I've decided that it's safest to let the images burn and wait patiently for sight to return.

A FEW MINUTES AGO I let Abbie go to town for supplies. She went back to Michigan City to get the car where we'd left it the night we came here by bus. We need bread and some cans of meat. She also plans to buy onions and tempt me with a special concoction. I was, of course, going to insist on going with her all the way, but, when I suggested it, her face went sad and hurt. "You still don't trust me," she murmured.

"It's not that, Abbie, it's simply—"

"That you don't trust me," she finished. She wasn't far from the truth, but I hated to let her see it so dearly.

"You don't know where to go," I said. "You don't know the roads."

"Nonsense. You lie quietly and I'll be back in an hour."

"You don't know what store to go to."

"I'll find one." She smiled patiently at me. "You need rest, darling, you look so drawn out."

She had me there. Of all the things in this world that a man could want, I want rest. I would like nothing better than to sit in this cool, cool cabin and think and relax and build up a little energy. But can I trust her alone?

I'M SITTING at my improvised box-desk, trying to set down my thoughts in an organized fashion. My wrist watch tells me it's seven-fifteen. Abbie left here before two o'clock. Five and a half hours. I can no longer tell myself that she's been delayed. I know it will be nine o'clock and midnight and tomorrow morning and still she won't come back. I know she's gone for good. For good.

How many times have I gone out to the high part of the road and peered down the long descent to the beer baron's home, watching the dusty road for my car? It's lonely out there as the sun begins to inch its way into the earth. The blasted wreckage atop the neighboring dune is like the ruin of some bomb-shattered city, desolate, blackened, splintered in a thousand untidy shards. I understand the South Bend man has no intention of rebuilding this season. I don't blame him. But standing there on the road with nothing for company but his wrecked house and the setting sun . . . that gets on a man's nerves. I've been out there half a dozen times and always a feeling of cold fear settles on my shoulders and I turn and walk back to the cabin.

I wonder when my body will be found? Will some vacationer pass by and have the curiosity to open the door? Probably not. It may be months before my body's discovered. I may not be found until winter. And why winter? I may not be found until the next season, when some passing fire ranger or sheriff's deputy finds the cabin and inspects it. By then there won't be enough left of me to identify. There will only be the driver's license in my wallet and the deed to the place and nothing else but . . . yes! There will be this manuscript. I must make sure that they find the manuscript with my body. I imagine the best plan would be to write until I can no longer hold the pencil or until my supply of paper gives out, whichever happens first. I must have some kind of container prepared, something termite- and water-proof. The Army footlocker under the bed. When I feel that I'm finally going to die, I'll stuff these papers inside, close the lid and lie on top of it. And most important, I'll lock the door from the inside. Supposing Abbie should return in mid-winter? I must keep her out of here. This is a poor kind of crypt. She could break down the door or a window. But will she come back after I'm dead?

Why shouldn't she? There's no danger in a dead man, just the basic nausea of his festering smell and the sight of the purulent flesh. There may be maggots, too. In this kind of place there undoubtedly will be maggots. It depends on how strongly she wants to return. She knows about the manuscript. Does she want it enough to face the maggots and the odor and the sight of me? I must find a better way to preserve the papers. I must think it out more carefully.

Now that my last chance is gone, I feel somehow better about everything. It's curious, but I feel relieved. I imagine it's the suspense of the thing. While I had that chance, I was tautly alert to find it, wary lest I fail to recognize a clue and let the chance pass unnoticed. That would have been too much, to have the chance and muff it. But this is almost better. She's tricked me. I wait now only for death.

If you can remember back to my first thoughts about the Dune-Dwellers, you will recall that I was baffled by their motive. What spurred them on? Was it money, hunger or love? Was it any of the other forms these catchwords take? Power fame respect, sex, recognition, prestige, satiety? It was none of these. It was something stronger, more basic, ancient as the race itself. Now I have the answer.

The motive is freedom. The obsessing urge of mankind, the spur that drives on over lust for money or power or food or love . . . the underlying motive of man's existence. Freedom.

If man can only master his bewildering environment, if only he can beat down the frustrations of his life, the whimsical, irrational setbacks, the plans that *gang aft a'gley*, the unreasoning, blind, unplanned misery of his life! If only he can rebel against this illogical authority of the world and become his own master . . . *that* would be the highest freedom. *That* would be the fruition of his most basic motive.

So he makes heroes in the image of his highest dream: godmen, symbols that infest his unconsciousness. The Arch-Rebel of the world, the prime image of man's thirst for freedom from the irrational. The Prometheus, the Lucifer, the man who takes his own fate in his own hands and *does* something about it. And on a smaller scale, the folk-heroes of the story-tellers, the Paul Bunyans, the Sinbads, Icarus and John Henry and Ulysses . . . taking their destinies in their bare hands and twisting a new shape to the tangled skein of unreasoning terror and dread. This is the archetypal dream of the human race, this quest for freedom. And, as it does in the highest and lowest of men, it emerges in the satanic rituals of the Dune-Dwellers, twisted, perverted but there for the seeing. I still don't know quite how they hoped to achieve freedom. Perhaps there is something to the imaginings of those who suppose a preexisting race of Earth-lings, since banished by divine anger, now hovering outside the planet, nebulous, monstrous, yet sensed in the bones of men as they maneuver and work, trying always to return to the globe they once inhabited.

Could a race of creatures pre-exist man and the chain of life that led to him? Could these . . . these *things* be the basis for all the magic, the witchcraft, the supernatural fears of the human animal? It seems unlikely and yet . . . Yet there is no proof. Neither for nor against. There is nothing but dark gaps of scientific guesswork, a series of blank spaces, like the unexplored regions of ancient maps.

My head is aching badly. I think I'll try some *Intra-caine*. There's no reason—now—to hoard it. The narrative now is more important than anything else.

I have only a few ampoules left.

I'VE BEEN WAITING for the stuff to take effect. The drumming in my head is like the roll of a gigantic parade.

It's been ten minutes since my application and I still feel no relief. I would like to muffle the pain in my fingers and arms. At moments that tricky business of the eyes reasserts itself and the written page writhes and glows like a churning mass of phosphorescent snakes.

I'll just rub the wet handkerchief on my neck again. It should work. Just a matter of time.

NOTHING YET. My eyes have steadied down a bit, but my head throbs with body pain. Can the *Intracaine* be spoiled? Is the potency diminished? I couldn't have built immunity so fast. Could I?

I have an overwhelming desire to let the pencil drop. I feel washed-out, drained empty of everything but this hammering pain. The swift finality of this day has suddenly piled up on me as I write. It is like sand, surging higher around me, walling me in, pressing against me from all sides with a steady mounting strength.

I wonder now if I've been fooling myself all along. Abbie's escape, and with her my final chance for life, has probably unnerved me more than I realize. I'm beginning to think all kinds of insane things. Why doesn't the damned *Intracaine* work? Have I been wrong about the nature of the curse on me, this peculiar spell that is sucking my life from me? Something as dark and evil as this must have a separate life of its own. It must exist outside the agencies that summoned it into being. It must live and act as a separate entity. I can almost feel it here in the room with me.

I'm going to shave the back of my neck. Maybe that's the trouble. And then, perhaps I'll rub the skin raw. I couldn't be immune already!

ALL DONE. The *Intracaine*—fresh ampoule—was like fire on my chafed skin. I had nicked it in places, and the drug sets each cut aflame.

But I think this will do it. I'm waiting.

Ten minutes. It usually takes less than forty seconds to work. I'll give it just a little more time.

HALF AN HOUR.

Well so that's that. All anger is out of me. I haven't the strength to shout or curse my fate. I knew immunity would come sometime. But why now? Why at this moment when I . . . when I need to think clearly, to reason? How can science work when the brain is a netted maze of screams?

I feel cold. The air is dead. My breathing is faster, my lungs ache cruelly. I feel very alone.

So this is what happens. This is how it goes. And all reason, all logic, all science can't help me. All that vaunted knowledge is powerless now. It can't help. Nothing can. I'm alone, all alone
now . . .

The light is gone from the sky and the air is chill. I could light the lamp but I haven't the will to, nor the courage. What good will light be?

I am not alone. There is something in this cabin with me. There is an invisible demon leeching my life from me in a single, steady withdrawal.

It is in this room. I can hardly see the paper before me yet my nerves are keyed to an acute pitch. Not alone. I cannot hear it or smell it. Something here. It makes no sound. Has no shape. But it must be here with me. Must be behind me now, waiting, watching, ready, as the vital essence of my life slowly sucks up into its maw. If I could—!

A noise! Rushing sound. Sharp, hissing, like a vast wind in an empty eternity of night. Closer. Approaching with frightening speed. Now—

Now stopped. Dead. Alone with it. Noises now, unrhythmic, irregular. Closing in on me. Crunching, brushing. Near me now. No help. Close. What are—?

"Darling?"

In the doorway, two figures. *Abbie!* And who . . . ? Abbie and my receptionist!

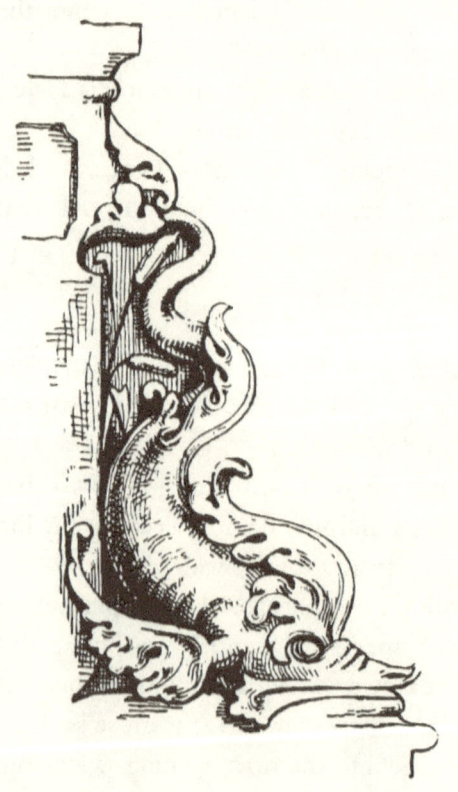

12 «◊» The Campfire Girl

SO COLIN WAS RIGHT. He told me what to do and I forgot and now it's taken two other people to remind me. "I made a mistake," I recall him saying that last night as the pain began to draw his life out of him, "I fought alone."

I really am very ashamed of myself, especially about my receptionist. It's such a warm feeling to have her here, despite her wisecracks, despite the smart-aleck stuff. She's a real person, that kid. She doesn't understand what's going on—not really—but she's willing to pitch in and do whatever she can.

I don't know how much Abbie told her on the trip back, or if she had to say anything at all to make her come. But the girl knows all the important aspects of the situation. How Abbie had the courage to bring her, I'll never know. But what is more amazing, the girl seems to grasp everything perfectly. I've always known her to be bright, quick to respond and eager to learn, but it's too much to expect that she should understand the devious meanderings of this case.

Yet she does. The idea of working with her is stimulating. She has a kind of dash to her, a vitality that can make mince-meat of a tough problem. She takes very little for granted, but she has tremendous confidence in her ability.

"Why shouldn't I help?" she asked belligerently when she arrived. "What's so special about you? I mean, from what I hear, you aren't doing so hot, are you?"

"Not so hot," I agreed. "In fact, ice-cold."

"We need new blood, new angles."

"That's why I brought her," Abbie put in. She still doesn't know whether I'm angry with her or not. How the hell could I be angry? She came back, didn't she? "We've got an idea and she has to help."

"Great," I said helplessly. *"You've* got an idea to make *you* talk."

"Terrific idea," the receptionist chimed in.

It's so simple I'm ashamed of forgetting it, just as I'm ashamed of ignoring Colin's advice. The only reason for my neglect, the only excuse I can offer myself is that I've been too close to this to see any but one or two elemental facts. I could see my death; I could see Abbie's guilt. Hazily, I knew that if she were telling the truth she really couldn't help me. Hazily, I had the feeling that the secret might be so thoroughly repressed that it could remain in its prison forever. But what the mind of man can do, it can undo.

There is a drug known as sodium *pentothal,* a sedative, a soporific, but with cautious under-dosage a drug that acts to release repressions. It is one of a group of drugs proved useful in a new technique called *narcosynthesis,* a shortcut technique that induces in the patient the mental state usually reached by astute psychoanalysis or reputable hypnosis, a state of mind in which the patient is powerless to withhold ideas purposely or unconsciously repressed. The Value of *narcosynthesis* is its speed, and its ease. Above all things, I need those two qualities.

"That was the first thing I thought of," my receptionist explained, not without a certain air of accomplishment. "Abbie here wanted to know about a drug that'd do the trick and the first thing I remembered was *pentothal*." She looked reproachfully at me.

"All right," I snapped back. "Okay, you're bright. I'm dumb."

"And how," she agreed. "The trouble with you G.P.'s is that you get in a rut. I worked for a guy during the war who delivered so many babies he forgot how to cauterize a dog bite. I mean, you have to stay hep. You have to keep up with the world."

"Okay, okay. Did you bring some with you?"

"Now where could I lay hands on *pentothal*? You'll have to write out a prescription. I brought some blanks along. Then we'll run into town and fill it. Don't strain the brain, Dr. L. Everything's under control."

I guess it is at that. She brought all the necessary equipment. Sterile gowns for Abbie, alcohol, swabs, a hypo and a set of needles, the rubber stricture tube, everything. I guess I'm losing my grip. This evening I thought I'd lost it. No, I *knew* I'd lost it. I was as good as dead, paralyzed by the *Intracaine's* treacherous failure, making plans for my demise, worrying about this manuscript, about maggots. Now I feel as though someone had placed in my hands a silver platter with my life on it. I know who the someone is and I'm ashamed of myself.

Thursday, 4:45 P.M. I don't know what to think. The *pentothal* has had some effect, but we don't seem to be breaking through the way we should. Administered some at 1:30 P.M., a trial dosage to determine Abbie's threshold of narcosis. She is sleeping off the effects now. My receptionist took down her words in shorthand and I'll read some of the evidence into the record whenever it seems important. I must perfect the administering technique before we can hope to break through. Meanwhile, here's what happened:

DR. LOOMIS: How do you feel?

MISS COWPER: Going away . . . fading.

DR. LOOMIS: Can you hear me?

MISS COWPER: Hear everything. Everybody. Not so loud.

DR. LOOMIS: Tell me about Chicago. Tell me about the time you worked in Woolworth's. Who did you know then?

MISS COWPER: Nobody. Johnny. Nobody at all.

DR. LOOMIS: Who is Johnny?

MISS COWPER: (indistinct)

DR. LOOMIS: What about your childhood? Tell me about the early days.

MISS COWPER: Hate them. Hate both of them.

DR. LOOMIS: Both of whom? Who do you hate?

MISS COWPER: The two of them. Lucy and . . . Lucy and him. And Alfred.

DR. LOOMIS: Who are Lucy and Alfred?

MISS COWPER: Hate them. I just hate them. Hate . . . (sleeping)

Friday, 8:30 A.M. The women awoke at dawn, ate sparingly. Abbie felt all right, no after-effects. We decided to try the *pentothal* early and perhaps get two sessions in today. It's probably dangerous to pile on treatment this way, but I have so little time. When I mentioned my doubts to Abbie she brushed them aside. Anyway, the second session went off better. She stayed coherent for perhaps fifteen minutes. I tried something different, something I'd learned about hypnosis. It didn't exactly come off, but it may with practice.

DR. L. Abbie, how old are you?

MISS C. Twenty-eight. Getting so old.

DR. L. No, you're only eighteen. You're eighteen and you're working at Field's, selling dresses.

MISS C. Yes, selling dresses. Mrs. Farrar comes in quite often.

DR. L. Who do you know? Who are your friends?

MISS C. Mrs. Farrar and Gloria Fine and Flo Morelle and Johnny Reiff and Jason and Maida and Mrs. Peterson from casual frocks and Mr. Kelk from women's shoes and Mr. Winternitz and Angie and Jerry *King* from wrapping. And Bev Riley and her boyfriend Mac and the lady who lives downstairs, Mrs. Pfeugler.

DR. L. How did you meet Jason and Maida and Mr. Kelk?

MISS C. Just . . . just met them. Mr. Kelk introduced me.

DR. L. And you met him in Field's? He works there?

MISS C. Yes. Women's shoes.

DR. L. How did you meet him?

MISS C. In the employees' cafeteria. He came up to me and sat down and started talking.

DR. L. What did he say?

MISS C. He asked me all about myself. He acted as if he knew me from a long time before. I told him everything I knew. I didn't mind telling him.

DR. L. Then he introduced you to the rest?

MISS C. Yes. They belong to a botany club. They go on walks in the country. They asked me to join but I don't care anything about botany. I joined.

DR. L. Why?

MISS C. Because. Because I joined.

DR. L. What do you do in the country?

MISS C. Why, we . . . We just walk. Picnics. We light fires and roast weenies. At night, that is.

DR. L. What else do you do?

MISS C. We talk. I fall asleep sometimes.

DR. L. Why do you fall asleep? Do they give you anything? Do they talk to you? Is that why you fall asleep?

MISS C. I don't know.

DR. L. Do they repeat things to you? Do they make you watch something closely and keep talking to you?

MISS C. I don't know. I just fall asleep. I mean, I don't remember falling asleep. But when I wake up they tell me I've been sleeping.

DR. L. And you don't remember falling asleep?

MISS C. I don't remember.

. . . I should add at this point that my receptionist thinks we're wasting time on Abbie's early Chicago years. She thinks we ought to go back to the North Dakota data and dig into the background there. But I have the feeling we can't rush this too much, even though time is vital. After this last session Abbie simply slipped off to sleep in the middle of a word. I feel guilty about it, but I'm afraid I'll have to put her under again this afternoon.

Kelk knew what she was just by looking at her. She didn't know him, yet she acquiesced in everything, joining the "botany" club, going on picnics. It's evident that these people can recognize their kind by some outward manifestation of their inward power or belief. What the sign is, I don't know. I doubt that Abbie does, either. Perhaps it isn't a sign at all; it may be a sensation. We've all had those feelings of friendliness or repulsion or fear when meeting new people. There must be something in these Satan-worshipers that goes *click*. This is it, something tells them. This is another of *my* kind.

What a tragedy for Abbie. She might have gone through life untouched by whatever is locked in her unconscious. But Kelk knew her for what she was, found her out and brought her to the group. If only she hadn't met him. But then, I suppose, there would have been others. There are always . . . others.

Friday, 11:00 P.M. This has been much more successful. Either we're getting better at administering the *pentothal,* or else Abbie is relaxing and opening more easily. I've found out a number of important things this time. The best way to report them is by reference to my receptionist's notebook. To wit:

DR. L. You're only twelve, Abbie.

MISS C. Twelve?

DR. L. Twelve. You're living in North Dakota and your parents have just died. They just died, Abbie.

MISS C. Why, no. They haven't died. They never died.

DR. L. But you said they did.

MISS C. I was lying.

DR. L. What did they do?

MISS C.   They're still alive. They'll never die. That's part of the plan. They can't die because they must usher the coming.

DR. L.   What do you mean, "usher the coming?"

MISS C.   It's the plan. Lucy is about twelve years old now, no—fourteen at least. And Alfred's died twice since. They put him into a steer. He's been slaughtered twice and now he's in an eagle.

DR. L.   Lucy is your mother and Alfred your father?

MISS C.   Lucy is my mother. I don't know about Alfred.

DR. L.   What do you mean, Alfred's in an eagle? And how is Lucy only twelve years old?

MISS C.   That's the plan.

DR. L.   Do they pass into the bodies of other things?

MISS C.   They do. If Alfred was my father, I do too. I hate him.

DR. L.   Don't you know if he was your father?

MISS C.   He says yes but Lucy says no.

DR. L.   Why do you hate him?

MISS C.   He's my master. I bring the whip to him.

DR. L.   What does he do with the whip?

MISS C.   Do you want to see my welts? The master-welts. I can't bring my whip to anyone else, not even Lucy.

DR. L.   What about the plan? What is the plan?

MISS C.   They told me once. They put it in the fire and I swallowed the ashes. It's in me.

DR. L.   What is the plan?

MISS C. (indistinct)

. . . Here she lapsed into that odd tongue I had heard the night of the explosion, the night they were to sacrifice Sam Olson. My receptionist had taken down some of it phonetically but it doesn't make sense. I'm sure she isn't getting the spelling right and I've told her not to transcribe it any more. But she did get a few phrases. They go something like this, phonetically, that is:

MISS C. *Yeodra nil gannirl parsigl* . . . *Yeodra an eckyrsteck* . . . *gn forsinl eeyorl nil eeyrna* . . . *Yeodranis an kriyorvn eckyrsteck.*

The vocabulary seems limited, many words taking different endings to form a kind of syntax. I imagine that with a few months' work I could break down enough of it by elementary means, pointing to things and asking Abbie the name for them, that kind of slow nonsense. But I have a better idea.

DR. L. Can you translate that into English?

MISS C. Translate? I don't understand.

DR. L. Tell me what you've said, but in English.

MISS C. I don't understand.

Her voice has gone up half an octave and her words are slurred now, the voice of a child. She sometimes makes grammatical errors and often mispronounces words. Her voice has a rushing, breathless quality as if she were struggling to get everything out as fast as she possibly can. At these moments her face contorts oddly—for an adult, that is—and she makes peculiar faces, some funny, some tragic, some as distorted as the facial writhings of a spastic. But during this session, which lasted almost an hour, she never seemed to falter except when she obviously didn't have any information to divulge.

DR. L. Tell me some more about the plan. What is "ushering the coming"?

MISS C. To bring them in. We have to guide them back. And the others, too. I mean they'd be mad, the others, only we have to make them not mad.

DR. L. What else did they teach you?

MISS C. The fire and the water and the rain. And all the masses. I know all about everything because Lucy and Albert told me. I'm smart too. I remember it all.

DR. L. What about the fire and water and rain?

MISS C. To call them. I know how, you bet. We have the best crops in the state. Wheat.

DR. L. Tell me about the masses.

MISS C. They let me say one for Nils. Old Man Kittleson. All by myself. I know all those things.

DR. L. What did you say for Nils?

MISS C. (gibberish)

DR. L. What does that mean?

MISS C. (gibberish)

DR. L. Tell me in English.

MISS C. I don't know.

DR. L. What happened to Nils?

MISS C. He died. Not all at once. He died, though. I did it all by myself. Lucy says I . . . But it's wrong to brag. I'm not supposed to brag. Or tell.

DR. L. How old were you when you said the mass

for Nils?

MISS C. I was seven. The rain age. When I was fire, they let me say for Websterville. It all burned down. I did it by myself, too.

DR. L. A town burned down?

MISS C. Yes. Websterville. They were mad at us. We have to make them not mad. Fire makes them not mad. I did it by myself. If I follow Abbie's thoughts rightly, she said a black mass for a Nils Kittleson when she was seven . . . and he died. The business of Websterville is astounding. Can they invoke fire to wipe out a whole town? I must have the sequence of ideas wrong. At any rate, her unconscious is loaded with this foul stuff. We have to get the last of it out.

My receptionist, clever kid, reminds me that it isn't enough to bring the data out into the open. Abbie must be made to remember it as though it were her name and telephone number. Must have it in her consciousness, ready, current. Otherwise, when the *pentothal* wears off, the whole business will slip back into the unconscious and be lost again until the next session.

When Abbie wakes up, I think. I'll try just that. I'll remind her of what she's been saying and we'll see what happens.

But the strain of this is getting me. If my receptionist weren't here, I'd have ruined the whole treatment a dozen times and gotten nothing for my trouble hut a lot of gibberish and half-uttered ideas. I can hardly contain myself when Abbie is under the *pentothal*. I want to shake her, force her, push her into more exact answers. But every time I begin to grow excited my receptionist leans over and pushes me back. I would ruin everything without her.

We're waiting now for Abbie to come out of the *pentothal*. My receptionist thinks of everything. She even brought a deck of cards and as I write I can look at one corner of the floor and see her laying out a solitaire hand. It's her favorite game, a baffling kind of business with everything in packs of four.

"What's it called?" I ask her.

"You'd love it," she responds. "It's called 'Idiot's Delight' and it comes out about twice a year if you play it every day."

Saturday, 9:15 A.M. Abbie woke up about eight-thirty this morning and I began throwing questions at her.

"Do you remember what we were talking about under the *pentothal?*"

"Nothing, I'm afraid." She smiled guiltily at me and I felt my heart grow sick with shame. She has given up trying to touch me. She used to make an attempt to smooth my hair or touch my hand. But I cannot stand to have anybody touch my flesh.

The impact on me is like a hot rivet. My skin seems to retreat from it, shuddering away in wide rippling pools of flesh. It isn't simply Abbie's touch.

Every time my receptionist pushes me back, I feel a kind of jolt and the front of my body crawls with nervous tension.

"Do you remember about Nils Kittleson?" I went on quickly.

"Nils?" She looked at me oddly for a moment. "I said a mass for him. When I was a child in North Dakota. Why?"

"What!" I felt a surging joy in me.

My receptionist woke up with a start. "What's the matter?"

"She remembers!"

"That's good." Very businesslike girl. "How about breakfast."

"She remembers, don't you see?" I turned on Abbie and my hands itched to hold her tight with gratefulness and . . . and love.

But not now. Not yet. "Talk," I ordered. "Tell me about the mass."

"Why . . ." She seemed bewildered. "It was the usual mass. Albert was my clerk. We—!" Now, suddenly, recognition filled her. I could see it well up behind her eyes like some dark fluid finding its own level.

"You see," I said, laughing. "You're remembering things you never could before."

"But that's fantastic. I don't remember doing anything when I was a child. I mean, I just grew. And now, all of a sudden, I remember things. Nils Kittleson. It took him four months to die.

They called it brain fever."

"I know." I glanced away. "Like Colin had."

"Like—?" Now she saw the whole thing. "And like you?"

"Now what's the ritual?" I asked quickly. "How does it go?"

"Why I . . . I don't know. I just remember saying it"

"Get the notebook," I snapped at my receptionist. "Read back some of that gibberish to her."

"Before breakfast? Look, Dr. L., I'm a growing girl. I need food."

"Plenty of time for that before . . ." I had a better idea. "Let's dope her up again and have her run through the whole thing. You take it down, as much as you can, and then, when she snaps out of it, we'll help her remember."

I felt a kind of thrilling, thrumming vibration in my chest. It wiped away everything—guilt, fear, everything. It was akin to the sensation of a man who has had no food or water for days, that keen, trembling quaver in the musculature that makes the slightest gesture a palsied quaking. "Fix a hypo," I ordered. "Quick."

10:45 A.M. All done. Abbie came through perfectly and would have gone on babbling for hours but I shot a little more *pentothal* into her and she dropped off to sleep. My receptionist's notebook is loaded with gibberish, all phonetic, but probably the most valuable collection of nonsense I've ever had.

I played my last card, too. I asked Abbie what could counteract the mass. The answer is all down there in the notebook. Whatever it is. It may simply be the cold statement that it can't be counteracted. But I have to take that chance. It's better to know the best or the worst as fast as possible. If Abbie isn't awake by nightfall I'll shake her awake. I have to know.

I'm like a demented man. I should feel sorry for Abbie, for the terrible punishment we're inflicting on her nervous system. But all I feel is a devouring eagerness. All this can't be in vain. It mustn't be.

Midnight. Now I know. But I'll begin at the beginning.

Abbie awoke at eight. The cabin was hot from the day's sun, a huge oven, and the pain inside me was a spit on which I turned, barbecuing slowly.

"Read off the first few words," I asked my receptionist.

She stumbled over them and corrected herself several times, but she got out about twenty or thirty words of gibberish before Abbie stopped her.

"Of course," she said, as though we had been telling her the earth was round. "I know that," she said, and proceeded to continue the ritual letter-perfect.

"Do you know what that is?" I asked her.

"I said that for Nils."

"Did you say it for Mr. Profit?"

"Yes. "

"For Colin?"

"Yes."

"And for me?"

Her eyes dropped as though for the first time she realized what she was saying. She turned away, picked at the blankets on the bed and then, seeming to make up her mind, she turned back. "That was what I said for you," she told me, repeating the words slowly, a confession of murder.

I stood up and leaned over her, tense, my head an echoing cavern of pain. "All right," I said, "now listen to this."

I motioned to my receptionist and she read off Abbie's answer to the question: "What can counteract the mass? What can save the victim?" The words rolled out into the hot, quiet room, strange words, fit for all manner of sorcery. She was reading more easily now and the words began to pick up a kind of cadence, as of a chant or incantation. Abbie sat stiffly, entranced. When it was over, I saw her eyes start up to my face, then stop, waver, shift and drop downwards again.

"What does it mean? What is it?"

"I . . . I can't explain," she said with difficulty. "It's

hard to translate. "

"I know, Abbie." I was being very, very patient. "But give me a general idea."

"I can't." Her lips were trembling strangely. What was wrong?

"Then a hint?"

"I . . ." She glanced up at me. "You wouldn't want me to." Her eyes were widening slowly, as though she were in darkness, the pupils dilating to huge proportions, so wide they threatened to swallow the irises completely. The febrile motion of her lips was spreading across her face.

She was nervous, distraught, poor kid. I shouldn't rush her so fast. I should be more disinterested. It was only my life . . . but I must sound calm and detached. "Think it over," I heard myself say in a choked voice. "Then maybe you'll find a way to tell me."

She tried. She sat there and thought. My receptionist slumped back in her chair and closed her eyes. The heat was tiring, oppressive. No welcome breeze rustled the leaves. The room was as quiet as a sealed crypt . . . mine. The three of us sat there silently and I kept my eyes on Abbie.

Something was building up in her, I could tell that. It was like watching the hot, bubbly fluid in a glass coffeemaker; frothing, building slowly in height out of a frantic internal chaos. It began, in Abbie, with her mouth. The quivering seemed to ripple slowly across her face, as though subterranean fires were crumbling the crust of her skin. The strange vibration spread to her neck. I had never seen her this way. It was almost as if she were being shaken apart from within.

Her eyes were huge, deep, unsteady. Her fingers shook madly and she seemed to be possessed by a gigantic, endless shudder. Then a countermovement started in her legs. She crossed them and seemed to be staring at her bare feet. Suddenly her torso stiffened erect and her head came back. The trembling was gone. She was rock-steady, immovable. What was going on inside that lovely body?

Then I saw what it was. It was neither thought nor sudden purpose that calmed her. Fear stiffened her body. Fear was mounting inside her, shaking her, then steeling her. It was fear that dilated her eyes to those mad holes of night. Fear of what? What did she know that there were no words to express? What couldn't she tell me? What clutched at her with such almighty pressure?

"What's the matter?" my receptionist wanted to know. She was watching Abbie curiously, almost sadly.

"It's all right," Abbie managed to get out. "I'm all right."

My receptionist looked at her wristwatch and rose. "Look," she said with an air of casualness that was overdone, "if there's nothing stirring yet, I'd like to get some air. Okay?"

I nodded without speaking.

"Fine. Be back in a little while." She paused at the doorway and waved at us. "Talk it over, kids." Exit.

I turned back to Abbie. There was no one here to restrain me now. I would get her secret out of her any way I could manage. "Tell me what that gibberish meant."

"But I can't, Joe. It . . . it isn't possible."

"Do *you* know?"

She nodded. "Yes." She took a breath and seemed to hold it. "I know."

"You've got to tell me," I insisted harshly. "You know how important it is."

She looked at me with a hooded expression. "To you," she said.

I was suddenly ashamed of myself again. "I'm sorry," I mumbled. "I don't mean to be so selfish but it's—you know. I get tightened up inside and I can't think of anything else."

"You shouldn't," she said softly. "You should think only of that one thing. It's the most important thing, Joe. I'm not angry."

"I'm sorry," I repeated. "I really am."

"I've done something horrible to you," she said musingly. It was as if she were finally putting her action into real words, almost as though she'd never phrased them quite so accurately before. "And you're the one I love," she went on slowly. "Isn't that monstrous? I must have been insane. I . . . I don't remember any of it but I must have been . . . I don't know. Possessed?" She considered the word. "That's what it was, I suppose. And now I've done this thing to you and you're . . ." She fell away with an abrupt movement, throwing herself face down on the cot.

"You're the only one I loved," she said indistinctly. "In all my life, the only one. And I had to—I" Sobs cut her off.

I went to her, although I hadn't wanted to. My arm went around her shoulders and I felt them shaking violently. "You couldn't help it," I heard myself say, "I know that."

"I . . ." her sobbing muffled the words, ". . . I had to do this to *you*. The one I loved. The one." It was like a refrain, a mournful chanting refrain. "The only one. The only one."

She turned toward me slightly and seemed to catch her breath.

"Joe," she said unsteadily, "there are worse things than being cursed. Much worse. It's . . . after all, it's something outside of you. It really isn't you, it's something they *do* to you. But there's something so much worse, darling."

"I know. It's what you have."

She made a funny choking sound. "What I have?" She was laughing wildly, crazily. "God, no! *I* don't have it Joe it has *me!*"

"We'll change it then."

"We?" She smiled at me, a soft, wonderful thing full of love and the exaltation of loving. "Both of us?" she whispered.

"We're not done yet," I said. "We'll both come through."

Her smile faded, wiped away. Her mouth moved soundlessly, spasmodically.

I felt my arm draw back from her. All of a sudden I understood. This was the translation of that infernal gibberish. "Then there's nothing?" I snapped harshly.

She looked up at me. Her face was wet, her eyes

liquid in the deep violet hollows around them. "I didn't mean that," she said.

"Then what?" My voice was ragged, demanding.

"I . . ." She pushed her hand gently against my chest. "Leave me alone for a while," she begged. "I can't think with you so close to me."

"Think about what?" I had to know, had to.

"Stop it, Joe. Please don't keep asking me!"

"But I—"

"Joe! No more questions. Later, not now."

I got up from the cot and went to one of the chairs. At that moment I would have throttled her if I had the strength. I couldn't stand her, the sight, the smell of her. It was like watching some loathsome slug inching its shiny way across my chest, like a sea-horror, all tentacles and claws, all slithering ooziness crawling and mincing across my body.

But she loved me. This misbegotten horror, this beautiful, breathtaking woman loved me. Or was she lying?

I think we must have sat there for almost half an hour and said not a word. We heard the car drive up, the door slam. My receptionist's voice came loud and cheery through the stifling heat. "Here I am!"

Neither of us replied. The girl swung in the door, looked at us, then stopped and stood there, hands on hips. "Well, hello." Neither of us felt like answering. "Hello," she repeated. "Then no hello? Hello, how are you? I'm fine. Nice weather. Terrible heat. How was the drive? Fine. Meet anybody? Not a soul. Glad you're back. *Thank* you." She sat down in a chair and watched us glumly.

"Little ray of sunshine," I murmured. The sound of my own voice reverberated in my mouth as though it were a great cathedral, arched roof bouncing back the words with penetrating precision.

"No soap?" the receptionist surmised. "No soap. Okay, we try tomorrow."

"Abbie," I said heavily, "says no."

"Tomorrow will tell," she assured me.

The women fell asleep much later, ages later. In the darkness the cabin was like a closed oven. The heat seemed to be aggravated by darkness. I craved light with which to see things, sense things, anything but this damnable heat, any sensation to blanket it, a noise, a taste, anything.

Then I had a sensation. It sponged the heat away from me in a single sharp swipe. It was a moan. And it came from Abbie. She turned in her sleep and I heard her moan again, a deep, throaty sound, as though her body were voicing itself through its very pores. What torment rode through her sleep-dazed brain?

Suddenly a great pity came to me. I knew a little of what it must be like for her. In that moan everything became clear. The torture of her soul, sinking into the nocturnal hell-house of her unconscious, falling, falling deep into the blackness of it. Can we ever really know the mind of another? I knew hers. In that instant when her soul shrieked in agony, I knew something of what her life must be.

I stood over her and felt her forehead. *Hot.* Hot as

live coals. I bent over and rested my cheek against hers. The inhuman crime of it, the monstrous burden of her soul!

She stirred. "Darling?"

"Go back to sleep," I soothed her. "Everything's all right."

Her voice was a bodiless murmur. "Darling . . . I love you."

God, what a crime! This warm, lovely girl, the girl I . . . there'd never been another like her. Not for me. There never would be. I kissed her hot cheek. "I love you too," I managed to say. "I love you, Abbie."

She sighed once, a tumultuous surge of breath. Then she rolled away from me slightly and dropped off to sleep again.

As I sit here now, making the pencil scratch over these sheets of paper, feeling every looping "e," every sharp stab as an "i" is dotted, the feeling of being prematurely dead is intensified. This lifeless cabin, given over to none but the sleeping and the dying is like some anteroom of a charnel house in which the victims, variously advanced on the road to death, sit or lie, awake or sodden with sleep, waiting for the end. It would make a good crypt.

I am tired of writing. The pencil hardly obeys me anymore. My hand muscles feel atrophied. It can only be a matter of days. Abbie can no longer help me. The great plan, the science, the drugs, the analysis, the synthesis, all a farce. Even our love can do nothing. I am alone with my death now, utterly alone. None of us can do anything. I wonder, though, if she can tell me the time of it? It would be good to know even this poor snippet of knowledge amid a howling world of irrational, unknowable things. A strange curiosity is gripping me. I must ask her. Even if she's asleep, I must wake her and ask her . . .

But she's gone.

The cot is almost undisturbed. How could she leave unnoticed? How could she make so little noise?

I have to find her. I have to ask her something. She can't have gone far. I'll go and find her. We love each other. She'll tell me.

. . . I have been to the turning of the road. The night is hot, dry as old bones. The ruins on the high dune seem to vibrate with the day's heritage of warmth, to shimmer in the moonlight. She is nowhere. I must try the other way. Into the woods. Towards her cabin, perhaps. If only there were people in this area to ask:

"Have you seen a woman pass this way?" The area is desolate, the cabins empty. This is a blasted, arid, hot and dusty patch of earth, reserved for demons and the ghosts of men. I must find her.

. . . She's nowhere. It's two A.M. by my watch and I must have covered the woods for half a mile around. If she wanted to run away, why didn't she take the car? Where can she go in this deserted area? Why did she leave me?

I see, too, that she's gone barefooted. Her shoes lie beneath the cot. She is clothed in a white dress, startlingly clear by moonlight. Why can't I find her? How far could she have gone barefooted? And why—now when we know our love—why?

I'm going out again.

. . . Two-fifteen. Nowhere. I'd . . . I'd wake my receptionist but I . . . I don't know. I want to find Abbie myself. I have to find her and ask her only one question. Why couldn't she have stayed long enough for that? I'll have to go . . .

There's something off in the woods. I can hear a faint rustling. I'll look out the window . . .

Yes, something there. Moving, light. Too big for Abbie. Something now crackling. I can hear it. Far, distant, huge. One moment . . .

The woods are on fire.

13 «◊» Epilogue

THIS IS APPROXIMATELY thirty-six hours later. Let's call them hours, anyway.

I can't write very well. No time for apologies. The story first.

I wrote before that the woods were on fire. The timber must have been kiln-dry. Tinder-timber. The leaves, greenish gray, were as close to death as they could be on living trees in summer. A week of heat had parched the forest to death in life. Somehow, and so easily, a fire had started.

I remember shouting. I remember running out of the cabin. I remember pounding through the woods, slashing past trees, bushes. I remember everything clearly: steady momentum, steady tempo, shoes pounding, legs tensing, up, down, forward, body lurching on over the stumbling action of my legs, toward the fire.

She was silhouetted against the flames. Abbie slim and erect an andiron of steel against the flames. She seemed to be of them but not yet in them. I shouted to her and she turned to see me. I saw her lips move, but her words were wiped out by the crackling advance of the fire.

"Abbie!" The word was hot and acrid in my mouth.

Smoke now. Crisp, snapping smoke from the pine and the terribly dry underbrush. These things spread like grass fire. "Abbie!"

Flames roar louder, deafening. Smoke and sparks, great sheaves of fire billow out at me. Fire yards, feet from me.

A louder roar now, above. Lightning? From the sky it comes, a huge shouting roar and a flash that breaks across the sky, a ragged gash letting in the fierce white flame of the heavens.

The heavy, belching grunt of thunder, rolling across the forest, matching sound and might with the advancing fire. Twigs snapping, the flames charging in on quick red feet.

"Abbie! Come back, Abbie!"

My eyes . . . She . . . her figure now white in the lightning flash, now black against the flames, retreating, dwindling. Must catch her. Legs bunch, pulse, throb. I must catch her.

"Goodbye!"

Her voice, out of the flame.

"Goodbye, my darling!"

Fading into the flame, laced with the tongue of the flame, speaking in its mouth, fading with it, flickering. Her slim, straight body against the flames. *In* the flames.

I, running, stumbling. Sparks burn my face. I fall, ground looming, smoke surging up into my face. The crashing impact of the ground. I . . .

. . . came to about three hours ago. They've given me a private room in the hospital, courtesy to a visiting professional, no doubt. When I regained consciousness a woman was watching me. I opened my eyes slowly and looked up into the face of my receptionist.

"Where's Abbie?"

"They're looking for her body." Her face paled and she turned away for a moment. "You really took the count," she said then.

"Can't they find Abbie?"

"Not a chance. Look," she continued briskly, "I had to haul you out of there by the heels. If you'll feel on top, you'll find a lot of hair burnt away."

I lay there thinking. Abbie? "Well," I said at last, "thanks. I—" My hand had been rubbing the top of my head, feeling about the thin hair and the few shaved spots where they'd taped up what had evidently been lacerations. "Hey!"

"What?"

"My *head.*" I could hardly get the words out. "My head!"

"What's with your head?"

"It—doesn't—hurt." Spaced out, like that.

Her eyebrows went up. "Oh?" It didn't impress her. "That's nice."

"Nice? Why—?" But it was no use. I could see she'd never believed I was going to die. She knew a lot of it, but not that. "Abbie?" I asked again.

"They haven't found Abbie," she explained. "No

sign of her. They combed the whole area, everywhere the fire was."

Of course not, I thought. Why would they find her body? Abbie, the campfire girl from way, way back. She was gone, back to her own flaming birth, back into the bottomless deep of fire, to the source and the power of her unknown existence.

Of course she was gone. It was her way of saving me. Locked in the reservoir of her unconscious was the answer to the curse, the answer we had so glibly read back to her, summoning it up out of her unconscious like a hoary monster of the night and shaking it before her terror-stricken eyes. And that was the fear, too. Because the answer was so simple . . . she had to die.

They were all dead, all killed. Had I murdered them? Had I raised Morelle's ambition to an all-consuming boil, destroyed Flye by dissolving his life fetish? And was it I who transmuted Maida's worship of the past into babbling idiocy, who drove the mute, brute Kelk to his death in an ecstasy of shuddering terror, who goaded Khereniev's omnipotent self-love to rocketing death?

There was nothing left now but the memory of one last death, a death that, on the balance of the world, upheld a life.

"Stop brooding," my receptionist said. "You look so . . . so lost."

"Not me."

"You know," she said, smiling at me, "you ought to get married."

I tried to muster a smile. It didn't hurt to smile any more. Inside my head there was only peace. I could smile or grin or laugh out loud. I could do anything I wanted to do. I could lower myself to the infinite depths, raise myself to the highest, most rarefied heights where the soul of man stands shoulder to shoulder with his destiny. I could do anything. I was free for the one thing given to all men together. Free to act with them, in them, for them, to the end that all of us might be free. And Abbie had freed me.

Bruin Asylum

Make Your Reservations Today!

THE WITCHING NIGHT
  BY C. S. CODY – BOOKING NOW

A GARDEN LOST IN TIME
  BY JONATHAN AYCLIFFE – BOOKING NOW

THE FUNGUS
  BY HARRY ADAM KNIGHT – JANUARY 2014

I AM YOUR BROTHER
  BY C. S. MARLOWE – MARCH 2014

THE MAGICIAN (EXPANDED EDITION)
  BY W. SOMERSET MAUGHAM – JUNE 2014